ChangelingPress.com

Arcane Island (Talents 3)

Angela Knight

Arcane Island (Talents 3)
Angela Knight

ISBN: 978-1-60521-847-2

Publisher:
Changeling Press LLC
315 N. Centre St.
Martinsburg, WV 25404
ChangelingPress.com

Printed in the U.S.A.

Editor: Jean Cooper
Cover Artist: Angela Knight

The individual stories in this anthology have been previously released in E-Book format.

Table of Contents

Arcane Island (Talents 3)
Angela Knight

Dave Frost died in combat five years ago, but his soul survives, magically bonded to the body of his partner -- a six-hundred-pound tiger. Dave can conjure a human manifestation, but nobody treats him as a man anymore. Especially not women. Until he meets Ariel, his costar, while shooting a reality TV competition in the Bahamas. The show's producers have assigned him to the beautiful witch for an onscreen showmance.

Ariel Piper's talent is strong enough to turn the competition in their favor. Unfortunately, she also has a condition that makes using her magic agonizing. When they discover Dave's touch kills the pain, he's driven to help.

Their showmance soon becomes the real thing, though Dave fears she'll dump him when the show wraps. Can Ariel convince this heroic, wounded man to trust her love before the show comes to a lethal climax that's not in the script?

My Feral Heart

Deep in my Feral heart
Where all my passions start,
I feel your magic's call.
I want to give you all,
All my Feral heart.

You make my hunger roar
All I want is more.
See the gold of my eyes?
I tell you no lies --
I'm the cat you're looking for.

I taste your Arcane kiss,
and feel your fire hiss
As your magic heats my skin,
You make me want to sin
Deep in my Feral Heart.

You make my hunger roar
All I want is more.
See the gold of my eyes?
I tell you no lies --
I'm the cat you're looking for.

See me stalk you in the dark
Listen to my passion growl
'Cause I wanna hear you yowl.
Feel your power spark
Deep in your Feral Heart.

You make my hunger roar
All I want is more.
See the gold of my eyes?
I tell you no lies --
I'm the cat you're looking for.

Chapter One

Dave

The cave reeked of black magic -- a combination of rotting blood from sacrificed chickens and the burnt metal pong of old spells. Overlaying that was the stench of fear, spoiled food, and guano from the bats I could hear fluttering and squeaking somewhere ahead.

It was also dark as the inside of a bear's hairy butt, except for a circle of illumination from my helmet flash. The light bounced across Bobby Nolan's back as he strode ahead of me, taking point. He was walking a little God damn fast, given we were hunting MEEDs -- the Magically Enhanced Explosive Devices the Caliphate's sorcerers liked to plant. Chances were good the bastards had arranged some nasty surprises in their cave complex once it became obvious we were going to overrun them. It would suck to step on something that blew us into orbit.

So I was less than thrilled Bobby had his attention elsewhere. Probably brooding about the fight he'd just had with his girlfriend.

Idiot.

But then, if he'd been smart, he wouldn't have cheated on Erica Harris to begin with. He'd hurt her, damn it, and I wanted to kick his ass. And I wasn't alone in that, either. We all liked our team Arcanist, who was elsewhere in the cave complex, using her magic to disable a MEED one of the Marines had found.

"Bobby, slow up," Jake Nolan whispered from behind me. We were moving in a stack, single file. "The idea is *not* to find the booby trap by stepping on it."

"Go fuck yourself," his brother snarled.

"Bobby, mind on the job, not on your dick," Lt. Kurt Briggs snapped from behind Jake. Our team leader rarely lost his temper, but when he did, his tongue could strip the paint off an MRAP.

Bobby's lioness rumbled a warning growl at Kurt, making the air vibrate with her magic. Kurt's cat, Stoli, and my Smilodon returned her growl with interest. Because there was a distance limit on melding, the cats rode a helicopter circling overhead just out of Stinger range while their minds fused with ours. Working together, Familiars and Ferals could create a mystical shell around the human's body. The bulletproof animal manifestation had the beast's strength, claws, and fangs -- with human intelligence. Which made for a giant combo plate of whup-ass.

They didn't call us Tooth Tanks for nothing.

Trouble was, if Bobby gave in to his cat's emotions, he could give the phrase "friendly fire" a *friendly fang* twist. I looked over my shoulder at Kurt, meaning to ask if he wanted me to take point instead. Before I could get the question out of my mouth, Bobby stopped in his tracks. I bumped into him.

All hell broke loose.

From the corner of one eye, I saw sigils flare on the tunnel wall Bobby had brushed with one shoulder. The blood-red light of a Caliphate booby trap blasted through the tunnel. In that fraction of a second, the spell grabbed his lioness' anger and drove Bobby into a murderous rage. Since he was already pissed, it didn't take much. He roared, the sound deafening in the tunnel's confined space.

His cat exploded into full manifestation right in my face, a glowing lioness sculpted of pure magic, one huge paw already swinging at my head. I didn't even have time to duck. Bobby hit me so hard, light exploded in my skull with a crack like a tree limb breaking. The tunnel wheeled around me as I went down.

"Frost!" Kurt's voice rang with horror. "Bobby, you fuck..."

I didn't even feel my body hit the tunnel's hard-packed dirt. I couldn't breathe, couldn't move as the world exploded into chaos. Bobby's blazing cat leaped over me, roaring in fury as she charged his brother.

I struggled to breathe as a single gunshot echoed between the tunnel's rock walls. The roaring cut off.

"Shit!" Jake screamed. "Bobby!"

I tried to move, but my head seemed disconnected from my body. I couldn't feel a God damn thing. Couldn't breathe. *Jesus, did he break my neck?* Blackness closed over me, and I realized I was dying.

Smilodon roared in terror and rage, but I was already falling into the infinite black. Something jerked me to a stop -- Smiley's magic. I clawed for him in sheer desperation, and we fought to hold on as death tried to rip me away.

The tiger's love and need flooded my consciousness as he hauled me to him. We fell into light, and I could breathe again. The air was full of the thunderous *whomp whomp* of helicopter blades. I sucked in a panicked breath and opened my eyes. Vertical lines filled my vision, and I stared at them, panting in fear and confusion.

Bars. The bars of a cage. *I was in a cage.*

Smilodon moaned, the distressed sound much louder than it usually was in our spirit link. Disoriented, I looked down. Instead of hands, I saw huge striped paws. Cold horror flooded me as I realized what had happened.

I'd fused with my tiger because my human body had just died of a broken neck.

* * *

I came out of the nightmare screaming. The sound emerged as an ear-splitting roar.

I opened my eyes to see the bars of a cage. For a bewildered moment, I thought it was still the day Bobby Nolan killed me.

No. No heavy *whomp whomp* of helicopter blades, though this was definitely the cargo bay of an aircraft. *The fuck…*

The cockpit door banged open, and I jerked around as a balding man stuck his head out. His round, stubbled face was white with fear and anger. "Shut the fuck up, you furry freak!"

I shook off the nightmare's sticky residue, recognizing Steve Mason, the pilot of the SC. 7 Skyvan flying me to Hammerhead Cay. The vibration of the old cargo plane's engines had stopped, and we were sitting still. I reached for my magic, solidifying part of my aura and using it to vibrate the air around me. A tiger's body doesn't have the anatomy for human speech, so I'd had to learn how to talk without moving my mouth or larynx. "Have we landed?"

"Yes, we fucking landed! Where the hell do you get off, roaring like that?"

"I was asleep. I had a dream. Look, could you unlock the damn cage?" Cages didn't normally bother me -- I'd spent a lot of time in them over the five years since I'd died -- but that dream always left me feeling raw.

Nothing like being killed to give a guy PTSD.

Piggy little eyes glittered. "Get used to it, *demon*. Once we elect us a Humanist president, he'll put freaks like you in camps to keep you away from decent people."

"You really need to go back on your antipsychotics." Smilodon sent me a mental image of throwing ourselves against the bars. The bastard would jump right out of his khaki cargo shorts. But since I didn't want to see his bare, hairy ass, I restrained us to a menacing growl. Menacing is one of our best things.

Mason sure thought so. He went white and jerked back before he caught himself and sneered. "On second thought, you won't get the camp. *You*, they'll put to sleep like the animal you are."

The prick was probably right. Humanists had a serious hard-on for all Talents, but they saved their worst hate for Melds like Smiley and me. "I'd rather be an animal than a bigoted asshole."

"An asshole with *hands*. Unlock your own fucking cage!"

"Good idea." I was tired of his shit anyway. I concentrated, drawing on the well of magic Smiley and I shared, then sent it pouring through the bars to form a glowing manifestation of my human body.

And just like that, I stood outside the cage on my own two feet. Smiley and I couldn't maintain the mystical shell for long, but I could use it like the body my folks had buried five years ago.

As usual, I'd clothed the shell in a copy of my Arcane Corps cammies. First, because nobody wanted to see my glowing junk. Second, I liked reminding dickheads like Mason that I'd died for my country while they were watching football and eating Buffalo wings.

Mason's jaw dropped as he went pale, even more spooked by ghostly me than he'd been by my toothy tiger smile. "How... how did you..."

"Do you really think any cage can hold me?" I took a step toward him, my manifestation casting a soft glow over the cargo hold. Behind me, Smilodon rumbled softly from our cage.

Mason plunged a hand into a pocket of his baggy shorts and whipped out an honest-to-Bella Lugosi crucifix. Waving it in my direction, he yelled, "Get back!"

I blinked, more bemused than pissed. "Who the hell do you think I am? Dracula?"

"Demon! Freak!"

"Moron." I took another step toward him. He dodged around me to run toward the back of the plane. He must have lowered the rear cargo door while I was asleep, because I could see white sand and coconut palms through the opening. Mason jumped out and lumbered off across the beach, graceful as a hippo in a grass fire.

"And they call *me* a pussy," I muttered. I turned to contemplate the cage.

A hefty padlock held its guillotine style door closed. Bending, I explored the lock with glowing fingers. It felt cold and solid against my mystic skin. I'd gotten so good with my manifestation, I could almost pretend I was still human. And there were some things I could do even better than before. Like picking locks.

Pressing the tip of my index finger against the lock's keyhole, I began to push, simultaneously weakening the mani's mystical field so it was no longer quite solid. A tendril of my magic snaked into the lock. Expanding the tendril, I probed until I found the slots for the key's teeth, filled them with my magic, and twisted. The padlock popped open as I withdrew the makeshift key, turning it back into a finger. Dropping the lock on the deck, I raised the guillotine door.

Smilodon padded out. He chuffed, lifting his head, and I reached down to scratch the itch I could feel behind our left ear. Then I banished the mani and let myself pour back into the cat's body.

"Did you *have* to scare the shit out of your pilot?" Tisha Jennings peered in through the open cargo door. Middle-aged, a bit plump, *Arcane Island's* showrunner had dark skin and a round, pretty face with warm brown eyes. She wore her graying curls in a short cap, a plumeria blossom tucked behind one ear. Her flowing emerald maxi dress swirled around sandaled feet, a pattern of pink plumeria rioting around the hem and halfway up the skirt. We'd become friends over the course of my Zoom auditions for the reality show. "How the hell are we going to get you home? He swears he won't fly you."

"Jerk's lucky I didn't bite him." I padded over to join her at the door. "And what were you doing hiring a Humanist pilot? I was afraid he'd shoot me in the head and drop my cage in the ocean."

"Hey, *I* didn't hire him. He works for Jackson Gilbert. Delivers supplies to the island." Tisha stood back, giving me room to leap down. To her credit, she didn't look a bit nervous at being so close to me.

I frowned. Jackson Gilbert was the billionaire who owned Hammerhead Cay -- along with a significant chunk of the Talent Broadcasting Network, Hammerhead Productions, Hammerhead Publishing, and Gilbert Air. And probably other shit I didn't even know about. "I thought Gilbert was supposed to be Pro-Talent."

"He is. Otherwise, he wouldn't be producing this project." Tisha turned and set off toward the coconut trees that ringed the small airstrip. "Come on, we're missing the welcome party. The company's laid out quite a spread."

"Good. I could eat a yak."

Tisha flashed straight white teeth in a grin. "Sorry, no yak on the menu. But we'll find something to fix you up."

I strolled beside her, drawing in the salt air, trying to flush the lingering reek of aviation fuel from my sensitive nose. The sand felt warm beneath my pads, and the breeze tugged my whiskers.

Tisha wasn't very tall, and she blinked as she noticed my back was level with her waist. "Damn, you're huge."

I smirked up at her and purred, "That's what all the girls say." If you make people laugh, they're less likely to see you as a six-hundred-pound murder machine.

Tisha laughed. "You have no shame."

"Life's way too short for shame." *Especially mine.*

* * *

Ariel

When you hear the words "Caribbean paradise," you probably picture something that looks a lot like Hammerhead Cay. Jackson Gilbert's private fiefdom was one of seven hundred islands that made up the Bahamas, and it was every bit as gorgeous as its brochure said.

Sand as white and fine as confectioners' sugar rolled down to meet a sea piercing and unearthly in its turquoise purity. Palm trees rustled as seagulls rode the cooling ocean breeze beneath a sky so intensely blue, it made the eyes ache.

I mean that literally. It felt like someone was driving steel spikes through my pupils. Squinting against my pounding headache, I walked toward the white canvas tent where the welcome breakfast was being served for the cast and crew of *Arcane Island*.

I'd gotten soft. Five glorious months on Aurarest had eroded my tolerance for the pain my magic could inflict. True, not every day was agony, even without the drug. Some days all I had to contend with were periodic acid stings in random places, like fire ant bites. When it got bad, though, it was like being trapped in a bag of broken glass.

Today was a sack of shards kind of day.

When I reached the tent, I broke step, frowning at the two men who stood on either side. They were dressed in khaki shorts and matching shirts with Hammerhead Cay Security embroidered on the pocket. Their hair was cropped military short, and they wore AR-15s slung over their shoulders.

One of them held up a clipboard to stop me. Like his buddy, he was built like a retaining wall, with about as much expression. "Need to check your ID."

I took off the lanyard that held my laminated ID card and handed it over, my eyebrows climbing. "We're on a frickin' private island. It's not like we have to worry about terrorists."

"Actually, we do," Guard Two told me. "We've gotten threats. Humanists have been talking about a hunting expedition to Hammerhead Cay to kill the 'demon possessed cats.'"

"Lovely." I'd like to think some keyboard warrior wouldn't actually sail to some billionaire's island to shoot people, but… They'd done crazier.

Guard One handed back my badge. "You can go in."

I stepped into the huge tent and paused to let my eyes adjust. Over a hundred people were queued up at the buffet or eating at the round tables. Stomach growling, I joined the line.

As I waited, I scanned the crowd. Everyone wore color-coded IDs on lanyards marking them as crew or production staff -- camera operators, staff writers, grips, gaffers, production assistants, carpenters, video editors. A couple of shooters with shoulder-mounted cameras worked the room, and a pair of audio engineers held boom mics over the crowd, documenting the event for the show's behind-the-scenes content.

Curious, I reached for my magic, ignoring the rake of pain. Instantly, everyone in the tent seemed to light up with currents of blue and green in the shades I associate with excitement. Flashes of yellow here and there indicated anxiety, probably pre-shoot jitters. A couple of people's auras swirled with bright sherbet orange. I took particular note of those, because they were lying like hell to somebody.

A few of the figures were dimmer. They'd be the non-Talented Normies who had no magic at all. Most of those who had magic weren't much brighter, since their power wasn't that strong.

Patterns in the currents corresponded to particular Talents. Those whose power concentrated in their hands were Arcanists like me -- they drew their spells with images or sigils. Bright eddies around the throat indicated Bards who worked magic by singing or speaking. Strong currents in the legs and arms meant Primos or Primas -- dancers whose every step and gesture could weave spells. Then there were the slight variations in the currents, signifying the Bards who wrote scripts or the Arcanists who worked magic through hair, costumes, or makeup. You didn't normally see so many Talents in one place, but Hammerhead Productions employed a lot of gifted people, even without the reality show's cast.

I even spotted an Alchemist, who stood at a tall, wheeled bar on the other side of the tent. A selection of potion ingredients stood arrayed in jars in front of him, along with assorted equipment and bottles of what looked like juice, PowerUp and soda. As an espresso machine hissed, magic swirled around his hands as he added herbs to a coffee cup for a woman who looked hung over.

Jackson Gilbert was paying an Alchemist to play barista? The guy was really going all out for this thing.

I went back to scanning the crowd, focusing on the couple of dozen folks who glowed much more brightly than the rest. Those were either my competition or the show's judges.

Brightest of all were the Feral Melds. The three men sat together at one of the tables, blazing like a trio of torches. Though none of them were fully manifested, I could see the ghostly glow of their animal spirits superimposed over their human bodies.

Tisha Jennings had pitched *Arcane Island* as a cross between *Survivor, The Voice,* and *America's Got Talent.* Sixteen contestants would form four teams of four, each with a Melded Feral, an Arcanist like me, a Bard singer, and a Primo/Prima dancer. The teams would compete in a series of challenges by combining their magical abilities, and the one with the most points would split the four-million-dollar prize. That was a big purse for a brand-new show, and it proved the Talent Broadcasting Network thought *Arcane Island* would be a huge hit.

If my team won, my cut would change my life. I was damn well going to make sure we won.

As if aware of my gaze, one of the magical animals, a liger spirit -- a tiger-lion cross -- turned and rumbled softly at me. I recognized both cat and man then, since Chris Freeman and I had served together. His Familiar, Kaiju, had been the biggest cat I'd ever seen. Ligers didn't have the limits on their growth that tigers and lions did, and Kaiju had weighed over a thousand pounds before his death.

Chris himself was an inch or two over six feet, with a powerfully muscled build, dark hair and a Feral's golden eyes.

I didn't recognize the two with him -- a big White guy not much smaller than his enormous glowing bear, and a lean Black man whose locs were almost as glorious as his lion's mane.

I wanted to introduce myself, but my growling stomach had other ideas. Reaching the aluminum serving pans, I started loading down a plastic cafeteria tray with fried chicken, pasta salad, veggies and mashed potatoes. The more magic you used, the more food you needed. I planned to Hoover up every calorie I could get into my mouth.

I headed over to the Alchemist, a thoroughly ordinary round-faced man in the khakis that were apparently the island staff uniform. His nametag read Nathan Sanders, Hammerhead Cay Staff. He had so much curly black hair, I figured he'd probably be bald if he didn't use his own products. I eyed the glowing bottles of PowerUp at his elbow. "Is that the Potion version?"

"Yep." He started to hand one over.

"Can I have two?"

Sanders studied my badge. "Well, since you're a contestant…" He handed me the bottles.

"Thanks!" I tucked them happily under one arm. The stuff tasted like cherry-flavored sweat thanks to all the electrolytes, but there was nothing better for recharging magical batteries. I'd gotten hooked on Potion in Afghanistan, but I hadn't had any since I'd left the CIA.

The Arcane Corps had invented the magical energy drink during Vietnam for use by combat troops. Coke had paid a shit-ton for the Potion license in the Eighties, and the civilian version was as pricey as top shelf whiskey. The Alchemists who microbrewed it were well paid, since you can't mass-produce magic. I hadn't been able to afford it since I'd left the CIA.

Balancing my loaded tray, I headed toward an unoccupied corner. My head still pounded, and I was desperate to turn down the volume.

As I knelt to put my meal on the tent floor, a bright glow caught my attention. A lioness sprawled in regal splendor a few feet away, demolishing the contents of a tray piled high with roast, turkey and chicken. In a reversal of the men at the Ferals' table, I could see the spirit of a woman superimposed over the cat.

Must be a combat vet. By law, the only way a Feral could get a large predator Familiar was by serving in the Arcane Corps. Yet the Corps rarely assigned Familiars that size to women. Leopards or jaguars, yes, but lions, tigers and bears were reserved for the most formidable warriors the USAC could produce. They were basically the Corps' answer to Navy SEALs. The woman must have been a badass before she died.

Another stab of pain had me reaching into my shorts pocket to pull out a soft pastel stick in azure blue. The stick's powerful mystic field resonated with mine until my fingers seemed to vibrate. I'd made it myself, blending pigment, clay and acacia gum with my own powdered blood in a ritual that had taken hours. The materials an Arc uses must include something of theirs -- blood, hair, bodily fluids -- to resonate with their magic. Blood was both traditional and gave the strongest response.

I eyed the tent floor, which was fortunately made of vinyl. Good, I'd be able to draw smooth lines, something impossible to do on sand. Moving quickly, eager for relief, I drew a circle around myself, then started sketching sigils around the inner ring.

An incredulous female voice demanded, "Are you *casting* in the middle of *brunch*?"

I looked up to see pair of metallic silver platform sandals planted just outside my circle, their owner's toenails painted royal blue. The woman wore a sarong skirt wrapped around her hips, the pale blue fabric printed with long peacock feathers. It was also sheer enough to showcase the kind of sculpted legs that made men bark at the moon. She'd paired it with a royal blue bikini that revealed a sapphire belly ring. Its top framed breasts that treated gravity as something afflicting lesser women.

She had an Angelina Jolie kind of beauty -- cheekbones that could have grated cheddar setting off a lush mouth that balanced her narrow nose and square, angular jaw. Long spiral curls tumbled around her shoulders in a shimmering honey-blonde curtain.

Too bad the Victoria Secret looks came with big blue serial-killer eyes.

I let my own eyes slide a little out of focus, curious about her Talent. Her magic swirled and eddied in the distinctive patterns of a Bard, glowing so brightly I figured she probably had a recording contract if her voice was as strong as her magic.

Bracing her hands on her knees, she bent to examine the sigils I'd completed. Several men at surrounding tables stared at either her breasts or her ass, depending on their angle of view. Their eyes went as glazed as Krispy Kremes.

The laminated ID swinging on a lanyard around her neck read *Zoe Maddox*. Like my own ID, a purple stripe across the top bore white block letters: *Contestant*. "That looks like a pain-relieving spell." Zoe might not be an Arcanist, but she could read sigils.

"I have a headache." Damn it, I really should've thought about what I'd reveal by laying down a circle in front of God and my competition. *Stupid, Piper. Really, really dumb.*

She raised her head, blond brow lifting. "Ever hear of Excedrin?"

"A time or two." I eyed the swirl of her aura.

Zoe glared back, apparently imagining we were in a staring contest. I was too busy analyzing her emotions to give a damn. There was a smug green tint to her field, along with swirls of sherbet orange that suggested deception. Not the kind of girl you should turn your back on if you were allergic to knives.

"Well, I do hope your little spell helps. It would be a shame if you were unable to compete." As she spoke, her power pulsed through her aura, adding a punch of magic to her voice. Probably trying to give me a case of self-doubt, judging by the way the orange took on streaks of lime green shot with violet -- malice and pleasure at inflicting pain.

I knew that ugly combo a little too well.

A blade-sharp stab of agony radiated from my grandmother's hand as she gave my shoulder a tender pat. The social worker beamed in approval, missing the cruelty in Dawn Aleister's eyes. I tried to scream, tried to beg not to be left with her, but I couldn't move, couldn't speak…

Luckily, Maleficent Maddox didn't have a

fraction of Granny's power-- or her raw viciousness.

But I did.

I gave Zoe my best cold psycho stare. "Lots of Caliphate sorcerers could tell you I don't have a problem rising to any challenge. Too bad they aren't around to reminisce."

Her eyes widened, then narrowed. "Are you actually *threatening* me?"

"Are you actually trying to spell *me*?"

Her gaze flickered as the smug green gave way to a spike of yellow unease. "I have no idea what you're talking about."

"I can see auras with my eyes open. *I just watched you cast.*"

The yellow intensified. "Good for you." She curled a lip, turned on a platform heel and strode away, her ass rolling beneath her sarong. The men nearby watched her go with longing.

I wouldn't, boys. As soon as she came, she'd bite your head off and crunch it between her mandibles.

My stomach growled. I went back to my spell. Might as well. Damage was done now. My dinner got cold as I worked. Concentrating through the raking pain, I laid down bursts of will and magic with every stroke I drew.

I was briefly distracted by a commotion -- some Normie asshole ranting about a demon-possessed tiger -- but my throbbing head got me back on task.

When I was done, I touched the circle and sent power rolling through it. The pain faded from screeching to a bearable ache as I went numb from the spell dampening my magic. Nothing would make the pain go away completely except Aurarest, and I wouldn't be getting any of that until I won the contest. *If* I won the contest. That was a pretty big if, considering the Arcanist heavy-hitters I was competing against.

I might have brooded about my chances, but my stomach growled like an impatient Familiar. Prodded, I picked up my tray and started eating. The food was cold, but with competition like Zoe, I needed the calories.

I was comfortably stuffed and sipping PowerUp when a sudden silence fell over the crowd.

Tisha Jennings and a tiger strolled into the tent. I couldn't see his human manifestation from inside my circle, but it had to be Dave Frost. Tish had told me he'd be competing.

Dave's involvement in *Arcane Island* was quite the coup for Hammerhead Productions. If the country had Talent heroes, Dave was one of them, along with his Feral buddies, Kurt Briggs, Jake Nolan, and their respective Arcanist wives, Genevieve and Erica.

Four years ago, they'd foiled a terrorist plot to assassinate President Andrew Roth and every member of Congress in an act of black magic. Good thing, too. Roth was a Humanist asshole, but if he'd died, we'd all be in camps by now. Humanists had been predicting we'd do something evil since Talents came out of the broom closet during World War II.

A year later, Dave and friends had foiled another plot, this one by Humanist politicians who'd hired an Arcanist assassin. Adrian Fleming had attempted to engineer lethal fatalities at a Humanist protest by driving Jake insane with a spell. The conspirators hadn't seemed to care that the Feral might eat some of their own voters.

Fleming had been captured and promptly turned state's evidence, outing the politicians involved. One of them was President Roth himself, who'd been forced to resign in the resulting shitstorm. The Humanists had taken a beating in the following election, though they were already regrouping for another try.

Hero or not, though, Dave was still a tiger. Everyone in the tent watched him with a combination of fascination and unease. Melds weren't the most predictable people, since sometimes their beasts didn't play well with others.

Still, he was breathtaking. His tiger was a gorgeous animal, easily twice the size of Valeria's lioness. And that was aside from the intelligence and self-awareness in the gaze he swept over the crowd.

Damn, I thought, *I wish they'd assign us to the same team. He'd make a hell of an ally.* From the way Dave blazed, he was far more powerful than the other Ferals -- even Chris Freeman's liger. We'd romp all over the rival teams. I sighed, knowing that was exactly why the producers would never do it.

Besides, I'd never been that lucky.

Chapter Two

Dave

As one does when a tiger walks in, everyone in the tent stared.

"Mason's not the only one you terrified with all that roaring," Tisha murmured.

Which sounded like my cue. I lifted my voice in my best imitation of a 1950's borscht belt comedian. "I just flew in from Florida, and boy, are my arms tired." To spruce up that hoary old joke, I manifested a pair of airplane wings protruding from my ribs, then added puttering sound effects. After years of practice manipulating sound with my aura, I could imitate everything from the metallic boom of car crashes to my former human voice.

Now I capped the airplane routine with a long, loud farting sound and added a snare drum rimshot. The crowd rewarded me with laughter and a chorus of groans.

Heh. You can't be scared of someone who makes fart jokes -- even if he does have three-and-a-half-inch fangs.

Someone called, "You need better material, Frost!"

Recognizing the voice, I looked around. Sure enough, three familiar faces grinned at me from a nearby table.

The Arcane Corps is a very small world. Most Ferals who served in the Caliphate War know each other, either from training or deployments. Like me, all three men were Melds, though their animals' spirits inhabited their human bodies instead of the other way around. Since humans tend to live a lot longer than their critters, you usually ended up hosting your

Familiar.

Unless somebody killed you first.

Tisha followed my gaze. "Why don't you go talk to the competition while I get you a tray?"

I looked at the serving line, where everyone and the caterers were eying me nervously. "Good idea."

"What do you want?"

"Meat. Lots and lots of meat. About twenty pounds should do it." When her eyebrows lifted, I grinned. "Sorry, Tish, a can of Happy Cat ain't gonna cut it."

"Guess that case of Savory Salmon is going back to Amazon." Chuckling, she made for the buffet line while I sauntered over to my fellow vets.

"Hi, boys. Been a while."

Oscar "Oz" Nichols smirked, Feral gold eyes crinkling. "Ready to get your fuzzy butt kicked?" Oz was a Kodiak Feral, so he wasn't just trash talking. Plus, he was a big man to begin with, built like a tank, six-four and blond.

"By you?" Smilodon chuffed as I drawled, "I'm going to eat you posers for breakfast." Heads snapped in our direction, and I raised my voice. "Metaphorically! Geez, some people."

"Can you blame them?" Tyrone Navarro wasn't as big as the other two -- six feet and leanly muscled, and his Feral gold eyes seemed to glow against his dark skin. He wore his hair in long dreads that remind me of his lion's mane. "Considering the way you scared the shit out of your pilot?"

"How'd you hear about that? I just ran him off twenty minutes ago."

"He dropped by the tent looking for Jackson Gilbert and whining like a little bitch."

"He had it coming. Idiot pulled a crucifix on me

and accused me of being a demon."

Chris Freeman snorted and forked up a bite of
sausage from his heavily loaded plate. His liger
Familiar was huge, which is why Chris had named him
Kaiju -- the Japanese word for monsters the size of
Godzilla. "Should've bitten him."

"Yeah, but then I'd have to lick my ass to get the
taste out of my mouth." As they hooted, I glanced
around and froze.

There she is! My heart began to pound. "Excuse
me, fellas. I see the woman of my dreams." I started
across the tent. Yeah, I wanted to win the million for
Briggs Feral Sanctuary, but I'd really come for *her*.

She sprawled in splendor in a corner of the tent,
alone, an empty tray in front of her. She watched me
coming, regal and intimidating. Feeling like a thirteen-
year-old at the middle school prom, I tried to come up
with something clever to say.

Manifesting in all my former human glory, I
extended a hand, hoping for a handshake. "Hi. Dave
Frost. You must be Valeria Sanz."

The lioness' eyes tracked from my face to my
hand. Suddenly I understood why people found my
tiger's lack of human facial muscles so disconcerting.
Except for the occasional snarl, it's hard to tell what
we're thinking.

Smilodon tensed and sent me a mental image of
claws streaking at our nose.

When Valeria spoke, her voice was cool and
lovely and very female. She did *not* manifest to take
my hand. "Mr. Frost, I'm judging this contest, so
fraternization is not allowed. I'm not even supposed to
speak to you unless we're on camera."

Feeling like an absolute idiot, I let my hand drop.
"Oh. Okay. Maybe after the show wraps?"

Valeria turned her head away, her tufted tail flicking, and made no answer.

If I'd still been human, my face would have been redder than a traffic light.

Smiley had been right. When a female big cat played hard to get, it involved bloodshed. I certainly felt like I was bleeding. Despite my scalding embarrassment, I turned and padded away as if I didn't GAF.

Feeling someone's gaze on me, I noticed a gorgeous redhead watching me with obvious sympathy. Oddly, she was sitting on the tent floor in a magic circle, an empty tray in front of her. What the hell was that about?

Had to be an Arc. I closed my eyes to see how much power she had...

Shiiiiiiit. Given the way she blazed, she was even more powerful than Kurt Briggs's wife, Genevieve -- and Gen had more magic than Gandalf. Had to be another competitor.

I frowned, staring through my closed lids. There was something seriously screwy about her magic. It looked... tangled somehow, seething as it roiled over her skin. By comparison, Genevieve's flowed in serene currents. I'd encountered a lot of Arcanists -- terrorists and assassins included -- and none of them had had auras that fucked up. "That looks painful."

"What?" Her voice was smooth, flavored with a creamy southern drawl. Charleston, maybe, with a little New Orleans for spice.

"Your magic. The pattern is..."

"Weird." She grimaced. "I know." Angling her head at Valeria, she added, "That didn't look like much fun either."

"Yeah, but I don't give up easy." I rolled my eyes

in mock ecstasy, deflecting pity with a joke. "Those eyes, that tail…"

"Those claws."

I gave her my best toothy smirk. "That just makes it interesting."

"Hey, Dave!" Tisha called from the end of the buffet line. "Are you eating or not?"

"Coming." I glanced at the redhead and purred, "Eventually…"

As I'd intended, the Arc laughed. I padded off, satisfied that at least I'd salvaged some dignity.

Back at our table, my fellow Ferals looked equally sympathetic. "Duuude. We saw the mushroom cloud from here," Oz said.

"We're not supposed to talk to the judges," Tyrone added.

Tisha walked up with a mixing bowl, followed by a muscular dark-skinned twenty-something in jeans and a red Beyoncé concert T. He carried a tray piled with slices of roast beef, turkey, and ham. "Dave," Tish began, "you're not allowed to…"

"… Talk to the judges. So I've been told. Repeatedly."

Both she and her helper hesitated, looking from me to the table. Knowing what they were thinking, I said, "I'd crush that folding chair like a Coors can. Gimme." I manifested an arm to take the bowl and put it down on the tarp floor in front of me. Judging by the faint glow of the liquid inside, it contained PowerUp. The kid knelt to set out the tray.

As I started to tuck in, a dark-skinned girl -- probably a production assistant -- rushed over to mutter something to Tish.

"Excuse me," the show runner said, and hurried off with the PA.

Tish's helper gave me a dazzled grin. He was a good-looking guy, with a long, angular face. His hair was cut in a trendy taper fade, the curly hair a bit longer on top. "I'm a big fan. Did you really do *all* the voices for *Medal of Honor*? I loved that game."

His enthusiasm made me smile, reducing the acid sting of Valeria's rejection. "Glad you liked it. That was a fun project." And it had paid well, too. Keeping Briggs Feral Sanctuary in catnip mice wasn't exactly cheap.

Kurt Briggs, my former lieutenant, had taken me in after my parents' neighbors tried to firebomb our farm. I was damn well going to help him provide for all the other big cats he rescued.

I owed him.

The kid licked his lips. "Could I... Could I get a selfie?"

"Ahhh..." I knew what to do with bigots, but star-struck Dave fans made me feel a little uncomfortable. "... Sure."

He started to reach for his back pocket, and his face fell. "Oh, shit. I don't have my cell." None of us were allowed to have phones for fear we'd leak the show's secrets on social media.

"Maybe after we wrap?" I suggested. Out of curiosity, I closed my eyes to check the patterns of magic rolling through his aura. "Primo, right?"

"Yep. Kordell Armstrong." Face lighting up in a grin, he stuck out a long-fingered hand.

I manifested an arm and shook it. Kordell returned my glowing grip with an enthusiastic pump as his name rang a bell. "You did that TikTok video with the dance that went viral. Moon something, right? That was nice work."

"You saw Moon Bounce?" His smile amped to

incandescent. "Yeah, I got a ton of followers off that. Shot my numbers right up. Nowhere near as many as you've got, but I was happy with it."

"It was good choreography. I'm not surprised it went viral. As to my channel..." I shrugged. "... Everybody shares cat videos."

"Yeah," Oz cracked. "You and fluffy, big-eyed kittens."

"You're just jealous."

"You betcha ass. Happy Cat never offered *me* a contract."

"You also didn't have to eat cat food on camera. That stuff tastes of ass and despair."

Ty Navarro smirked. "Not asking how you know how ass tastes."

"Tiger. I eat all kinds of things. That blonde in the blue bikini looks especially yummy."

Laughing, Kordell waved. "I'll let you get back to your breakfast. Catch you later."

Watching him go, Oz said, "We were never that young."

"And if we were, it wasn't for long," I agreed, hoping Kordell's experiences on *Arcane Island* didn't burn all that bright enthusiasm into bitterness.

Of course, he wouldn't have to kill anybody. That should help.

Smiley went to work on our pile of food with his usual single-minded intensity, pinning down slabs of meat with our paws and tearing off strips. I let him take care of refueling while I went right on bonding with the boys.

As we ate, my gaze fell on the Arc with the tangled aura, who was sipping a bottle of PowerUp and watching me as if fascinated. "Who's that redhead Arcanist? She glows like a welder's torch."

Chris followed my gaze. "Ariel Piper. Went on a couple missions with my team in Afghanistan, defusing MEEDs. She's scary as hell."

Coming from a guy who could manifest a thousand-pound cat, that was saying something. "Scary? She looks like the Little Mermaid." And what the hell had her parents been thinking, naming her Ariel?

"You haven't seen her work. One time we were patrolling this village. Piper always took point because she can see spells without closing her eyes. Somebody in a burqa steps out of this house, almost runs her down. She whirls, plants her hand in his forehead, and *POW!* Burqa boy goes down. And doesn't get back up."

"Burqa *Boy*?" Burqas were the long black robes worn by women in conservative Moslem countries. Since those folks weren't in the habit of competing on RuPaul's *Drag Race*..."Suicide vest?"

"Yep," Chris said. "He was wearing enough explosives to kill us -- and everybody else in the surrounding block. Piper punched his ticket before he had a chance to set it off. Disrupted the explosives too, just with that one pop on the head." He shook his head. "It put her flat on her ass for a day afterward, but we'd have all died otherwise."

Tyrone's brows flew up. "She killed the guy by *touching* him? I've known Arcanists who could deal some nasty jolts that way, but I've never heard of one being able to send you on a dirt nap."

"Even Indigo Ford couldn't do that," I agreed, remembering the terrorist who'd made our lives hell four years ago. "Thank God. That bitch did enough damage is it was."

"Yep. Ariel was reassigned after that. Rumor is

she got attached to a CIA wet-works team. We missed her -- best Arc we ever had. Seeing magic is *handy*."

"Huh," I said. "Usually people with that much power aren't that sensitive."

"Ariel's the exception."

"So why is someone like that competing on a reality show?" Oz asked. "She could be pulling down six figures in the corporate world."

"Yeah, but a million bucks is a million bucks," Ty pointed out.

As we watched, Tisha came back in the tent and headed over to speak to her. The Arc got up and followed her to our table. Looking uncharacteristically nervous, Tish said, "Dave, if you're finished eating, I was wondering if we could have a few minutes of your time?"

I glanced down at my tray. While I'd been running my magical mouth, Smilodon had demolished our meal. "Yeah, we're done." I rose. "See you guys later."

They all said their goodbyes and we followed Tish out. As we walked, Ariel extended a hand to me. "Ariel Piper."

"Dave Frost." I manifested an arm to give her a firm clasp. Pain stung my mani's mystical fingers as if there were razors jutting from her skin. After the Burqa Boy story, my instinct was to jerk away, but I'm a stubborn SOB. I tightened my hold instead.

And the pain faded. Closing my eyes to check what was happening, I saw the currents of her aura lose their jagged contours, untangling until the magic flowed more smoothly against mine.

When I opened my eyes again, Ariel was staring at me, her lips parted as if stunned.

"What's going on?" Tisha gave Ariel a

sympathetic look. "Your magic giving you fits again?"

"It was." There was wonder in her pretty blue eyes. "Not anymore."

* * *

Ariel

The tiger looked up at me, blazing with the combined magic of Familiar and man.

His manifested hand released mine, and my aura slowly began to kink again, stinging like a mild sunburn. Still, it was far less intense than it had been. I had to fight the impulse to grab for him, hungry for more of that cooling relief. Even my blocking spell hadn't killed the pain so completely.

Somehow contact with Dave Frost's powerful aura had stabilized mine.

Tisha eyed us, then shook her head as if dismissing an inconsequential mystery. "We need to talk."

She led us out of the tent and across the beach toward Jackson Gilbert's Bali-style main house, currently serving as the production team's headquarters. It was a stunning structure built of bamboo bent in long curving arcs, its roof thatched over teak support beams. The whole island had an eco-tourism vibe, right down to its wind-turbine-generated electricity.

Not that I gave a fuck about the decor. I was too busy trying to figure out exactly how Dave had just done what he had. And was it something he could do again?

A guard nodded at Tisha but didn't stop us as she led the way up the steps to the house's wide veranda. A cluster of fiddle-leaf fig trees in ceramic pots screened a pair of rattan grand peacock chairs with fat cream cushions. I dropped into one of them, settling against its high fan-shaped back, my gaze fixed on the tiger as he sank to his belly on the bamboo flooring. He really was enormous -- his head was easily three times the size of mine.

Hmm. His ears were angled back. If it meant the same thing as when my cat did that, he was uneasy about something. His tail flicked back and forth like a metronome.

"So we've got this idea," Tisha began, leaning toward us in her seat. She lowered her voice until I had to strain to hear her over the sound of the wind and the screech of seagulls. "We want to do a showmance."

That jolted me out of my Dave fog. I'd researched reality shows when I'd decided to do *Arcane Island,* and I knew a showmance was a romance between two cast members. *She can't possibly mean...*

"Me and Valeria?" Dave asked, sitting up. His ears rotated forward like Floofinator's when she heard the can opener.

Tisha shot him an impatient look. "I told you, you can't even talk to Valeria except when she's judging. I mean you and Ariel."

I'd been afraid of that. "You're kidding."

"Nope. We want you to have a showmance with Dave."

The tiger's mouth dropped open, exposing impressive fangs as his eyes rounded. "Are you out of your mind? *Too many legs!*"

Tisha frowned, clearly puzzled. "What?"

He manifested a hand and waved it. "Private joke. Which wasn't very damn funny to start with. This is even less so."

"Do I have to remind you that bestiality is illegal?" I demanded, thoroughly disgusted. I should have seen this coming. Any deal that sounded this good was bound to blow up in my face. That was the way my luck always ran.

"We're not talking about having *sex*," Tisha said impatiently. "You'd just kiss his manifestation. The visuals would be amazing."

"So would the death threats on my Twitter feed."

Tisha's dark eyes narrowed, taking on a black-ice glint. "May I remind you, *you signed a contract*. You agreed to attempt the challenges you're given. You're being paid well, even aside from the shot at the million. Plus, we footed the bill for your Aurarest for the past few months. If you back out now, you're going to owe the company fifty thousand in reimbursement for drug costs, because that shit doesn't come cheap. And that's aside from the judgment when we sue your ass for breach of contract. Which you will lose."

"Drug costs?" Dave's tail twitched as he looked from me to the show runner. "For what?"

Glaring at Tish, I growled, "I have Kimura Syndrome."

"That's what's causing the thing with your aura?"

"That's the one."

"And the treatment for it costs ten grand a month," Tisha said coldly. "Which Hammerhead Productions has been paying for since she signed the contract."

He eyed me. "Did the meds stop working or what?"

"I had to get off the Aurarest to compete. It blunts my abilities too much."

"That sucks."

"If you break that contract, you'd better get used to the pain," Tish said. Yeah, Hammerhead

Productions' rep for playing hardball was well deserved.

My stomach clenched as I realized I couldn't afford to tell the showrunner to go fuck a coconut tree. Even aside from being sued, I needed that prize money. And not just so I could afford my prescription. It was my only chance to get out from under the parade of ruthless assholes who'd made my life a living hell since I was thirteen. "Fine, God damn it," I spat. "I'll do it. I can't take much more of this shit."

"And you *knew* that." Dave stared at Tisha, his gold gaze so menacing, I found myself edging back. "You figured that of the female contestants, Ariel was the one who'd agree to the *Beauty and the Beast* bit. Because she's just that desperate."

Tisha winced. "Look, I'm sorry. It wasn't my idea. Jackson thought…" She flicked a hand. "… It would humanize the Ferals. People are suckers for romance."

"As I recall," the tiger drawled, "the reason Humanists gave for opposing gay marriage is folks would want to marry people like *me* next. They'll lose their fucking minds."

I snorted. "How would you be able to tell?"

Tisha leaned her elbows on her knees and dialed the earnest up to eleven. "Dave, I wouldn't push this if I didn't think it would help the Talent cause. If we can show that you're like any other guy, just trapped in a tiger's body…"

"Yeah, right. We'll be lucky if they don't start burning crosses in front of BFS again. That crap is why I had to do this to begin with. Donations go in the shitter when you're picketed by assholes with AR-15s."

Tisha glowered. "I'm telling you, this show will make you so popular, they won't dare give you any trouble."

"Don't piss on my head and tell me it's raining." His ears pinned flat against the huge skull in question. *"I don't like it."*

I'll give her one thing: she didn't back down from all that enraged tiger. Either she had ice water in her veins, or she thought Dave was a lot more harmless than I did. "Will you do it or not?"

Rumbling a deeply pissed sound, he turned to give me a long look. "If I say no, what happens to Ariel?"

I blinked. What did he care? He didn't even know me.

"You'll both be in breach. And we'll sue the shit out of you. *And* your Tiger King buddy, since he gets the money for his cat sanctuary."

A familiar grating voice screeched, "I'll get you, my pretty. You and your little dog, too!" Sounded exactly like the Wicked Witch from *The Wizard of Oz.* I'd heard Dave do imitations on his YouTube videos, but I hadn't realized how startling it was in person.

"Well?" Tisha demanded, refusing to be distracted.

He looked away, his tail lashing so hard I expected to hear a bullwhip *crack.* "All right. Fine. Yeah, I'll fake your fuckin' B story."

"Thank you," Tisha said, her tone too polite. She glanced down at her watch and rose to her feet. "Look, I've got to set up for this afternoon's production meeting. I have to go." She paused, looking down at us, frowning. "I really am sorry about this." Then she vanished through the double doors into the house.

"'I have to set up for the meeting,' my striped ass," Dave growled. "She wanted to get out while the getting was good."

"Probably. I..." Suddenly it felt as if a knife had plunged into my guts and twisted. The shock of it bent me double, swearing, as pain scoured my skin like steel wool.

Alarmed, Dave jolted to his feet. "What's happening? Do I need to get Tish to call the doctor?" Reality shows had to have an on-site physician to get insured.

Clinging to the rattan chair arms, I concentrated on breathing through the pain. "No, there's... there's nothing... there's nothing they can do. Whenever I get... get upset, it can trigger attacks." The pain intensified, and I clenched my teeth against a scream.

Glowing hands caught my wrists. Instantly, a wave of cooling relief surged through me.

Astonished, I looked down at the shining fingers and watched my tangled aura smooth. The burn snuffed out as if hit with a fire extinguisher. "Wow."

I looked up. Dave had manifested, his human form shining against the background of the palms. I stared at him in wonder. He'd probably never been handsome, but he'd have been striking with that long, strong-featured face and leanly muscled build. Especially clad in an Arcane Corps uniform.

Dave blinked, probably at my awed expression. "What?" He frowned. "What's going on, Ariel?"

"Touching you makes it better. Why does touching you make it better?"

Dave looked down at where his hands gripped my arms, then closed his eyes so he could see my aura. "It does seem to help. Weird. Wonder why? I mean, I'm not *trying* to do anything."

"Probably something about the way our auras interact." I sighed. The relief almost made me feel dizzy. "Hell, who knows? I don't understand what causes the problem to begin with."

His manifestation's lips tightened. Unlike the rest of Dave's angular face, his mouth looked soft. "Maybe I can teach you some of the techniques Genevieve Briggs and I developed when we were fighting those terrorists. We might be able to figure out a way you can control your Kimura's, too."

"What kind of techniques?"

"Gen can use me as a battery whenever she's doing a particularly tricky spell. She came up with it when Indigo Ford was trying to break Gen's ward so her husband could eat us. Trust me, you don't want to be a polar bear's chew toy."

On sheer impulse, I reached up and cupped Dave's manifested face in my hands. He felt as warm and solid as flesh and blood. Yet my aura swirled at the contact, its normally jagged contours sliding across my skin like skeins of silk. "That's really kind of you." I thought of the showmance Tish wanted. *Maybe this won't be all that bad after all.*

Impulsively, I leaned forward and kissed Dave's manifestation right on his glowing mouth. His eyes widened. The taste of his magic flooded over my tongue to roll down my throat like brandy mixed with warmed honey -- thick and sweet. Every hair on my body rose in a wave of erotic heat. I hummed in delight.

Dave jerked away as if my lips had burned him. "Don't do that," he said roughly. "Don't do that unless it's for the cameras. Not like it's real." He slipped from my grasping fingers like the ghost he resembled. His manifestation vanished as the tiger whirled and leaped off the porch.

I jumped to my feet. "Dave! I didn't mean…"

But he'd already disappeared into the trees.

Yet my pain didn't come back. For the first time since I'd been fired from the CIA, I felt hope. Maybe there was a way to win this thing. Maybe just this once, there was a way not to lose.

* * *

Up on the balcony overlooking the front of the great house, Jackson Gilbert watched the tiger race away from the porch. *I'll need to ask Tish what's going on. Could be something I could use there.*

He'd miscalculated badly in sneering at the Humanists who were so convinced Talents had a deal with Satan. Now throwing his financial weight against their movement had come back to bite him on the ass. Yeah, they were idiots. But they were also idiots whose support he needed.

He was so fucking *bored*.

When Jackson had been young, making money was the ultimate high. It had also been a necessity if he'd wanted to escape the grinding poverty of his childhood. And he'd done just that. Of course, he'd had a lot of help from Ray Jennings, who could talk anybody into anything, legal or not. Between Ray's Bard gift and his own brilliance, they'd been millionaires by age twenty-five.

Too bad about Ray, really. He'd been useful, but he'd also been a bit *too* good.

For years, getting richer had been Jackson's favorite game, especially if he'd had to skirt the law a bit to do it. The danger had just added spice. Besides, risk was manageable if you had someone with sufficient Talent on your side. Though of course, you had to make damn sure they didn't turn the tables on you. That, too, had been part of the buzz.

People saw Bards as harmless entertainers strutting around in sequined costumes. Ray had proved a good Bard was more dangerous than any Arc terrorist. All the terrorist could do was kill you. A Bard could change your mind, whether you wanted it changed or not. That was, ultimately, why he'd had no choice but to get rid of his old friend.

Thing was, making money no longer excited Jackson as it once had. He was one of the richest men on the planet. With his investments, he could make millions just sitting on his ass. He needed a fresh challenge. A new risk. The bigger the better.

There was the traditional wealthy pastime of philanthropy, but Jackson had never seen the appeal in giving human flotsam his hard-earned money. Though making people grovel *could* be entertaining. For a while, he'd contemplated going up against Bezos, Branson and Musk for control of the space tourism business. Thing was, he'd never gotten that worked up about technology. He liked pitting himself against other humans.

But politics -- now *there* was an interesting challenge. He'd seriously considered getting involved with the Constitutionalists, but they had no instinct for the jugular. They were too handicapped by trying to manage the vast herd of cats -- figurative and literal -- who made up their voter base. He didn't have the patience for the bullshit. Too, they already had their anointed one all picked out.

Besides, the real energy and passion lay with the Humanists. Any group that hated that hard could be useful if you harnessed their energy. Though you did have to be careful the unintended consequences didn't bite you on the ass afterward.

That could be exciting in itself. The first challenge would be convincing them his political 360 was genuine. He hadn't exactly made a secret of his low opinion of their collective intelligence.

Satan? *Really*?

The Humanist Party badly needed someone sane in charge. The idea of putting Talents in camps was a prime example of how loony tunes their current leadership was. Exterminating Talents was the equivalent of destroying America's nuclear arsenal. Everyone from Putin to the remnants of the Caliphate would start launching magical attacks within weeks of the camp doors clanging shut.

Besides, did they really think the Talents would go down without a fight? Given that the most powerful Arcanists and Ferals were all combat vets, they could do real damage. The result would be chaos. Wall Street wouldn't like that at all. Even Jackson might lose money, and he'd gotten richer during the Great Recession.

He really needed to take the reins for the good of the country.

But pulling it off would require a big, showy change of heart. He'd need to give them a reason to believe his conversion was genuine. Something that would allow him to announce -- with suitable sorrow -- that he'd had no idea of the evil Talents could do.

The Humanists would eat up that idea with a spoon. For one of the richest Constitutionalists on the planet to admit he was wrong -- that the rabble had been right -- they'd *love* that. They'd flock to his banner.

Just in time for his presidential run.

His heart beat faster just thinking about it.

Chapter Three

Dave

I stalked through the coconut trees, trying not to remember the brush of Ariel's lips against mine. It had been the first time in five years a woman had touched me, *looked* at me as if I were a man and not some combo plate of a ghost and an animal.

And what a woman. Even when I'd been human, the attention of someone like Ariel would have dazzled me. I hadn't been a hunk like Kurt or Jake even when I was alive. Now... Yeah, I sometimes got fascinated stares -- hell, I was a *tiger* -- but none of those women would have given my human body a second look.

Yet for one glorious moment, Ariel had gazed at me with gratitude and desperation, as if I were her salvation. I'd always wanted someone to look at me like that.

Which was the whole problem. She didn't want *me*, she wanted an end to her pain. I was the equivalent of that ten-thousand-dollar prescription she couldn't afford. She'd probably look at a free bottle of pills the same way.

The trouble was, that kiss had meant a hell of a lot more than that to me. I remembered the way her lips had felt against mine -- soft, hot. *Real.*

If I wasn't damn careful, I'd fall in love with her. Then I'd really be screwed.

What I needed was Valeria. Yeah, she came with a big neon *Beware of the bitch* sign, but at least she was my own kind. The minute Ariel got access to her meds, she'd drop me like a six-hundred-pound rock. The illusion of being seen as a man and then having it ripped away would be more devastating than never having it at all. I'd be better off with Valeria. Assuming

I could get her to give me anything beyond a sneer.

But I also couldn't stand to deny Ariel whatever help I could give her. One look had told me she was clinging to the ragged edge by her fingernails. I knew what that kind of desperation felt like. When I'd first melded with Smiley, I'd felt the same. My dad had to lock up the guns to keep me from self-medicating with a bullet.

At that thought, Smilodon gave a pained moan of distress.

No, I'm not going to do that to you. It wouldn't have been fair to steal whatever time the cat had left in our short life. It wasn't Smiley's fault that I'd gotten myself killed. The cat wanted to live enough for both of us. Suicide was a purely human concept...

I heard an all-too-familiar sound -- a gasp of terror. I looked up.

And there on the sandy path ahead of me, stood Raven Garland, the woman who'd supplied the soundtrack of my childhood. When I was a kid, Mom had owned every CD that Bard had cut. I'd gotten my first kiss to Raven singing "Magic Hands," in that pure, haunting contralto with its three-octave range. Even now, I had a Spotify playlist just for her stuff.

Raven was older now, of course -- about Mom's age, though she looked little older than she had when her videos dominated MTV. Somewhere there was an Arcanist with one hell of a facelift spell. I'd have to ask Gen if Raven was her client.

But even as I grinned in delighted recognition, Raven's green eyes went huge. She started backing away, her face paling until it almost matched her spikey platinum hair.

Oh shit, just what I needed. "I'm a huge fan." I sounded a little panicky even to myself. "Can I have your autograph? Mom would never forgive me if I…"

The soundtrack of my childhood whirled and hurried off through the trees. Not running. Quite. It was hardly the first time somebody taken one look at me and ghosted, though this time the sting was sharper than usual.

I sighed. This was why I had no illusions a relationship with Ariel was even remotely possible. Didn't matter how she looked at me. I still had too many legs.

Smilodon made a questioning rumble. Illusionary fur seemed to rub against my skin as if the cat curled around me. *Don't sweat it, Smiley.* I manifested a hand to scratch myself behind one round ear. It wasn't the kind of thing I did in front of people, even Kurt. But Smilodon enjoyed it, and the tiger deserved whatever strokes I could give him.

Just as I turned to start the other way, a young Black woman ran up, clipboard in hand. A pretty girl in her early twenties, she wore the standard PA uniform of jeans and an *Arcane Island* T-shirt. A walkie-talkie crackled from a clip on her lush hips, and her wildly swinging lanyard ID read *Jenny Stone, Production Assistant.* "There you are! You're needed for the briefing about tomorrow's shoot, Mr. Frost."

Of course I was. "Lead on."

* * *

After going through the gauntlet of security guards again, we assembled in the craft tent as Tish went over the schedule. First, we'd shoot the team assignments all morning before our lunch break. Then in the afternoon, we'd confront our first challenge with our new teammates. In the evening, we'd learn our scores from the judges before the teams would adjourn to our bungalows for the night.

It was going to be a hell of a day, so I was more than ready when PA Jenny guided me to the teak stairs that led to the house's second-floor bedrooms. Most of the cast were sharing rooms, but those of us with fur got to sleep alone.

"I'm a Talent too," Jenny told me. "A Bard. Nowhere near powerful enough to be on the show, of course, but I'm a good writer." She started describing the script she was working on, and I realized she was pitching it to me. Like I'd have any pull at all because I'd played a Feral sidekick in a movie.

I contained my sigh and listened politely. When you're a fuzzy murder machine, it's a good idea to establish yourself as a nice guy. Could reduce the size of the inevitable torch-wielding mob.

The room she showed me to looked like a giant bird's nest. An egg-shaped space with woven wicker walls and bamboo flooring, it held a nightstand, a TV/bureau combo, and a tiger bed. The bed was the same basic shape as the house cat version, except ten feet across and made of thick rubber over a tough, padded core. Three-inch claws are hell on bedding, especially given the nightmares.

"Tomorrow we'll move your bed to the bungalow you'll be assigned to with the rest of your team," Jenny told me, eying it dubiously. "Is it okay? It doesn't look that comfortable."

"You'd be surprised," I said. "I've got one just like it at home." My folks had spent far too much on the bed shortly after I'd had to move to BFS. They'd been feeling guilty about the debacle at our horse farm. I have no idea why. It wasn't their fault one of the neighbors firebombed the place. We were lucky we got it put out. As it was, we lost a horse barn and ten Familiar horses.

The memory still pissed me off because those assholes *knew* me. They knew I wasn't a fucking Satanist. When I'd been a kid, Mom dragged me to church every Sunday. They'd watched me get baptized. I'd literally *died for my country*, and they'd still tried to burn the farm down. To add insult to injury, the fucker who'd done it was acquitted a year later.

No way could I live with my folks after that. I knew one of the bastards would try again. I'd been lucky Kurt's dad had offered me a place at BFS when he'd heard about the fire.

Fred had founded Briggs Feral Sanctuary in the 1990s as a home for retired Familiars, though he'd ended up opening the sanctuary to regular big cats too. The no-nonsense old bastard had given me a reason to live and helped me get my head on straight. Even though I'd been a foul-mouthed, bitter prick at first, he'd never lost patience.

Then he'd been murdered, despite everything Kurt and I had done in a futile effort to save him. But this time I was going to repay Fred, Kurt and BFS.

I was damned well going to win that million. Even if it meant risking my heart to the emotional buzzsaw that was Ariel Piper.

* * *

I woke the next morning to the sound of a fist hitting the bamboo door in demanding thumps. "Mr. Frost? Mr. Frost, it's time to assemble in the craft services tent for the morning briefing."

"Yeah, yeah," I muttered, peeling my eyes open and dragging myself out of the tiger bed. Smilodon produced a low, moaning grumble of irritation. Tigers slept a lot more than humans and trying to force my cat's biological clock to match human hours never went over very well. "I'm up."

There was a long pause outside the door. "...
Good." Judging by the thoroughly freaked-out note in
the man's voice, he was disconcerted by Smiley's
grumbling. "We really need to head to the tent, Mr.
Frost. You don't want to be late."

"Give me a minute. I need to brush my teeth. I
have morning breath like you wouldn't believe."

"You do that?" Then hastily, as if afraid of
offending, he added, "Sure. I'll be right here."

Manifesting an arm, I absently reached back to
scratch an itch on Smiley's furry ass as we padded over
the laminated bamboo floor into the suite's bathroom.
As I'd requested, there on the teak vanity sat a tube of
the toothpaste specially formatted for use by Familiars
and Melds. We reared up on our hind legs, braced our
paws against the vanity, and bared our fangs. I
manifested hands, squeezed toothpaste onto the brush,
and went to work brushing our thirty teeth.

I smiled, remembering the first time I did this
job. Smiley had been a cub and I'd been a green recruit,
insanely proud at being assigned a tiger of my very
own. Cat in my lap, I'd gently brushed the six-week-
old's needle fangs while he tried to gnaw on my
fingers. Now I had even more reason to make damn
sure he didn't lose any teeth.

The mint toothpaste tasted odd, since Smilodon
didn't perceive flavor as I once had. A cat has only
about 500 taste buds compared to a human's 9,000,
though Smiley's acute sense of smell made up for a lot.
The fact food no longer tasted the same had been one
of the toughest things to get used to.

As I pushed the door open with a glowing arm
protruding from one tiger shoulder, the production
assistant stepped back. A skinny redhead in jeans and

an *Arcane Island* shirt, he had nervous eyes and a scraggly beard that fought valiantly to cover his chin.

"Hi," I said, hoping to set him at ease. "How you doing, Tim?"

His eyes widened. "How'd you know my name?"

"You're wearing an ID badge."

"You can read?" The kid instantly froze, looking horrified at the taste of the Converse Chuck Taylor he'd just shoved in his own mouth.

I sighed and set off down the hall in the direction I'd come the night before. "Don't sweat it. Everybody else is surprised too."

"Uh… I'm really sorry." Tim hurried after me, all but babbling. "The set and equipment are all in position for the morning shoot. Each of the contestants is assigned a shooter who's supposed to focus just on you. There are other cameras assigned to get the wides, along with the Steadicam guys. We've even got drones for the aerial shots."

It wasn't yet dawn outside, and safety lights illuminated the crushed shell path to the craft services tent. We had to wait in line for the guards to check our ID. Evidently they thought a Humanist tiger terrorist might menace the island.

As we stepped inside, the PA asked, "What would you like for breakfast? I'm supposed to get it for you."

"Scrambled eggs and all the meat you can get your hands on," I said. "Oh, and get me a bowl of PowerUp from the Alchemist, would you?"

"Will do." He joined the long line that wound past the buffet.

I'd turned toward the table where Chris Freeman was sitting -- the other Ferals were still in line -- when a familiar voice asked, "Dave?"

Ariel stood holding a tray and looking a little anxious. When I closed my eyes, her magic looked even more snarled than it had the day before. "Morning, Ariel."

"I… Uh… wondered if you wanted to sit with me."

"Sure." I felt a little bad about running out on her. She might be using me, but I couldn't really blame her. That kind of pain is maddening. "How long did last night's treatment last?"

She flashed me a tight smile. "Until I woke up this morning. It's pretty bad right now. Stress tends to do that."

And with the challenges starting today, she'd be under a hell of a lot of stress.

Ariel led me to the back of the tent where she sat down with her legs crossed tailor fashion. This put my head above hers, and I blinked at the gesture of trust. Plunking my furry butt on the vinyl, I settled down on my belly.

Leaning forward, Ariel braced her elbows on her knees, her gaze flicking across my face as if studying the swirl of my aura. "They're probably going to put us on the same team, given this showmance thing."

I tried to ignore the tempting cleavage her position displayed. Her shorts and low-cut crop top were cotton, both in a pink floral pattern. Probably a good choice for shooting on a sunny day in the Bahamas.

I just hoped my furry face wasn't showing anything incriminating. Like lust.

"Look," she began earnestly, "I'm sorry about yesterday. I wouldn't like it either if someone forced a kiss on me."

I blinked. "You didn't exactly *force* it on me."

"If I hadn't, you wouldn't have been so upset."

I inhaled, breathing in her scent, which held none of the acridity of a lie. She really was embarrassed. There was also a bitter top-note of pain running over the floral odor of her shampoo. Smilodon moaned softly, drawing alarmed glances from those at nearby tables. I ignored them and manifested a hand. "Don't worry about it. Let's see what I can do."

"Thanks, I appreciate it." She looked so relieved, I realized she hadn't been sure I'd help.

"I wouldn't leave you in pain just because I got pissed."

"Some people would."

"I'm not that kind of asshole." I let an artistic pause fall. "I'm a whole 'nother *species.*"

She grinned as I'd intended. "What species is that?"

"*Panthera Tigris Prickasaurus.* Gimme." I waved my glowing fingers. She put her hand in mine. I willed my aura to slide around hers, applying psychic pressure. Her blue eyes widened.

When I closed my eyes to check, the furious churn of her magic had already begun to slow, its currents unkinking, smoothing. "When we get a chance, I can show you those techniques Gen and I came up with."

"I've got your dinner, Mr. Frost." The PA hurried up with a mounded tray across one arm, a bowl of PowerUp in the other hand. He paused, looking uncertain as he tried to decide how to put them both down without spilling them.

"Here, I'll take that," Ariel said, and took care of the tray with her free hand. The PA put the bowl down and retreated.

I let Smiley attack our breakfast and gripped her slender fingers, concentrating on slowing down the grind of her aura. A few minutes later, Ariel relaxed and drew in a breath. "Thank you." Her voice sounded a little rough.

"No problem." Having her gratitude made me feel way too good. *Bad idea, Frost. We're talking a stick-a-fork-in-a-light-socket level of dumbassery.*

"Listen up, people." Silence fell as Tisha Jennings rose from her seat, a microphone in one hand. "Welcome to *Arcane Island*. We'll be assigning your teams today, and you'll face your first magical challenge." Her dark eyes swept over the crowd, picking out the contestants. "I don't have to tell you how important this show is, not just to you personally, but to the Talent community. This is our opportunity to make the Normies see us as real people instead of the satanic 'Other' the Humanists accuse us of being."

She paused, as if allowing each of us to remember exactly what it was like being on the receiving end of those accusations. Most of us had encountered them a *lot*, even the ones who weren't furry. "If they can see us work and strive to succeed, they'll start to care about us. Maybe even like us." Her face went grim. "And you don't put people you like in camps."

The tent went still. Not even the silverware clinked.

"Over the next six weeks, we're going to ask you to do some things that will be difficult and challenging -- and which will probably piss you off."

The crowd laughed, though I noticed the Talents with contestant IDs looked more tense than amused.

"Today's challenge will be a case in point." Tisha walked to the whiteboard someone had set up on an easel. "We'll spend the morning shooting the team assignments, then this afternoon we'll move on to the first challenge." She picked up a dry erase pen and began to sketch. "We've constructed four cages in the bay…"

As we listened to her description of the challenge, Ariel leaned toward me and murmured, "This is going to suck."

I could see why she'd think so: the toughest element of the challenge was going to be up to her. "You can handle it," I said, and hoped to hell I was right.

* * *

With breakfast over, the sixteen contestants got wired for sound as the audio engineers showed us how to attach tiny lavalier mics and waterproof battery packs. The humans hid them in their clothing, but a tech presented me with a wide collar rigged with both a mic and its battery. It also had a set of plastic windows on either side I suspected was for a name card.

The poor tech looked so spooked I took it away from him and manifested to buckle it on. Smiley didn't even twitch an ear, used to tolerating indignities from our days in the Corps.

That done, we all assembled out on the beach in the center of a small forest of lights that were to fill in the shadows cast by the rising sun. A couple of audio teams held boom mics overhead to catch any sound the lavaliers didn't. Five or so armed guards stood around, wearing flat expressions I suspected concealed extreme boredom.

And that didn't even count the cameras. We were surrounded by enough shooters to make even me blink, despite my movie-making experience. The equipment ranged from the kind of shoulder-held cameras you see in television news to tripod-mounted ones to the expensive Steadicams that create a gliding effect. The Steadi operators wore elaborate harnesses to support the cameras' ungainly gyroscopic systems, making them look like futuristic cyborgs. Meanwhile, drones buzzed overhead like giant Jurassic mosquitoes.

Ariel joined me and my fellow Ferals as we gathered in a tense little knot.

"They didn't have this many cameras on *Feral Revenge*," I told her, remembering the blockbuster I'd worked on a couple of years before. "We won't be able to scratch our butts without it being captured for posterior."

Ariel grinned. "You mean posterity."

I smirked up at Oz. "Not with this many assholes."

Oz eyed me. "The pun is the lowest form of humor."

"Only to those without the wit to make them." God, I love a good straight man.

"That leaves you out, then," he shot back.

"That's not what your mother said."

We killed time snarking at each other like that while Candice Green, the director, arranged us contestants to her satisfaction.

Between us and the ocean stood four narrow vertical banners arranged in a half circle, each in vivid colors with the name of one of the show's four teams: Wizards, Sorcerers, Oracles, and Mystics. In the bay beyond stood four huge cages on stilts -- the sets for the day's challenge.

"Quiet on the set!" Assistant director Anton Boyko called, as the show's host, Amelia Sharp, prepared to launch into her opening spiel.

Sharp was a stiletto-slim brunette who'd hosted two cable reality shows. She had a smile that never reached her eyes and ambitions of being the next Jeff Probst.

Someone moved to the front with a digital timecode slate and snapped it, producing a sharp clap the video editors would later use to sync the footage and sound.

"Action!" Green called, and the host smoothly launched into her opening. Sharp was a Bard, and as she spoke her magic rolled over the contestants, who went still, listening to her intently. Even I felt the tug of her power.

As we'd anticipated, Ariel and I soon found ourselves standing under the same turquoise banner. It read "Mystics" in a spiky peach font that suggested sigils.

Sharp handed her a turquoise and peach Mystics T-shirt, and Ariel put it on over her top. Since I'd been the first assigned, I'd already slotted a pair of Mystics name cards into my collar.

Our third teammate turned out to be Kordell Armstrong, the hero-worshiping Primo who'd asked for a selfie. I smiled as he slipped on his T-shirt and trotted over.

"I can't believe we're on the same team." Kordell grinned wide enough to show his gums. "Wait'll my folks find out."

I was considerably less pleased when Sharp called Raven Garland's name.

Raven didn't move, staring at me as she went dead white. "That's not going to work!" The Bard's voice was tight with strangled panic.

"That's putting it mildly," I murmured in

disgust. "This is going to be a problem."

Ariel frowned at me. "What?"

Raven hurried over to Sharp, her shooter following, and started arguing with the host in a low, desperate voice.

"What's she saying?" Ariel demanded. "I can't hear her over the surf."

"Shhh," I said, listening with my far more sensitive tiger hearing.

"You don't understand," Raven protested. "I can't. I *told* Tisha what happened to Roger…"

Roger? Something teased my memory, but I couldn't quite pull it up.

"Team assignments aren't up for negotiations," Sharp snapped, her voice pitched to carry clearly. "You're going to have to deal with your fear or you can kiss that million goodbye."

"It's not that easy!" she wailed. "I still have nightmares, and it's been thirty years. I could handle one of the other Ferals, but that tiger…"

"You'll have to make it work, because you're either on Team Mystics or Team *nothing*." Sharp stabbed a finger at us in a gesture that said the argument was over. She thrust the Mystics shirt at the Bard, who took it and reluctantly put it on over her trendy powder blue cotton T.

As the singer turned, she caught sight of all the cameras focused on her. Her eyes widened. Blanking her expression, Raven pulled her shoulders back and stalked across the sand like the diva she was.

With a sigh, Smiley and I lay down and tried to look as harmless as we possibly could -- which, okay, wasn't very.

"What's going on?" Kordell asked, confused.

Ariel stared at the woman intently, probably

reading Raven's emotions from her aura. "She's terrified and pissed off."

"But *why*?" the Primo demanded.

"I'd say it's got something to do with me." Raven Garland was going to be a huge pain in my striped tail.

"She's scared of you?" Kordell looked offended on my behalf. "That's ridiculous. You're a hero. The Fords would have thrown the whole country into chaos if they'd assassinated all those politicians. Not that Roth would have been a big loss, but still."

"I don't think she cares. There was something that happened to her band when I was a kid, but fuck if I can remember what it was." I glanced at Ariel. "You got a clue?"

"Nope. Thirty years ago, I was four."

The Bard reached our group, but instead of joining us, she planted herself beside the banner and proceeded to ignore us. I sighed and manifested. Leaving Smiley lying beside Ariel, I walked over to have a try at reassuring her. "Look, I can tell you're not happy about this…"

"It's fine," Raven said with frigid dignity, not looking at me. "I signed a contract, and I'm going to abide by it. And this is a terrific opportunity for me. Though I had no idea they'd…" She broke off.

I shook my head. She really should have seen it coming. "You know any reality show's goal is to engineer as much conflict between the cast as they can. Conflict equals drama, and drama is good TV."

"Until somebody dies." She clamped her mouth shut.

"I'm not going to hurt you, Raven. You or anyone else. I've been melded with my cat for five years now, and I don't lose control of his instincts anymore."

"And I don't lose control of mine," she retorted icily. "I'm fifty-eight, not twenty. I'm a professional. I'll do my job."

"You telling *me* that, or yourself?"

Her lips drew into a tight line.

Shit. Well, there was nothing to do about it but hope she could keep it together.

Chapter Four

Dave

We spent the next couple of hours shooting confessionals -- the reactions of the contestants to their new team members, along with whatever plans they'd formulated for the first challenge of the contest.

My own shooter and an assistant producer took me aside and tried to get me to bitch about Raven's freak-out. I didn't oblige them, mostly because I understood where she was coming from. Hell, a Feral had *killed* me, not that I told them that. It wouldn't exactly help. "I deal with people who are afraid of me all the time," I told the camera. "In fact, it's more surprising when somebody *isn't* afraid. I'm just going to have to handle it the way I always do: prove that I won't hurt her and have a little patience."

"But aren't you worried she'll cost you the contest?"

I twitched an ear. "Like she said, Raven's a professional. I'm confident when push comes to shove, she'll act like it." Which was an out and out lie, but the nice thing about having a face covered in fur is that it makes your emotions hard to read.

* * *

I stared at the rubber raft we were supposed to row out to one of the four giant cages standing on pylons out in the turquoise water of the bay. "Well, crap."

Eyes narrowed in pain -- the treatment I'd given her that morning had worn off -- Ariel fisted her hands on her hips as she stood beside me. "No way in hell you can get into that. You'd sink it."

"What are we going to do?" Raven asked. She was standing as far from me as she could get, a grim set to her jaw.

Fuck, I wish I'd known she was going to be on the show. I'd have Googled her and found out what her deal was. Now it was too late -- I didn't have either a cell or access to the Internet, thanks to the show's rules.

Beside her, Kordell shot Raven a look, then gingerly reached up and laid a hand on her shoulder. Instead of biting his head off -- as he seemed to halfway expect -- the Bard hesitated, then shifted a fraction closer. He looked pleased and gave her shoulder a little squeeze.

I was usually the one who played emotional support animal to the various high-strung Talents in my orbit, but if the kid was willing to take her on, God bless him. It was obvious I couldn't do it.

"This is basically a race," I said, thinking out loud. "First team back to the beach wins the challenge. When the buzzer goes off, y'all pile in the raft, grab an oar, and start paddling. I'm gonna jump in and tow you." I tilted my chin at the boat. "Just throw me the mooring rope."

Raven gave me a tight little smile. "I thought cats don't like water."

Appreciating the effort at a joke, I told her, "Tigers wear fur coats in jungles. A swim's usually the only way to cool off."

Noticing that Ariel looked as white-faced as Raven, I closed my eyes to check her out. And cussed under my breath. "I've yarked hairballs with fewer tangles than your aura. Gimme." I manifested an arm.

Giving me a grateful look, Ariel took my hand. I concentrated. When I'd done this with Gen, the idea had been to amplify her magic by feeding my own power into it. In this case, I had to grip Ariel's aura with my manifestation and slow down the churn.

At first our magic seemed to kink, and Ariel hissed as if I were making the pain worse. Hastily, I shifted my magical hold until the currents slowed and began to flow more smoothly. She rewarded me with a low moan of relief that sounded way too sexy for my peace of mind.

To distract myself from the dreamy expression sliding over her face, I glanced around. The other teams were tensing under their respective banners, waiting for the buzzer.

I turned my attention to the cage marked with the Mystics flag. We'd have to row out to it, scramble up the ladder to its mesh roof, and then drop through a hatch. Once we were all inside, the spell laid by the show's Arcanist ward specialists would activate, and we'd be trapped. Ariel would have to break the ward so we could open the exit door located in the cage's side, leap into the water, and swim to shore. We'd earn points for every section of the challenge.

"Raven," Ariel said, "I can't start breaking the spell until it activates, which it won't do until we're all in the cage."

"With Dave." She'd bitten her lip until she'd managed to chew off her lipstick. "I know."

Getting into a cage with a tiger would freak out people who *didn't* have her issues. Whatever the fuck they were. I was going to have to get that out of her. "You think you can do it?"

"Yes," the Bard replied, her tone determined even as she shifted from foot to foot.

Kordell squeezed her shoulder again. "Hey, I studied the video for 'Heartbeat' for one of my classes. That was some nice choreography. How did you… ?" He went to work distracting her with questions. I was starting to adore that kid.

Finally Amelia Sharp began the countdown. We all tensed. When the buzzer sounded, I dove off the dock with a huge splash. By the time I came up for air, Ariel and Raven were piling into the raft as Kordell steadied it. It rocked under them as they scrambled for the paddles lying on its rubber floor.

Kordell was the last aboard, untying the raft and throwing me its mooring rope. I snatched it out of the air with a manifested hand, stuffed the rope in Smiley's mouth and bit down on the knot in the end. We began to swim for all we were worth.

Glancing back, I saw the team grab the oars. For a minute, they all paddled in different rhythms, making the boat slew back and forth and resisting my efforts at towing them. Right behind us, a raft full of camera operators were having a good ol' time shooting the resulting clusterfuck. *Assholes.*

Raven yelled, "We all have to paddle in sync. Watch me. Like this... Stroke, stroke..." Evidently she must have done some canoeing. They got themselves sorted out and started paddling in unison as I swam toward the cage, all four legs churning. I'm strong as hell -- tigers have been known to drag prey twice their body weight up trees -- so we quickly took the lead.

The problem was going to be that ladder. I had no idea how I was going to climb it, since my manifested arms don't have the strength to support my tiger's weight, and my paws couldn't grip the rungs. But as we drew closer, I spotted a narrow metal platform just below the ladder. It was, just barely, wide enough for me to stand on.

I'd have to jump from the platform to the top of the cage. I could leap sixteen vertical feet -- I'd done it in the shows we gave for the tourists at BFS.

Unfortunately, judging by the ladder's rungs, this jump would be farther than that.

Adding the cherry to the shit sundae, I'd have to land on *top* of the cage. If I had a few feet to make a running start, it would be no problem, but there wasn't room. *And* I had to avoid sinking the damned raft, either by landing on it when I fell or capsizing it by falling into the water.

Either would thrill the fuck out of Raven.

* * *

Ariel

We were making good time toward the cage, thanks more to Dave's tiger strength than our own paddling. When I glanced across the bay at the other teams, I saw we were well in the lead.

Unfortunately, I knew we wouldn't keep it. There were two problems: getting Dave on top of the cage, then getting Raven to jump *into* it with him inside.

Knowing Dave, he'd manage his part. It was Raven who worried me. I eyed her, wondering whether Kordell and I should just pick her ass up and drop her inside whether she liked it or not. Unfortunately, that kind of stunt that could crack the team wide open. She'd never trust us again.

Plus, I was willing to bet Dave would not approve. He had that whole chivalry thing going. How the hell he'd managed to fight a war like that, I had no idea.

I was going to have to trust Raven to overcome her phobia. I just hoped she could do it.

Dave reached the platform, manifested arms, and tied off the mooring rope. Then he grabbed the platform with paws and glowing hands and scrambled aboard. We could only sit and watch -- there was no room for all of us.

Dave coiled his ten-foot-long body, craning his head back as he stared fixedly at the top of the cage. The shooters' raft bumped ours as they trained their cameras on us all. One of the drones buzzed closer, hovering to get a good view.

The tiger launched off the platform like a rocket in a magnificent leap, extending full length as his powerful forepaws stretched for the cage roof.

And didn't quite make it.

He caught the roof with his claws as his rear legs scrabbled at the side of the cage. For a moment, I thought he was going to lose his grip and fall.

Then not one but *two* pairs of arms shot out of his ribs, gripping the bars until one of his rear paws got purchase on the edge of the cage top. With a furious heave, he climbed onto the roof.

"Damn, Frost!" I yelled up at him. "What the heck are you, Octo-Tiger?"

Dave grinned down at me. "I can manifest any damn thing I want. You should see my giant glowing…" He broke off in mid-double-entendre, glancing over at the competition with his tail lashing. "What are you still doing in the raft? The Wizards have reached their cage."

I cursed and scrambled toward the cage side of the raft. Kordell had already jumped onto the platform, but instead of heading for the roof, he waited to give Raven and me a hand. Once we crowded aboard, he swarmed up the ladder.

When I checked on Raven, she was staring wide-eyed into the cage. Dave was already inside and sniffing its metal floor, his lips stretched wide in a grimace as he drew in air. The expression bared a whole lot of really big teeth.

"I'm smelling three separate magical signatures here," he called to me. "You're going to have your hands full. Better get in here."

I didn't answer, my attention on Raven. Her pretty, ageless face had gone white under her flawless makeup. "You can do this," I told her. "Gotta be easier than making the Billboard Top Ten."

"Good point." Flashing me a tight smile, she grabbed the ladder and started climbing with easy strength, me scrambling after her. She'd obviously stayed in shape. But then, if your job is singing and dancing *at the same time*, you'd better be good at cardio.

Dave had left the roof entry door open. I sat down and dangled my legs, hesitating a bit over that eighteen-foot drop. He'd manifested, stretching glowing arms up toward me as his tiger watched. "Let yourself drop -- I'll catch you."

"Here, I'll help." Kordell, who'd waited for us, took my elbows.

Raven watched as he lowered me into Dave's arms with easy strength. "Your folks must have been big believers in chivalry."

He smiled as Dave took my weight. "That and lots and lots of church."

I barely heard him. Dave had his arms around me, his manifestation feeling as warm and solid as flesh against my body, golden eyes staring up into mine. Magic flowed through his aura in a thousand subtle shades, beautiful and unearthly, even as all that concentrated power made my brain buzz. My nipples hardened as my senses came alive in a response so carnal, my breath caught. The memory of that impulsive kiss sizzled through me, and I lowered my head…

Dave set me on my feet and stepped back, looking away.

Damn, I was surprised how much that hurt. I made myself turn...

And looked right into the lens of the camera focused on me from the crew's raft.

Great. He'd just rejected me in front of millions of people. Assuming that many tuned in this fall. I jerked my chin up and glared into the lens, ignoring the directions they'd pounded into our heads: *Don't look at the cameras except in the interviews.*

"I can't!" Raven's voice spiraled, sounding a little frantic.

Shit! I spun.

Dave's human manifestation was staring up at the Bard, who sat on the cage roof, dangling her legs through the opening, clinging to the edge of the trap door with white-knuckled hands. "Get back!" she told him. "I'll jump down."

"Forget it. That's an eighteen-foot drop onto a steel floor," Dave told her patiently. "You'll break a leg, and we can't afford that. But I *can* catch you."

Raven's gaze swept over to the corner, where Dave's tiger was stretched out on the floor, his big head on his paws, pointedly not looking at her. When I checked her aura, it blazed a bright yellow, right on the edge of white. A splash of bright red in the center of her chest throbbed with desperate speed: her heart, beating so fast it hurt. She was having a full-fledged panic attack.

Fuck. I'd been afraid of that. Sucked to be right.

My own heart began to pound, and I turned to eye the spell around the cage floor. Though it wasn't active yet, Dave had been right. There were three rings of sigils, forming a mystical barrier -- a ward -- that would keep us from being able to get to the trap door. I couldn't even begin to break the spell until the sigils activated so I could see the working's structure.

I glanced through the bars toward the nearest cage in time to see Zoe Maddox drop into Oz's grip. Zoe saw me watching and smirked. The minute her feet hit the cage floor, the ward spell flared. Their Arcanist hurried over and got to work.

Mentally swearing, I glanced around and saw all the other cages were glowing with active spells. "Get your ass down here, Raven," I snapped, as my head throbbed in reaction to my anxiety. "Everybody else is inside their cages and working. We're going to lose this."

"Raven, I will not hurt you," Dave said patiently as Kordell murmured encouragement.

I stalked over to him. "Get out of the way. I'll catch her." Somehow, though she was taller than I was and probably outweighed me.

With a moaning rumble, the tiger rolled over on his back and dangled his paws in the air, as if trying to convince Raven he was a kitten. Unfortunately, he was the length of the cage, which kind of blew the illusion.

I reached up, trying to ignore the rake of my aura.

With a sigh, Dave stepped in and took hold of my shoulders. Instantly, the pain decreased. I wanted to lean back into him, take shelter in his cooling magic. He stroked his big hands up and down my arms, and I shivered.

Get your mind on your job, I told myself sternly, and looked up at Raven. "Come on, I'll help you down."

She stared at Dave, her eyes huge. "I can't! Roger..." All the fragile dignity she'd called on before was gone, lost to stark panic.

Shit. Shitty shit. "Take my hands!" I demanded, extending both arms. "I can help you beat the fear if you'll just let me touch you." Even as I said the words, I felt a blast of magic roll over me. I glanced toward its source. The Sorcerers' team Arcanist crouched, working to break the two remaining rings of the ward.

Zoe blew me a kiss. I really wanted to give that bitch a smack like my dear old granny's. The kind that doesn't leave any marks, but makes your skull vibrate for two days. I gritted my teeth and said, "The Sorcerers just broke their first ward ring. We're running out of time."

In my ear, Dave began to sing *"Magic Hands,"* in a dead-on imitation of Raven's voice. A guitar and drums joined in, complete with backup singers. It was an impressive bit of magic, though it lacked the gripping emotional intensity contributed by her Bard Talent. *How does he do that?* Other Ferals could do imitations, but I'd never known anyone as good with sound as Dave Frost.

Raven looked down at him, her eyes widening. "You really do know my songs."

"I meant it when I said I was a fan," Dave's manifestation said, even as he went right on singing. "I'm not going to hurt you." He smiled up at her, all charm. "America -- and my Mom -- would never forgive me."

Raven's expression softened before she switched her gaze to me. "Okay. Okay, I'm coming down." She pushed off as Kordell gripped her under the arms, lowering her into my grip. I braced myself as I took her weight and tried like hell not to drop her on her ass. And felt myself stagger. Shit, I wasn't going to be able to…

Dave caught her arms in his and took her weight. She stiffened, but he lowered her to the cage floor and stepped back fast.

I whirled and rushed to the side of the cage. Kordell grabbed the trap door and jumped down as Raven leaped out of the way. The door clanged shut. As the Primo's feet hit the floor, the triple ward rings snapped up around us, flooding the air with the ozone scent of Arcanist magic.

As if that wasn't nerve-wracking enough, I felt two sets of magical wards simultaneously break. The other two teams were gaining. My magic writhed and bit over my skin, reacting to my screaming tension until the pain stole my breath.

I fought to ignore the vicious throb and *focus*. Three sets of sigils orbited us -- intricate shapes in blue, green and gold leaving a comet tail of light as they moved. I reached out a hand, brushing the inner ward's cobalt glow. A magical snap sounded, and I jerked back, cursing, and shook my singed fingers.

That ward was *not* just for show.

I studied the spell, watching the way the rings interacted, searching for flaws, weaknesses I could use to pry it apart.

Another burst of magic rolled over the water as one of our rivals dropped another ring. The Sorcerers had one ring left, while the Oracles and Wizards each had two.

"Can you do it?" Dave murmured.

"I've broken worse. Now, can I do it in time?" I ground my teeth. "Doesn't look good. We're too far behind."

Raven winced. "I'm sorry."

"Well, fortunately there's something you can do about it." Dave said to Raven and Kordell. "We can help feed Ariel the power she needs to break the wards."

"Yeah, that is the point of the show," Raven said tartly. "But how?"

"Touch my manifestation and sing your little lungs out. I can collect that power, add my own to it, and pour it into her aura through mine."

Raven frowned. "You know how to do that?"

"Basically. And Genevieve, Erica and a bunch of Bards used Kurt and Jake as amps to control that humanist riot a couple years ago." He turned to Kordell. "Can you dance touching me?"

The Primo frowned. "It's hard to generate much power with movement that limited, but... Maybe Tuzelity?"

Whatever that was.

"Good man. Come on, Raven, I'll sing backup."

She bit her lip. "You're not a Bard."

"I don't have to be -- I just have to amplify your magic." The familiar guitar riff of "Magic Hands" sounded again.

I glanced back to see Raven throw a look at all the cameras focused on her. Her eyes narrowed, as she probably realized how many record sales this could net her. She put a hand on Dave's glowing shoulder, gathered her magic and began to belt out the song with all her Grammy-winning talent.

Every hair on my body rose, reacting to her sheer power. Pushing sixty or not, the woman was one hell of a Bard. Kordell planted one hand on Dave's other shoulder as his leanly muscled body started an intricate series of hopping cross steps and kicks. When I shifted to magical sight, I could see the magical energies the two Talents produced whirling around them.

Then Dave's free hand closed over my shoulder, and I felt his magic pour into me, rich with the power I felt every time he touched me.

I drew in the energy and began to weave it into my own as I turned back to the rotating sigils.

Magic exploded through my senses, and I heard a triumphant shout. There was a distant clang as a cage door slammed open, followed by splashes as the opposing team dove into the sea.

Too late. I'm too fucking late! The first damn challenge, and I'd already lost. Just the way I *always* lost.

For a moment, I felt the brutal cold of the icy holy water baths I'd endured when I was thirteen. Remembered the whip of my grandmother's power slashing my face. I saw the Caliphate sorcerer's eyes as I drove my power into his brain, watched him drop while I fought to keep his MEED vest from detonating. Heard the CIA section chief tell me, "Sorry, Piper. The President believes you're a security risk the country can no longer afford."

No, damn it. Not this time. Not this fucking time! Rage blasted over me -- rage at the producers who'd deliberately stuck my team with someone who was terrified of Melds. Rage at my parents. Rage at my government. Most of all, rage at my psychotic bitch of a grandmother.

I knew what I was about to do was risky as hell. For one thing, I could pop an aneurism that would kill me. I didn't care. I studied the intricate weave of the three warding spells. A dip in the brightness revealed a spot where tiny faults in all three spells lined up as they rotated. It wasn't there long -- just a split second before the rings rolled out of alignment again. I waited, barely breathing, for the faults to sync for the second time. And gathered all my power, all *Dave's* power, all the magic Raven and Kordell were feeding him. Aaaand… The light dipped.

There! I blasted all our combined mystical energy right into that spot. The triple ward exploded in a silent, blinding detonation like a MEED going off. When the light faded, I couldn't see anything at all. I heard startled shouts -- my teammates, even the Arcanists in the other cages, shocked by the sheer intensity of the blast.

"You did it!" Dave crowed. His hands tightened, pulling me away. I heard the metallic screech of the cage's side door being wrenched open.

Splashes, excited yells that sounded like Raven and Kordell jumping out of the cage. I didn't really know for sure because I couldn't see a damn thing. My ears were ringing, and my head felt like it was going to blow right of my shoulders. "Dave, I can't…"

"Backlash? Don't worry, I've got you." I felt a big, furry body press against mine. "We've got to get to the beach."

A manifested hand pulled me after him through the opening. At least the door wasn't as far up. We hit, and I barely held my breath in time as my head went under. I kicked blindly until I broke the surface, salt stinging my eyes. "Dave, I… can't see!" A cold, salty wave slapped me in the face, and I sucked water into my lungs. Gagging, I sputtered and coughed, on the verge of panic. "Can't see *at all!*"

"Damn it!" An arm wrapped around my waist as I went into a coughing jag. My skull felt like it was going to detonate like a truck bomb.

"Kordell," Dave snapped, "I need some help here!"

"Crap! What's wrong?" Kordell demanded.

Splashes sounded.

"Is she okay?" A note of genuine worry rang in Raven's voice.

"Blinded herself with the backlash from taking down all those wards at once. Should be temporary. Help me get her on my back."

Three sets of hands grabbed my arms and legs, helping Dave drape me astride the tiger. I was surprised Raven was willing to get close enough to the cat to help.

But the darkness was intensifying, growing heavy, thick as tar. Until it sucked me right down.

Chapter Five
Dave

"Crazy wench!" I growled as Ariel went limp across Smiley's back. If I wasn't damn careful, she'd drown before we even made it back to the beach. Manifesting the upper half of my body like a backward-facing tiger centaur, I hooked one arm around her chest and gripped her chin with the other hand to keep her head up. Smilodon began swimming hard, his legs churning the water.

To my surprise, Raven swam beside us, keeping an eye on Ariel. Evidently the frantic task of breaking the spell had distracted her from the panic cycle of her PTSD. Or maybe it was the intimacy of blending our magic. Either way, I hoped it continued.

"I've never seen... an explosion of... of magic like that," the Bard panted between strokes as she swam. "And I've hired... some of the most power... powerful Arcanists in the... the business for... for my concerts."

"It was amazing," Kordell agreed, frog-kicking next to her. Apparently keeping an eye on all three of us. The kid really was a born caretaker. "Think she... hurt herself?"

"She'll be fine," I said, hoping I wasn't lying. "She just blew everything she had breaking that spell."

"Which she wouldn't... have had to do if... I hadn't lost... my shit," Raven said grimly.

It took entirely too long for Smiley's paws to find sand. We burst out of the water, me still holding on to Ariel for dear life. Our teammates reeled to their feet and staggered out after us. Both looked totally fried -- which wasn't surprising. They'd fed me a hell of a lot of magic under truly shitty conditions.

I laid Ariel down on the sand, trying to ignore all the cameras pointed avidly in our direction. Overhead, drones whined a grating note.

Glancing over my shoulder to check on the location of the competition, I saw our camera crew beach their raft and rush toward us.

Amelia Sharp ran across the sand, a worried frown on her pretty face. "Is she okay?" Probably afraid of the bad publicity from killing one of the show's contestants.

"Don't know," I told her. "She needs to be checked out. Where's the doc?"

Sharp dropped to her knees beside me as her PA began muttering into her headset. It was Jenny Stone, who'd guided me to my room the night before. She listened a moment, then told Sharp, "We got a problem! The doc is busy with the Arcanists who erected the Mystics' ward. They've got such a bad case of backlash, one of them went into cardiac arrest."

Crap.

I closed my eyes to check Ariel's aura. To my relief, her magic still glowed. She was alive, though the currents of magic were snarled all to hell. When she regained consciousness, she was going to hurt.

Just as I was trying to decide what to do, she groaned and coughed a spray of seawater. I turned her over on her side so she wouldn't aspirate it.

One slender arm hooked over my manifested leg as she coughed. Smiley pushed past me to sniff her and chuff. I caught her scent through his nose -- seawater, her own feminine scent, and so much Arcanist ozone, she smelled like a lightning strike.

"Oh, God!" Ariel wheezed, and flopped over onto her back. Her blue eyes met mine, looking huge and dazed. Her beautiful face was dewed with drops of seawater. The tip of her pink tongue slipped out, licked away a drop. "Dave?" Her voice sounded throaty.

"How are the eyes?"

"Coming back. A bit blurry, but at least I'm not in the dark."

Without even intending to, I glanced down. Her T-shirt was sopping wet over her bare-midriff top, revealing the lush curves of her breasts and the lean contours of her body. Her legs looked incredibly long in the sopping wet shorts. Her sandals hung half-off her feet with their pink toenail polish.

But she was okay. Thank God, thank God, she was *okay*!

And she was looking at me like I was human -- like I was a man. A handsome man who'd saved her. And under that dazzled stare, I forgot I wasn't.

Wasn't handsome. Wasn't a man. Wasn't alive.

I leaned down and took her full mouth in a kiss of sheer relief. For a moment, her tangled magic stung me, and I realized she must be in pain. Smiley made one of those low moans, sending his magic pouring into me. I gathered it up and directed it into her, willing the jagged tangles to smooth. She sighed into my mouth, her wet arms lifting to slide around my manifested neck. Hunger hit me, sensual and wild, and I kissed her harder.

She moaned. That deliciously female sound sent arousal burning high and hot through me. Smiley rumbled, the sound hungry. I drew away an inch or two, staring down at her. She stared back, her eyes dazed, more than a little high.

Judging by a very familiar sensation, my manifestation had an erection. It felt exactly the way it had when I'd been alive. It took an effort not to jerk back and look down. Instead I clung to her, my breathing rough.

Unable to help myself, I glanced around. Sure enough, three cameras were pointed at me. I immediately got a mental image of my glowing dick being blurred out on national TV. I'd be lucky if Human Heritage didn't drag me out of BFS and lynch me the minute the show aired. Assuming Smilodon didn't eat one of them.

Ariel's eyes widened, and I realized she'd felt my problem. She cleared her throat and said to Sharp, "Did we... did we make it?"

"Sorcerers hit the beach first, but part of the score is based on the way you broke the wards. We won't know that until the judges rule," Sharp said, looking as feline and pleased as Smiley contemplating a twenty-pound turkey. Probably imagining the ratings.

Yeah, well, she wasn't looking at bestiality charges.

Ariel lifted her head and breathed in my ear, "Thank you. I thought my head was going to blow off my shoulders."

Damn it, that moan had been a sound of relief, not pleasure. Because of course it was. *Fucking idiot.* My magic hardon deflated like a soufflé when you slam the oven door. I pulled away from her and sat up, telling myself I was grateful. Smiley gave a low, distressed moan, reacting to my humiliation.

Ariel frowned, looking up at me. Probably reading my emotions from my aura. "What's wrong?"

I didn't answer.

* * *

Ariel

An hour later, we all stood under our respective

banners on the beach to hear the judges evaluate our performance. The sun was setting, a ball of flame sinking into the darkening ocean, spilling layers of vibrant red, orange and pink across the horizon, shading into violet and dark blue higher up. The view probably would have been glorious, but my head was pounding viciously, and the light seemed to stab into my eyes. The huge banks of studio LEDs only intensified my misery.

Bracing my feet apart in the warm sand, I concentrated on staying upright. Dave/Smilodon looked up at me and planted himself against my hip. Without a word, he began spilling his aura over mine, and the pain eased off.

Unfortunately, even his magic couldn't affect the brutal weight of my exhaustion as the four judges launched into a critique of the Wizards' performance in merciless detail. God knew when we'd get our turn.

Yeah, this is going to be fun. Like one of Granny's little "hugs."

By the time they moved on to the Oracles, my knees were shaking. I planted one hand on Smilodon's furry shoulder and braced my knees. It reminded me of Basic Training in the Corps when our instructors had played sadistic games while we stood at attention.

"Oh, for God's sake," Dave muttered. "This is ridiculous. Sit down before you face-plant."

"He's right," Raven said. "This is going to go on for a while." When I glanced at her, I was surprised to see anger on my behalf. "The least they could have done is judge us first. You blacked out, for God's sake."

Kordell moved to my other side and took my arm. He frowned down at me, and I realized he was an inch or two taller than Dave's manifestation. "You're shaking. Dave's right, you're about to keel over. Sit down."

"Do you need the doctor?" Raven asked.

Oh, hell no. "I'm fine," I said through my teeth.

Her frown got deeper. "I don't like your coloring."

"Neither do I," Dave growled. Literally -- Smiley embellished his manifested voice with vibrato from six hundred pounds of irritated feline.

"I'll live." But my shaking was getting worse, so I yielded to reality and sank down on the sand.

"I'm going to get you a couple of bottles of PowerUp." Kordell walked off.

"Oh, for God's sake," I grumbled. "It's just a headache."

"It's backlash," Dave corrected. "Which can be serious. I knew a guy in the Corps who died of a stroke from that. He was twenty-five."

Yeah, I knew people who'd died from it too. There were better than even odds I'd eventually be one of them, given my Kimura's.

The Primo came back a few minutes later with the show's Arcanist doctor, Barbara Kingston. She was a graying middle-aged woman, thin as a thermometer in her white capris and pink tunic, an old-fashioned doctor's bag in her hand. She eyed me. "Got a case of backlash, do you?"

She knelt beside me and pulled out a blood pressure cuff and stethoscope. She took my temp with a digital thermometer, then made me squeeze her fingers with both hands, checking for the uneven grip that was the sign of a stroke.

"I'm fine, damn it," I snapped, pain making me bitchy. "This is just the usual shit. I do this all the time."

"Your heartbeat and blood pressure are

elevated." She shone a penlight into my eyes, frowning. "Pupils are even, though. Looks like a migraine with a side order of hypoglycemia from breaking that spell." She handed me a PowerUp and a package of crackers before turning to Kordell. "If she gets worse come get me, but I think she's fine."

As she walked away, I noticed cameras pointed in our direction. *Figures.*

* * *

"Mystics, front and center," Sharp said at last.

Dave manifested and helped me to my feet with Kordell's assistance. Grimly, eyes shuttered against the merciless studio lights, I followed my team as we walked to the judge's table and the cluster of cameras around it.

"That was an impressive performance, breaking all three wards at once," the Arcanist judge told me. Jaylen Payne was a big man who looked as if he was pushing sixty, balding with a graying mustache. Given his iron posture, I'd be willing to bet he was former Arcane Corps. From what I understood, he'd been creating magical special effects for the movies for the past thirty years. Arcs were cheaper than computer animation, and their work let the actors see what they were interacting with. With CGI, you often got two ping-pong balls on a stick as a stand-in for the digital effects they'd put in later.

I dipped my head. "Thank you."

"It was also dumb as hell," Payne added coolly. I jolted in surprise, then wiped the expression off my face. "A million dollars is a lot of money, but it's not worth risking a stroke. You're not in the Corps anymore, Ms. Piper. You're not required to sacrifice your life to break spells. If I were you, I'd approach your future challenges with a little more wisdom and discretion." He shook his head. "Still, I doubt I could have broken all three wards at once. Two, maybe, but not three." He gave me another long look. "By the way, what's wrong with your aura? It looks like my wife's necklace collection -- snarled all to hell. Except with spikes. Is that as painful as it looks?"

I managed a tight smile. "Pretty much. I have Kimura syndrome."

He winced. "You need a prescription for Aurarest."

I snorted. "Why do you think I'm here?"

My knees were shaking again, damn it. I stiffened them again.

Evan Hall, the Primo judge who was a Broadway choreographer, told Kordell that though he'd been working under difficult circumstances -- having to maintain contact with Dave while dancing -- he needed to work on channeling his magic more effectively.

Kordell just nodded, though I saw pain whirl through his aura in shades of aching red. The yellow tinge of self-doubt rolled in after it, and I silently swore at the damage to his confidence.

Next, it was Raven's turn.

"You realize you almost cost your team that challenge?" Lilly Gardner asked. A legendary R&B singer, Gardner was over seventy, though every bit as gorgeous and ageless as Raven. Her skin was a deep, rich bronze, and she wore her hair like a crown, twisted in thick braids, some pure white, the others black. "I'm surprised at you, Raven. You used to be more professional than that. What's the problem?"

Raven flushed red across the cheekbones, but when she spoke, her voice was level. "In 1994, I hired a Meld for a music video I was shooting. We didn't realize he wasn't fully stable. Gary Handle had been trapped in his tiger when the helicopter he was on crashed during combat exercises. We had to do repeated re-shoots because he couldn't seem to get the choreography. And Roger Timmons, the director..." Her lips almost twitched. "Roger thought he was MTV's answer to Hitchcock. Lost his temper and ripped into Gary, and the tiger just..." She broke off as her lips pulled tight. "... Lost it. He attacked Roger. There was so much... so much blood. So much screaming. He tore Roger's arm off, and then he turned on me. He'd have killed me, but my bodyguard... he shot Gary. Killed him." Her hands worried each other, fingers clenching, winding. She was dead white now.

Lilly was looking a little sick now. I suspected she was sorry she'd brought it up. "I... I had no idea. I'm sorry, Raven, I... Heard of the attack, of course, but I didn't know the details."

"The Corps wasn't doing a particularly good job with ensuring Melds were psychologically stable back then," Valeria said from the other end of the judge's table, where she sat on her haunches on a metal platform. "We worked to get transition care improved, though I'm afraid things backslid during the previous administration. Still." She cocked her head and eyed Raven. "You knew there was going to be a Feral on your team."

"But I thought they were all going to be human." Dave winced.

"We *are* human," Valeria told her coolly.

Her eyes widened. "I didn't mean it like that. I..."

"I know what you meant. Look, it takes melded Ferals time to learn to deal with the emotions of their cats." Despite the no-nonsense phrasing, Valeria's tone was surprisingly kind. I hadn't known she had it in her, considering the way she usually treated Dave. "All Melds must learn to manage their Familiars, but the problem is particularly acute when you occupy the animal's body instead of the other way around. Both Familiars and Ferals find themselves dealing with entirely new bodies they don't understand. Imagine being thirteen again, except with fur, fangs and claws. Then there's the fact that you recently died. Not everyone who survives combat deals with PTSD, but every Feral who *dies* in combat does. There is no worse trauma. We died violent deaths and found ourselves no longer considered human. Half the population wants us in camps, and the other half sees us as pets."

Raven lifted her chin. "I'm aware."

"But Dave has been stable for years. He didn't even kill Virgil Ford, who thoroughly deserved it. Considering the Fords had just tried to kill him and Kurt Briggs -- and *had* murdered Kurt's father -- that says a lot about his self-control. I'd say he's probably the safest Feral in this competition, four-legged or not. So he's not going to be the problem here."

"Yes," Raven said steadily. "After the way he handled today's challenge, I realized that. He kept his head when I, for one, was freaking out. And he didn't lose patience with me, even when he'd have been justified."

"I'm glad you realize that," Valeria said. "But until you conquer your phobia, you're a drawback to your team. Your actions forced Ariel to risk her life to make up the ground you cost them. Three more Arcs were injured from backlash when she took down their wards like that. The show's doctor had to use a defibrillatoron one of them. All that's on you."

Raven's lips thinned. "It won't happen again."

The lioness sighed, sounding almost human.

"Look, I don't blame you for being scarred by your experience. What happened to Roger was horrible. But you should have been in therapy years ago. Instead, you denied your problems, and now your chickens have come home to roost. I suggest you get your act together. And when the competition is over, you need to seek therapy."

Raven didn't look away. "I will."

Valeria turned to Dave. "You, on the other hand, went above and beyond on this challenge. Frankly, I was surprised you were able to get Raven calmed down at all -- I could smell her terror from the beach. And your magic is impressive. Keep up that kind of work, and you could win this thing."

I glanced at Dave to see him staring at her with his mouth hanging open in complete astonishment.

In the end, the judges awarded us fifty-three points -- a tie with Zoe's Sorcerers. Though we were second to the beach, they gave us additional points for my ward work.

Good thing they didn't deduct them for almost killing one of the Arcs. Next time, Sharp informed us, the Arcanists would watch from a protective circle.

As we all high-fived under our flag, my attention fell on the competition. All of them looked frustrated and depressed to various degrees.

But Zoe looked downright enraged, her narrow blue eyes so dry-ice frigid they practically emitted fog. I considered blowing her a kiss, but I'd probably look like a bitch to the cameras.

Oblivious to any of that, Dave wore the terrifyingly toothy expression that was his version of a grin. "Valeria said I was impressive!" he breathed, sounding dazzled.

I felt a stab I realized was pure jealousy. *What the*

fuck is wrong with me?

* * *

Dave

With the shoot wrapped for the night, we handed over our lavalier body mics and battery packs to our audio tech.

Jenny Stone was showing us the way to our bungalow when we ran into Zoe and her team.

The Bard offered one hand to Ariel. "Well played," she said, a smile on her face that didn't go with the acrid note in her scent.

"That was really impressive," the Sorcerers' Arcanist agreed. A tall, dark-haired man, he had the erect build of former Corps and an ID badge that read Kieran Grant. "It looked like the Fourth of July when you blew all those wards at once. How did you do that?"

"Sheer desperation," Ariel said dryly. There was a tight line between her eyes that suggested the effects of my last treatment had already worn off. I really needed to find a way to make it last.

Zoe studied her, her gaze sharp, weighing. She turned and extended a hand to Kordell, who took it for a perfunctory shake.

I manifested out of sheer manners, not because I had any desire to make nice. That's the problem with being raised to be a gentleman. I didn't trust her as far as I could throw her, but Bards, unlike Arcs, couldn't do anything to you with a touch. I extended a hand. Zoe's gaze flicked down to it…

And she turned away.

Well, motherfucker.

Ariel made a low, pissed-off sound as anger spiked in her scent.

Zoe didn't seem to notice as she smiled sweetly at Raven. "Don't think *you* are going to have as much luck. Oh, I won't deny that back in the day, you were one of the best Bards out there. But that was a quarter century ago, wasn't it? A lot of years of wear and tear on the vocal cords. I mean, why else did you lose your contract?" Ozone reeked in the air. When I closed my eyes, I saw her magic engulfing Raven like an amoeba.

I had underestimated the little bitch. I shouldn't have. I'd heard what Bards could do. Kurt Briggs's Bard mother had used her voice to keep Fred from noticing she was cheating -- and Fred hadn't been anybody's sucker.

This bitch thinks she's going to fuck Raven over right in front of me? The thought sent such a wave of rage through me, Smilodon and I both growled.

Oz manifested in a blaze of sparks, his bear towering ten feet tall as it encased his human body. "Step off," he snapped, glaring at me in a sudden fury. "Touch her and you're dead."

My growl died of sheer astonishment. I'd known Oz since Basic. We were friends. I closed my eyes again and spotted something overlaying his aura that didn't look like Feral magic. What had the bitch been doing, and when had she had the chance to do it? They'd only been a team a few hours.

Raven made a strangled sound of sheer terror. Her PTSD was kicking up again. From the corner of one eye, I saw Jenny Stone head for the trees. Not that I could blame the kid.

"You back the fuck off!" I snarled up at the big man. "You're not going to terrorize my teammates. And you need to take a hard look at what *yours* is doing to *you*."

His eyes widened, and he blinked at me through

the shell of his bear before glancing at his Bard.

"I haven't done anything," she declared, voice ringing. "Dave's the one threatening *me*."

Backlash migraine notwithstanding, Ariel stepped right up into her face. "I warned you about this, Zoe. You're about two seconds from finding out what I can do when I'm *really* pissed."

Oz growled -- and not with his human voice.

Ariel turned her glare on the bear, and my heart clenched in my chest in sheer terror. In his right mind, Oz would never hurt her -- he'd been melded with his Familiar for a couple of years now, and he was stable. But Zoe must have been working on him for hours now. I moved in close enough to encircle Ariel with my manifestation if things went sideways.

Raven whimpered, the sound terrified. Without looking away from Oz, I reached back, grabbed her hand and dragged her closer. She huddled against Smilodon's furry side.

Kordell stepped in front of Raven like the hip-hop knight he evidently was. "Only an asshole threatens women," he told Oz with frigid dignity.

The Feral looked down at him through the glowing shell of his manifestation. Kordell was tall, but Oz still had three inches on him even without his Kodiak. "You smell like you're going to piss yourself." He smiled, slow and ugly and nothing like the man I knew. "You got good instincts."

Just as I was trying to figure out what the fuck to do -- I couldn't shield all four of us...

"The fuck is this? You know the rules," Tisha snapped, charging from the trees, Jenny at her heels. Bless the PA, she hadn't rabbited, she'd gone for help. "Any Feral that loses his shit is off the island. And that goes double for anyone I catch using magic to incite trouble." She glared at Zoe, then included Ariel for good measure. "This is going to be a safe set. I will not let a bunch of hotheads sabotage a project that could do us all some good. Now get to your God damn bungalows and stay there until tomorrow's shoot."

Oz growled, but at least he sounded more human this time. He banished his manifestation and turned away. As the rest of the Sorcerers team started to follow, Ariel curled a lip. "Don't fuck with my people again, Zoe."

"I'm terrified," she sneered.

Ariel's eyes narrowed. "You should be."

The Sorcerers' Bard whirled and stalked off in long strides.

"Jesus," Tish growled in disgust. "Did you not hear what I just said?"

"I heard," Ariel said. "But you'd better make sure Zoe did, because I will not let her play those games with my people."

Tisha's brows shot up. "*Your* people?"

"Yes," Ariel said, meeting the showrunner's gaze. "My. People."

And Tish, who wasn't even afraid of an Amur tiger, took a step back.

* * *

Jackson stood in his office, watching the playback on the screens as Frost kissed Ariel after hauling the half-drowned Arc out of the ocean. It was a hungry kiss, using plenty of tongue. Neither of them appeared aware of the tiger standing over them, ears rotated forward, tail lashing.

The Humanists were going to love that. The Outrage Machine would be in full roar for at least two or three months if he played it right. He smiled, imagining telling the hosts at Heritage News how shocked and horrified he'd been.

"I had no idea of the sheer perversion of Ariel Piper and Dave Frost, or I never would have had them on the show. And we all called Frost a hero! I was shocked. I've always believed in admitting when I made a mistake, and in supporting Talents, I made a big one. You were right, and I was wrong. These 'people' can't be trusted."

Oh, yeah. They'd swallow it hook, line and sinker.

Chapter Six

Ariel

Between its dome-shaped thatched roof and the bamboo walls bent in curving lines, our bungalow would have looked right at home in Black Panther's Wakanda.

The theme continued inside with rattan and teak furniture padded with fat cream upholstery. There were four bedrooms, an efficiency kitchen, a bathroom we'd have to share, and a sunken living area.

And cameras. Lots and lots of cameras. Lenses glittered everywhere we looked.

"The only place that doesn't have cams is the bathroom," Dave grumbled after he, Kordell and Raven looked the house over. "And *that's* probably wired for sound."

I'd collapsed on the couch and propped my feet on the slab of carved teak that was the coffee table. I'd felt better after the dose of soothing magic Dave had given me on the beach after I came to, but the benefit had faded by the time we'd clashed with Zoe and her buddies. Maybe I could get Dave to give me another treatment...

Remembering his impressive hard-on, I wondered what else I could get out of him. To distract myself, I slitted one eye open, despite the way the light seemed to drill straight into my skull. "Apparently, when they were ripping off shows, they got a heaping helping of Big Brother."

Dave snorted. "Given Zoe, I smell some Real Twatwaffles of the Bahamas too." He wasn't manifested, but I could make out his human half superimposed over his tiger. He studied me. "Head hurting again? I thought you were doing better."

"I was, but it came back." I closed my eyes and sighed. "Though I still got off easier than that poor Arc. I'm going to have to avoid blasting their wards like that again. It would suck to kill somebody." Not that it would be the first time, but those Caliphate fuckers had deserved it, whereas some poor Hammerhead Productions Arcanist did not. "You know those Japanese drummers with that big *taiko* drums? Feels like one of 'em is giving me his all." I squeezed my eyes shut.

Suddenly the coffee table I'd propped my feet on slid out from under them, and my heels thumped on the floor. The impact made me yelp at the reverb that shocked through my feet, up my spine, and into my skull. Before I could pry my eyes open again, a weight landed on my bent leg. I cracked my eyelids to see Smilodon's big head propped on my knee, golden eyes staring into mine. Instantly, I felt the currents of my aura begin to slow their vicious churn as Dave went to work on me.

Whimpering in relief, I sagged back into the couch cushions. Without thinking, I laid a hand on his head. His fur felt thick and surprisingly soft, if coarser than my cat's. Absently, I smoothed my hands back and forth. Realizing I was petting him as if he were Floofinator, I snatched my hand back. "Sorry."

Dave opened one eye. He'd closed them as I stroked. "Don't worry about it. Feels good." His eyes closed again.

I hesitated, then rested my hand on his head again. His magic poured over my body like warm honey in a way that didn't remind me of Floof at all. The room ceased its dizzy rotation.

Someone was rattling around in the kitchen. "Well, at least the pantry's well-stocked," Raven called.

"Who wants a sandwich? Dave, there's a couple of big Tupperware containers of ham here. I gather that's for you. You hungry?"

I opened my eyes at that. Given her assorted panic attacks, this was one hell of a 360.

"I'm pretty much always hungry," Dave said, without opening his eyes. "Running human software on tiger hardware burns a fuck of a lot of magic."

Kordell came out of the bedroom he'd claimed and went to join her. "Here, I'll give you a hand."

"Our next big challenge is Friday," Raven told the Primo as they started constructing sandwiches. "That's the first dance competition thing. Have you given any thought to what you're going to do?"

"I had this whole bit choreographed," Kordell said, amid a *clunk clunking* sound that suggested he was cutting something. "But now I'm worried it isn't good enough. I was going to use Rap Daddy's 'Big Time.'"

Raven paused as if considering what to say. "You can do that," she told him at last, "but you need to remember I've got to sing whatever song you choose. Me chanting a string of double entendres about the size of my dick is not going to fly."

Smilodon chuffed. It sounded surprisingly like laughter. I wondered if that was all Dave's amusement, or if his tiger got the joke.

Kordell looked at Raven, frowning. "Well, yeah, I can see that would be a problem. But I thought I'd be performing to a recording."

"The point of the game is that we all have to use our magic to enhance your act. Besides, even a good Bard recording isn't as powerful as in-person magic."

"Oh, yeah, I didn't think of that."

"I could do the rap part," Dave pointed out, his

voice sounding lazy and little rough. "And in my case it would be apt, given my long, furry..."

"Nope," Raven interrupted.

"... Tail."

She carried a tray of sandwiches into the living area, Kordell lugging Dave's supper on a turkey platter. "Still a little too X-rated for prime time," she pointed out. "Besides, you're not a Bard. Yeah, I can sing backup, but that still wouldn't give Kordell the full benefit."

Raven set the tray down, then looked at the tiger and hesitated. She went a little pale, but her jaw set as she deliberately sat down beside me on the couch, her eyes glued on him.

Dave sighed. "You don't have to do that."

"Oh, yes, I do." Raven picked up a sandwich and bit into it, chewing with a certain grim determination. "I'm done with being a coward."

"You're not a coward. You got in the fucking cage. You confronted your fear and you beat it. You even sang."

The Bard snorted. "I sang so I could concentrate on the music instead of your teeth."

"Doesn't matter *how* you did it. Point is, you *did*."

I took a bite of my own ham and cheese. "I didn't expect a woman who'd won sixteen Grammys to fix dinner."

She snorted. "You should've known me during the '90s. I could have out-diva'ed Mariah Carey. But once you go from packed arena shows to nobody returning your calls, the diva gets scraped off pretty fast." Then she turned to Kordell, who'd settled beside her. "What's wrong?"

I glanced at him and saw what she meant. He sat slumped, staring blankly at his sandwich. "What if I fuck it up? I mean, let's face it, I'm the weak link in this team. The rest of you -- you're powerful. I don't suck, but I'm not in your league. If we lose, it will probably be because of me."

The tiger sat up. Raven jerked, but Dave didn't acknowledge her reaction. "To start with, that's a really good way to psych yourself out."

"He's right." Swallowing, the Bard turned toward Kordell with obvious determination. "You've got more than enough magic, and you'll have the rest of us backing you up. Ariel..." She jerked a thumb at me. "... will provide special effects that will knock the judges' socks off. Furboy can provide an entire orchestra..."

"Furboy? You're getting cocky," Dave drawled. "I like it."

She ignored him. "And you and I will find a song that will show off my sick pipes and let you soar."

I listened as Raven, Kordell, and Dave began brainstorming. I felt way too drained to come up with a damned thing.

But even as Smilodon polished off the last of his food, I was aware of the big paw he'd planted on my foot and the slow, rolling surge of his magic keeping the pain away. I let my head fall back, half-dozing.

"She's asleep," Kordell said softly. I didn't have the energy to correct him.

"Wiped herself out," Dave said. "She's got a Wonder Woman complex. I'm surrounded by heroes back home, so I can spot 'em a mile off."

Raven snorted. "Ever look in the mirror?"

She's got a point, I thought, and dropped into sleep.

* * *

In their bungalow, Zoe shifted under the gaze of

her teammates.

"Was Piper right?" Oz demanded. "Have you been using your power on us?"

Fucking Arcanist, she thought, a bead of sweat rolling down her spine. There was anger in the big Feral's eyes. *I definitely don't want him to realize what I was doing while we were locked in that cage.* Gathering her magic, Zoe met his eyes and poured power into every word. *"She was lying."*

"Was she?" Kieran Grant asked softly, an icy note in his voice.

Oh, shit, the Arc has his eyes closed. Even their Prima, Nichole Hunt, looked suspicious as hell. The hard expression looked odd on her delicate, porcelain-pale features. The girl might look like a music box ballerina, but Zoe had already discovered she had a core of solid steel. It was all Zoe could do to influence the dancer at all.

I've got to nip this in the bud or I'm in deep shit. "I didn't do a God damn thing to any of you," Zoe said, willing magic into every word and spinning it around her teammates. *"Them,* yes. I don't know about you, but I want to win this fucking game. *But you're my partners."* As she threaded a purr of seduction into her voice, both men's eyes slid out of focus, their expressions taking on the tightness of desire.

"You're on my team," she continued, pumping power into every word. "I'd never do anything to hurt you."

And they all relaxed, suspicion draining away as they bought it. Even Ballet Bimbo Nichole.

Of course. Zoe was powerful as hell. She'd have a multimillion-dollar contract by now if that Sony asshole hadn't blacklisted her. Stupid Normie. If it hadn't been for his fucking Arcanist bodyguard blocking her influence, she'd have had the bastard giving her anything she wanted.

Which was why she didn't think Piper was as powerful as she claimed. Otherwise, the bitch would be making a couple million a year working for some label, keeping Bards like Zoe from "victimizing" poor widdle studio execs.

Thanks to the Sony thing, Zoe had been forced to scrabble at the edges, self-producing on iTunes, YouTube and TikTok to build her audience. She was making a decent living now -- she had a couple of good sponsorships. But nothing like she'd have pulled in with a big contract.

Arcane Island could change all that by letting her prove how good she really was. All the Sorcerers had to do was win. And they fucking well would if Zoe had anything to do with it.

There was a knock on the door. Nichole got up and went to answer open it, moving like the prima ballerina she was.

Zoe snapped to attention.

Jackson Gilbert stood on the other side, wearing khakis and a Hawaiian shirt, a pleasant smile on his gray-bearded face. Three big, brawny men in staff khakis stood behind him, all of them armed. Gilbert must be paranoid as fuck.

"I'd like a word, please, Ms. Maddox," Gilbert said, smile pleasant, eyes cold.

Zoe tensed as her heart began to pound. What did the asshole want with her? Oh, hell, she was probably in for another chewing out, as if Tish hadn't already handled that job. "What about?"

"I was wondering if you'd take a walk on the beach with me." When she hesitated, his stare went arctic. "That was not a request."

Oh shit. She got out of her chair.

Oz started to rise, but Jackson shot him a lordly stare. "Your presence is not required."

Instead of backing down, Oz looked at her. That wasn't even due to her magic -- he was just wired to be protective when it came to women. *I can use that.* She licked her lips and eyed the billionaire. *And I may need to.*

Apparently reading her anxiety, Jackson's smile widened, though it still missed reassuring by a mile. "You have nothing to worry about. I just wanted to tell you how impressed I've been with your work."

What did he mean by that? But her curiosity was aroused. Jackson had a hell of a lot of money. Maybe he also had something interesting in mind. "It'll be fine, Oz," she said, without taking her speculative gaze off the billionaire.

Oz frowned, but he didn't object as she sauntered over to join Jackson. The billionaire turned and led the way out of the house and onto the beach.

He signaled the dark-haired bodyguard, who stepped closer as the other two watched. "He'll be watching for any signs of magical influence," Jackson warned her. "He's an Arc, and he'll be watching for magic. If he sees something, I won't take it well." His smile thinned. "Oh, by the way -- he's deaf, so don't think you can influence him."

A chill stole over her. "I wouldn't…"

"Save it. Besides, I think you'll be interested in what I have to say."

Huh. What the hell is this? She gave him a toothy smile. "I'm already interested."

* * *

Dave

The next morning, we all trooped out on the beach just beyond our bungalow to begin practicing for the next challenge under the watchful gazes of our camera crew and audio engineer.

Raven and Kordell had agreed on a song the night before. "I want to do 'My Feral Heart,'" she'd said.

I'd frowned. "I don't remember that one."

"I never released it." The Bard's expression had flattened. "It was the one I was working on with Roger."

Kordell's eyes widened. "Uh, hey... Are you sure that's a good idea? I mean, it sounds... traumatic."

"Yeah, but Lilly's right. It's time I got over it. Besides, I can't think of a better tribute than dedicating it to Roger."

She'd gone to get her guitar and started playing. Five bars in, we'd agreed it was perfect. All she and Kordell had to do now was hash out the choreography.

Raven said she also planned to release a single of the song the same week the episode aired in the fall. Despite Zoe's sneering comments about her age, the woman knew how to build buzz.

It took more to succeed as a Bard than pipes and magic.

Ariel and I had settled down in the shade to watch Raven and Kordell start working on their moves. "Huh. Wonder what she wants?" Ariel murmured. I followed her gaze to see Tish emerging from the trees. Jenny Stone followed, lugging a huge wicker basket.

"Sorry, no goofing off for you," the showrunner said. Today she wore a pair of cream shorts and a matching cotton top printed with huge yellow frangipani blooms. "While Raven and Kordell work on their act, I want you to shoot more of your B-story. Which today is a picnic." At her gesture, Jenny put the basket down in front of us.

Smiley and I eyed her. "I gather this is supposed to be a nice *romantic* picnic."

"Of course. There's this gorgeous man-made lagoon with a waterfall in the middle of the island. It'll make terrific visuals." There was something hard in Tish's eyes that warned refusing wasn't an option. "You'll want to change, Ariel. It's a great place to go swimming."

We exchanged a look, sighed, and headed for the cottage.

* * *

Tisha had been right about the waterfall -- it *was* a beautiful location.

The rocky outcrop itself was natural, though the falls tumbling down from the jutting stone had been piped up there, just as the pool below had been dug out. The water circulated constantly, pumped out of the pool to the cliff top, then released to tumble down again. Great mounds of flowers surrounded it in a riot of reds and pinks and yellows.

There was a wide, flat black stone near the water's edge that had to be ten feet across. You could almost see the giant neon sign, complete with flashing arrow: *Picnic HERE*. Smiley bounded onto the warm stone, and I put the basket down with the hands I'd manifested to carry it. I swirled into a full manifestation as Smilodon turned to look up at me.

Smiley sent me a flash of imagery. "Go ahead."

The tiger raced across the artificial beach and leaped out over the water, hitting with a terrific splash. Instantly, I felt cooler as he rumbled in relief, paddling happily.

"That looks like fun!"

I looked around to see Ariel drop the long green lace cover-up she'd worn. Her suit was technically a one-piece, but it had all kinds of interesting cutouts that revealed diamond-shaped sections of bare skin. Her navel was pierced with something green and glittering that matched the suit.

I damn near swallowed Smiley's tongue.

Celtic-pale skin gleamed under a wise application of suntan lotion, freckles dusting her lean shoulders. Her body looked strong and long-legged, all elegant curves. I'd regretted dying a lot over the years, but never so much. I wanted to fill my hands with all that luscious femininity and do things you couldn't do in front of that many cameras. Not unless you were shooting porn.

Even my own cameraman had his lens trained on her. Reacting to my flash of possessiveness, Smilodon growled.

The shooter's head whipped toward me at Smiley's rumble, and his eyes rounded. I'd have felt sorry for him, but he carried a distinct stench I knew a little too well: fear and loathing. *Humanist. Great. Just great.*

His *Arcane Island* T-shirt and baggy khaki shorts revealed a wiry build, one long, ropy arm bracing his camera on a skinny shoulder. If there'd been such a thing as a were-ferret, he'd be it. He had that kind of long-nosed face, complete with beady brown egg-sucker eyes. He'd scraped his shoulder-length hair back in a graying ponytail.

Paling under my stare, he seemed to consider bolting. As satisfying as that might be to watch, I decided it wouldn't be good politics to freak him out. "It's okay," I called. "Smiley's not going to do anything. I won't let him." FerretCam had more to worry about from me, but I didn't think mentioning that would help.

Ariel started swimming laps, and we returned to watching her, floating placidly in the water. Smilodon sent me several *Animal Planet* images I didn't want to enact for the cameras. Especially not FerretCam. *Sorry, we're not her type,* I told him.

He chuffed, disagreeing.

Ariel picked that moment to roll over on her back and float, beautiful breasts thrusting from the water like emerald hills.

Jesus God, was she *trying* to drive me crazy? Remembering the kiss she'd given me, I had to wonder. I'd known women who teased as a power play before. Not only did they never deliver, they smirked as they walked away. True, they didn't owe me shit, but why promise at all if you weren't going there?

The thought Ariel might do that pissed me off. But... No. There'd been too much passion in her kiss for a woman playing cock tease to a dead man.

When she reached me, Ariel stopped swimming and floated, her eyes closed, her features serene, for all the world as if she didn't have cameras trained on her.

Hell, there was even a drone buzzing overhead. I gave serious thought to manifesting a catapult, grabbing a coconut, and knocking the little fucker out of the air. I suppressed the impulse. Pissing off Tish was not a good idea, especially given Ariel's need for Aurarest.

"Mmmm," Ariel said softly, eyes still closed. "It's been so long since I wasn't either numb or in pain. Aurarest never felt this good." She tilted her head in the water until she could meet our tiger gaze. "Thank you."

She said it so sincerely, I knew she meant it. *Nope, not a cocktease.*

Ariel closed her eyes again. "It eats at you. Being in pain all the time. You start feeling like you'd do anything to stop it."

Like romancing a cross between Tigger and a Ghostbusters *extra?* "Better than being terminal. Like me." I sounded a little mean, but I refused to be ashamed. I needed some distance, needed to shut her up before she made me want something I could never have. "I've got five more years at most."

Her head jerked out of the water as she shot me a wide-eyed look. Flipping over, she swam closer. "Wait, what? Why? What's wrong?" The alarm sounded genuine, and not just the self-interest of someone worried about her magical prescription running out.

"Tigers only live about twenty years, even in captivity. Smilodon's fifteen."

She stared at me, her lips in a soft, tempting O. "I... I didn't know that. I mean, yeah, I knew tigers didn't live as long as people, but..."

"That's the whole reason I'm here," I told her. "BFS -- that's my friend Kurt's Feral sanctuary -- isn't collecting as many donations as we used to." I curled Smiley's lip, exposing a lot of frustrated fang. He was emitting a constant rumbling growl, reacting to my anger. On the shore, FerretCam looked twitchy -- but fuck him. "Picketers with AR-15s are bad for business."

"So you're doing this as a fundraiser?"

"That's why it's so important we win this thing. The million will buy Kurt a little breathing room." I figured the chances any of that rant would make it on the air were virtually nil, but I felt better for saying it. If I had to live my life in a fishbowl, I might as well get something out of it.

"I'm sorry," Ariel said quietly. Cupping the side of my face, she leaned in and kissed me. Her mouth felt tender and sweet on mine.

By the time we came up for air, I was rock-hard beneath the waterline. Remembering our audience, I shot a wary look toward the camera crew. *Oh shit.*

Both shooters had their lenses trained on us. The woman assigned to Ariel looked excited. But FerretCam...

"I don't think your guy likes Talents," Ariel murmured. "His aura is all hot reds and sickly yellows. That usually means anger and disgust."

I couldn't see emotions in auras as well as she did, but I recognized the acrid scent of revulsion on the air. "Yep, Humanist. The smell gives 'em away every time."

She sighed. "Guess we won't be able to play, not with our judgy little friend capturing it for posterity."

I eyed her, breathing in her scent, rich with arousal and need. She wasn't just pulling my chain -- *she wanted me.*

I hadn't made love to a woman in years. Damned if I was going to blow this chance because of a bigot. "Let me worry about FerretCam."

Smiley rumbled in my mind, sending me a series of images. I grinned. *Go for it.*

"Hey! Hey, hey!" The Humanist's voice held a note of panic. "What are you *doing*?"

Smilodon had slipped out of the water while the crew was distracted by our kiss. Now he slunk toward FerretCam, who backed away, lens pointed skyward as Ariel's shooter got it all on video. "Frooossst!" The man's voice spiraled toward a squeak. "Frost! Frost, make him stop, for fuck's sake!"

"He won't hurt you," I called. "He just wants to play."

"What a coincidence," Ariel murmured. "So do I."

The drone operator guided his little machine down to get a shot of Smiley's slow-speed chase, though his face was dead white. Probably wondering if he was dessert. The boom operator followed, though he obviously wished his mic pole was longer. To be fair, I could see why he wouldn't want to get closer to Smiley's inquisitive rumble.

Right on cue, Smiley roared and made a mock lunge at Ferret.

Who squealed like a little girl, whirled and ran, as one does from an Amur tiger that is deeply pissed-off. The other shooter charged after them. You had to admire her commitment to her craft.

Meanwhile the boom operator and the drone pilot sprinted in the opposite direction. They were either less committed or had a stronger sense of self-preservation.

"Alone at last," I said when the yips faded. None of them would be back for a while. My furry wingman would see to that. I turned back toward her. "Where were…"

I didn't even get the last word out before her mouth was on mine. I inhaled in surprise as she plastered herself against my manifestation, all long legs and arms and desperation, kissing me like the world was ending.

Our magics surged together and fused. It wasn't like the times I'd intentionally smoothed her aura. This felt… deeper, more profound than that. For a moment I could *feel* what she felt.

And what she felt was need. Not just for sex, but

for an end to her loneliness and suffering. Not just the physical pain of Kimura's either. There was a sense of aching loneliness. My life hadn't been a picnic, but I had family and friends who loved me. She just... didn't.

With her tongue swirling hungrily over mine, our auras meshed. Ferals could form psychic bonds with animals, but it was virtually impossible with humans. Yet I could *feel* her bitter loneliness, her fear over her future, the sense of helplessness in a world hostile to everything she was.

I could feel her skin, smell her, *taste* her through our joined magic as vividly as if my manifestation was flesh and blood. I knew that was an illusion created by our blending auras, but it felt real. And it made me feel alive in a way I hadn't in the past five years.

With a soft growl, I wrapped my arms around her and kissed her back.

* * *

Ariel

I closed my eyes, the better to concentrate on the softness of Dave's mouth, the feel of his strong hands as he stroked me, kissed me. He felt as steady in the water as a concrete pylon sunk into the lake floor.

His manifestation glowed against the darkness of my closed eyes, shimmering colors flowing in whirling currents of our magic. The contact made my aura settle, though I could tell he wasn't doing it intentionally. His touch alone did it.

Euphoria rolled over me, intoxicating and joyful. And it wasn't just from the pain flowing away.

I've had lovers -- I even had a Feral lover once -- but they'd never felt anything like this. Dave's manifestation seemed as warm and solid as living flesh and blood. The impression was only heightened by the delicious currents of his magic.

Then there was the way he kissed me, held me, lips clinging and stroking mine. I could sense his hot need. Like a prisoner on a diet of bread and water who'd been given a feast.

So I kissed him back with all the hunger in me, soul-deep, sliding my tongue into his mouth, savoring that hot whirl of power. It made me imagine his cock thrusting into my pussy. Made me wonder how his magic would feel pushing deep. He hardened, going thick and urgent, pressing against my stomach. As if he were flesh and blood instead of solidified magic.

I slid my hand lower, seeking his hard-on through the thick fabric of his uniform pants. And there it was, pressing hard against his fly, a deliciously rounded column. I purred in pleasure and rubbed down his length, pressing, teasing. The violet of his arousal flared brighter as his cock bucked hard against my palm.

"God, you feel so... good!" I breathed. My nipples had pulled into tight peaks and my pussy felt swollen and slick.

Dave drew back a fraction. Beneath the water, one hand closed over my breast. His thumb flicked back and forth over the tight jut of my nipple, his aura simultaneously playing over mine. Magic swirled through his manifestation, beautiful and unearthly.

Pleasure spiked through me, more intense than anything I'd ever felt from breast play before. I groaned. "God, how are you doing that?"

His smile was slow, hot and very male. "PFM -- Pure. Fucking. Magic." He leaned in to lick and bite the shell of my ear. Somehow his mouth felt wet, though I knew that was impossible. The erotic tickle made me throw my head back in delight, imagining what he could do to other erogenous zones.

He began to nibble his way down the sensitive cords of my throat. Under the water, his hand tightened on my breast, thumb playing the nipple, driving my need higher.

I wrapped my legs around his thighs and held on as I launched my own exploration with both hands. Unfortunately, I was blocked by illusionary uniform trousers. "I don't suppose you could change all this fabric into something more accommodating?" I murmured. "I want to touch you."

He drew back and gave me a pirate's smile. "If you insist."

And just like that, my hands were touching bare skin. He felt deliciously hard against me -- not bodybuilder bulky, more like a marathon runner -- long and lean... and able to go and go and *go*. I'd be worried about somebody wandering up and getting an eyeful, but the water was just cloudy enough to defuse the light. Between that and his glow, you couldn't see what was going on below the surface.

"I'd like to put my mouth on your pussy," he breathed. His glowing eyes were narrow with excitement, and his aura had gone deep violet, shot with swirls of rose pleasure. "It's not like I'd drown..."

"Oh God, I'm tempted," I panted. "But with my luck, Zoe would show up, and we'd never hear the end of it."

Dave snorted. "We could just sic Raven on her. The Diva would shut her right up." He slid a hand between the spread thighs I'd wrapped around his ass. His palm felt warm through my suit as he cupped me, pressing hard until I shuddered, my arousal spiraling.

"I've... gotta get... rid of this suit..." I gasped.

"You underestimate me," he breathed, and his fingers sank right through the fabric as if it wasn't even there. I might as well be naked.

I stiffened with a gasp, staring into his glowing face as he slid a forefinger between my vaginal lips, teasing the opening. "I can do all kinds of things with my manifestation." His thumb found my clit and began to stroke.

I shuddered, impossibly aroused. "I've heard of magic hands, but sweet God..."

He grinned. "Good one. Try this." His forefinger began to widen until it felt more like a cock, stroking in and out as he teased my clit.

I swore, surprise and arousal making me writhe. Seemed nothing was impossible when it came to Dave Frost.

I could feel his hard cock trapped between us, and I reached down to wrap my fingers around it. It felt warm and hot and real, and I stroked it. Not just with my hand, either. I willed my aura to swirl over it, and I felt him jolt, his eyes widening. "Damn, Ariel. You really are Talented..."

"So to speak..." I stroked him with firm pulls, dizzy and hot as he played with me. His free hand teased an aching nipple, squeezing and flicking right through the fabric of my top. Hungry, feeling wild, I kissed the strong column of his throat, bit and licked and suckled.

An orgasm began to build, gathering low in my belly, coiling tighter and tighter, on the razor edge of a pulsing explosion.

Then, with a wicked grin, he grabbed my wrist and pulled my hand away from his cock. Before I could protest, he angled the thick shaft and drove himself into me right to the hilt, swimsuit or no swimsuit.

Apparently his dick mani considered the laws of physics mere suggestions.

"AhhhH!" I gasped, and he clamped his mouth over mine, muffling the choked scream of delight. His arms encircled my hips, lifting me, grinding me down. Fucking me hard and fast while I writhed, climbing the peak. I squeezed my eyes shut, watching our magic roil around us like the sun's corona, spiraling in hot coils, boiling as we gasped against each other's mouths.

I came, and he followed me a heartbeat later. Magic rained around us in literal fireworks, hot burning rose and blazing violet.

Shit, I'd never done *that* before.

I clung to him desperately as the light show faded, dizzy and quivering in every muscle.

In the distance, I could hear the Normie squalling for Dave. "We're going to get in so much trouble," I murmured against his mouth, as I fought to catch my breath.

Dave pulled away to give me a rakish grin. "Fuck them. They got their kiss. Anyway, this is *Arcane Island*, not *Voyeur Island*."

Chapter Seven
Ariel

We walked back hand in hand, strolling like any two lovers. That is, if you could ignore the fact that one of us was glowing like a lightning bug.

I was trying very hard not to dwell on Dave's statement that he had only five more years to live. It didn't seem possible. Especially with the currents of his power rolling gloriously over my magical senses like ocean waves. It made me want to reach out to him. Establish a connection again. "I've never felt anything like that."

Dave slanted me a look and smirked. "I'm sorry to hear that. You certainly didn't seem inexperienced to me."

I eyed him. "Is that a slam?"

The humor slid away from his face. "No, it's me deflecting with humor. Old, bad habit." More quietly, he added, "I've never felt anything like that either. Hell, I never expected to. The dead aren't exactly known for their love lives. And when they are, it's creepy."

"You're not dead, damn it," I snapped. But even as I glowered, I registered the vulnerability in his eyes, as if he was trying to protect himself from an experience that had meant more to him than he was willing to admit. "What are you so afraid of?"

He snorted. "Not a God damn thing. Once the worst happens, you don't have a hell of a lot to lose."

Somehow that stung. I wasn't even sure why. Maybe because an experience that had rocked my world hadn't even seemed to even lift his mood.

Dave glanced at me and did a double take, eyes widening. "I didn't mean that the way you obviously took it."

"You have no idea how I took it." I tried to pull my hand from his.

"I'm sorry, I..." His fingers tightened, clung. Taking a deep breath, he said quietly, "Being with you... I'd like to do it again. That's why I'm scared." His smile got nowhere near his eyes. "I'm afraid you'll say no."

There was such vulnerability in his golden gaze, I felt my anger drain. "I have no desire to say no." Suddenly I needed to give him something. Something *else*. "Like you said, I'm not exactly a virgin."

"Now wait, that wasn't at all what I was implying. I was just being a smartass. Anyone who knows me will tell you that my default is pretty much set to *asshole*."

I gave him a long look and decided to take a chance on honesty. "I don't form connections easily. There's stuff in my past that..." I shrugged. "Though I guess there's stuff in everybody's past. Point is, it makes it hard for me to open up. Hard for me to trust."

He just... *looked* at me. Seeing entirely too much. Seeing enough to put a flash of pity in those glowing eyes. I felt the knee-jerk urge to retreat and say something hardass, but I was coming to realize Dave was even more vulnerable than I was. After all, whatever nasty shit I'd endured, I'd managed to survive.

He hadn't.

I lifted his hand and looked down at our laced fingers -- the flesh ones and those that glowed. "There's always been this distance between me and the world. It kept me safe. But when you touch me... I feel what it's like being *safe with* someone. It doesn't make sense -- we've just met. But I... You can't know what that means to me. To know that someone's not going to hurt you. That's..." I shrugged. "... That's a new thing."

"What happened?" The words came out rough and sharp. His glowing eyes locked on my profile. "Who did that to you?"

I tried to meet them. Didn't happen -- I had to look away. If he'd been anyone else, I'd have told him to fuck off, as I often did when I didn't want people to know just how broken I was. Fact was, I probably wouldn't even have been accepted into the Arcane Corps if I hadn't been able to fool the psych eval.

But part of me *wanted* to tell Dave. I opened my mouth...

"You terrorized your fucking cameraman into quitting!" Tisha barked. We both jumped and looked around to see her steaming toward us, trailed by Elaine, the boom operator, and the drone guy.

Fucking *awesome*. Just when I was making a little damned progress.

"Turn off those cameras," Dave ordered in such a cold voice, Elaine immediately pointed her lens at the sky as the boom operator switched off his mic. Even the drone dropped into its pilot's hand.

Dave turned the glare on Tish. "You got your kiss and you got your video."

"And *you* almost gave that shooter a heart attack!" Tish blazed.

"But I saved him from throwing up in his mouth. Which was what he was on the verge of doing. Why do you keep pairing me with Humanist assholes?"

Tish frowned. "Dick's not a Humanist."

Dave snorted, rolling his eyes. "Of *course*, his name is Dick. Who didn't see that coming?"

"How did you *not* know he was a Humanist?" I

demanded. "There's so much anger and disgust in his aura, anyone with the power of a Christmas tree bulb should have seen it."

"That doesn't mean he's a bigot," Tish protested. "Maybe he just…"

"… Objected to bestiality?" Dave asked in a silken voice, eyes narrowing. "Somebody get the phone, *because I fucking called it.*"

Smiley rumbled behind Tish. Even she flinched this time, turning to face the Familiar. He stalked regally past her to lean against my hip and give her a flat predator stare.

"There was way too much hate in his aura," I told her. "You really need to assign Dave to a shooter who isn't a bigot."

"And who doesn't piss himself whenever Smiley starts channeling Sher Khan," Tish muttered.

Dave's mani stepped right up to her and lowered his head until he was all but whispering in her ear. I still heard him. "We'll give you your B story," he said in a low, iron voice. "But you're going to give us a little privacy afterward instead of shoving a camera in our faces, trying to shoot something you can't show anyway."

She looked up at him, her gaze flicking from his face to mine. I felt my cheeks go hot. I tried to make up for it with my best icy glare, but she seemed impervious.

Instead of the disgust I'd half expected, a grin lit her face. And not a dirty grin either. She looked pleased, as if she were happy for us. "Fine," she said. "But no more terrorizing the shooters."

"Agreed." He lifted a brow. "What happened to Dick, anyway?"

"Flew off with your erstwhile pilot."

Dave snorted. "I'm sure they'll be very happy together. Assholes of a feather pucker together."

"Eeeeww," I responded, unable to resist.

Behind him, Elaine snickered, and the boom operator grinned. Evidently, they liked Dick about as much as we did.

Tish ignored them. "Get back to the beach. You need to practice your act."

* * *

We all worked with Kordell for the next three days. Elsewhere around the island, we could hear the other teams at work too, their Bards' voices rising and falling, punctuated by the occasional roar of a Feral. I was acutely aware of the skin-prickling sensation of magic being thrown around like rice at a wedding.

Kordell was a nervous wreck, cycling between excited confidence and his deep fear that he was going to lose the game for all of us.

Raven and Dave took turns talking him down. I even tried my hand at it a couple of times. He was too polite to tell me I wasn't a performer and had no idea what I was talking about, but I could almost see the thought balloon hanging over his head.

Kordell's nerves only grew as the first two teams performed. In order to take advantage of the magical light shows the Arcs and Ferals would create, we were shooting at night using low-light cameras.

All the members of the staff and crew who weren't actively involved in the shoot were seated on folding chairs facing the part of the beach that was to serve as the "stage." They were supposed to provide audience reactions for the cameras. I even spotted a couple of guards in the crowd, for once without their guns.

Our fellow contestants sat in chairs under their

team flags, positioned to either side of the performance area.

The Oracles went first. Debora Allison's voice soared over the pitch-dark beach in the first exquisite notes of Leonard Cohen's "Hallelujah."

Then the bard herself appeared, riding sidesaddle on Chris Freeman's liger as she accompanied herself on a guitar. Her full-skirted white gown spilled down the huge cat's side to swirl in his wake as he prowled along the beach. You had to give her points for guts, though I heard Dave snickering at the long-suffering angle of Kaiju's ears.

Primo Finlay Barton leaped out of the dark, clad only in black tights and body paint as he began to dance around the glowing cat and his rider. Barton was a principal performer with Cirque du Soleil, and he paired raw physical power with exquisite grace. Maruyama Kiri's spell globes swirled around his lean, muscled body, cycling through the spectrum in time to the music and shedding comet trails of sparks. His acrobatic leaps made you wonder if his secret identity was Clark Kent. Their combined magic spun a spell of awe and joy so intense, even I had tears in my eyes.

Unfortunately, the judges weren't impressed by Kaiju's horse imitation -- Valeria told Chris he should have taken a more direct role. The Oracles weren't happy with the thirty-four points they were awarded.

The Wizards did better. Devyn Allison sang Imagine Dragons' "Wrecked" in a deep, grieving rumble as Blake Sanders carried out a desperate, agonized pursuit of his lover's "ghost." Lasya Dheer had sculpted the image of the dead woman so skillfully, she appeared to be flesh and blood, only to disappear in swirls of magical smoke whenever the Primo touched her.

Tyrone's glowing lion stalked Sanders, playing the role of death. At the song's climax, he leaped on the dancer. Dheer's magic exploded around them, looking like a gout of flame.

I wasn't surprised when they got the show's first perfect score.

Then it was our turn. As we all took our places on the sand, Kordell looked downright serene thanks to the cool layer of Bard magic swirling around his head. He'd asked Raven to give him a boost to help him control his stage fright.

He walked out on the beach with regal grace, broad shoulders squared. He wore only a pair of snug black Speedos that displayed the elegant contours of his lithe body. His long feet looked bare and dark against the white sand.

The near nudity wasn't just for sexy effect. I'd spent two hours today applying his magical body makeup, though it was currently invisible, waiting for my magic to trigger it. All that showed was the gleam of oil on his skin as Kordell fell into his opening pose.

Sitting in my circle, I reached for my magic as I felt the power of my team began to gather. Smiley waited beside me for his cue.

I was staring at Kordell so intently, it took a moment before I spotted the anomaly on the sand just beyond him. A faint patch of light lay in his path, so dim I was probably the only one who spotted it. I stared, frowning, not even sure what I was looking at.

Then I knew. It was a spell -- not activated yet, but definitely there. Instincts I'd honed in Afghanistan disarming MEEDs made the hair rise on the back of my neck.

One of the production assistants snapped the slate, and the director called, "Action."

I heard the hiss of Raven's indrawn breath, felt Smiley gather himself. *Now or never.* "Wait!" My voice rang out across the sand as I leaped to my feet.

Raven shot me a frown. "What?"

Amelia Sharp glared. "His time has started. You can't…"

"I'm calling a safety halt," I snapped, striding from the circle toward the glowing patch, Dave at my heels. "Unless you want some really ugly publicity, I'd suggest you listen."

"What's going on?" Dave murmured.

"Not sure yet," I whispered. "Something."

"What's the problem?" Sharp demanded.

I dropped to one knee in front of the glowing patch of sand. It was so faint I might have wondered if I imagined it -- except my instincts knew otherwise. "Somebody's planted a booby trap. Right here."

The Arcanist judge, Jaylen Payne, walked over to join us, bending to examine the sand with his eyes closed. "I don't see anything."

"Of course not," Zoe called from beneath her group's flag. "She's grandstanding to buy time because she knows her team is about to get their asses kicked."

Payne looked up at me with narrowing eyes, his mouth setting. He believed the Bard. Of course, he did. The bitch was influencing him. I was beginning to get a serious hate-on for Zoe.

"Let's find out." I slapped my hand down in the center of the spell. As I did so, I felt the faint outlines of the working -- and instantly knew what it was supposed to do.

Back in Afghanistan, disabling a trap like that would have taken an hour or more, since they were designed to enhance the power of explosive devices.

I didn't have to be that careful, so I hit it with a

whip of aura. It exploded.

Across the sand, I heard a startled cry of pain.

I jumped to my feet and stormed toward the Sorcerers' banner, my fists clenched. Pain shot through my skull, partly triggered by backlash, partly from the intensity of my rage. I broke into a run. "Really, motherfucker? Really?"

I knew that dance backward and forward, and I remembered what move Kordell had intended for that particular section of sand. The choreography called for a soaring leap that came down exactly in that spot. "He's a God damn dancer!" I snarled at the Sorcerers' Arc. "He would have landed right in that fucking spell, and it would've broken both legs. It might have done worse if he landed badly afterward." I had one fist drawn back, ready to hit Grant, who'd fallen to his knees, gasping.

Before I could land the punch, Oz stepped into my path and grabbed me. Since he was six-five and built like the bear that was his Familiar, I wouldn't be breaking his hold. "You're out of your mind! You think I would've let them do something like that?"

"Then why is he on his ass?" I snarled. "Looks like Backlash to me."

"I don't know, but he didn't cheat!" The big man shoved me back so hard, I stumbled.

I glared up at him. "Of course, *you'd* think so. You're under her fucking influence." I jerked my chin at Zoe, whose aura swirled with smug pleasure despite the expression of shocked outrage she wore.

"That's ridiculous!" the Bard protested. "I wouldn't use magic on my own team!"

"Oh yes, you would, you manipulative bitch." I scanned Oz's aura. As I expected, there was a haze of orange smoke hanging around his head. I grabbed his face between my palms, meaning to break her influence.

Eyes widening, the big Feral tried to jerk away. "You're nuts, lady!"

"Oz, *stop her!* She's crazy! God knows what she'll do!" Zoe's voice rang hard and urgent.

I saw Oz's eyes narrow. A spell flashed over his mind. *Oh, fuck, she's been working him!* For hours, maybe days, she'd been using her voice to soften him up, turning him into a weapon she could trigger on command.

I felt the rising burn of a manifestation and knew I had no time to break whatever spell she'd laid.

His aura blew right past the red of rage into stark, searing white. He was about to lose his shit and manifest. Then I'd be well and truly fucked.

I called up a different blast of magic than I'd intended -- the spell my dear old granny had so often used on me.

Then I rammed it right into the center of his skull.

Gold eyes rolled up in the middle of a savage growl, and all six-and-a-half feet of him toppled straight backward to hit the sand, out cold.

"What the hell did you do?" Payne demanded, staring at the unconscious man. "And how did you do it?" He dropped to his knees beside the Feral and checked his pulse. "He needs a doctor! Where's the..."

Dr. Kingston bustled out of the crowd and pushed Payne out of the way. "Give me room." She shot me a glare. "What did you do?"

"Stunned him. His aura blew white. He was about to manifest and rip my head off." I jerked my chin at Zoe, who'd lost the fake outrage and was starting to look uneasy. "She's been working him, using her magic to lay the groundwork to make him go nuts on command."

"The only one nuts here is you," Zoe snapped.

"No, she's not," a rich female voice said.

We looked around as Valeria padded up. "I saw his magic gather. He was about to manifest." The lioness lowered her head and sniffed. "Whether he'd have hurt her or not, I can't say."

"I can," Dave growled, his tail lashing in fury. "I can smell it. And believe me, I know the reek. That's how I ended up with four legs and a tail. Except Ariel doesn't have anywhere to go. If he'd broken her neck, she'd be dead." He was staring at Zoe, who took a step back from his murderous tiger stare and swallowed.

I turned toward Tisha as she jogged up, looking alarmed. "Yesterday you said if any of us tried this kind of shit, we were off the island."

Her eyes widened and her lips thinned. "I'll have to discuss this with Jackson."

"What do you mean, *discuss it?*" Dave demanded. "She could have killed Ariel just now."

"I didn't…" Zoe exploded.

"Shut up," Tish snapped, then gave us a frustrated glower. "We don't know what would have happened, but I can't believe she intended to do permanent damage."

"When a berserk Feral is involved, damage has a way of becoming permanent," Dave rumbled.

"He's right," Valeria said, glaring at Zoe, who was now looking just short of panicked.

"However, it did happen during a challenge," said a deep voice, interrupting Zoe's protests.

Jackson Gilbert pushed his way to the front of the crowd, looking deceptively laid-back in a Hawaiian shirt and khaki shorts. "The rules allow contestants to use magic on the other team during challenges."

I stared. "Even if your victim ends up in wheelchair?"

"Or dead?" Dave's tail lashed.

"It wouldn't have put him in a wheelchair!" Kieran snapped, harried, his eyes narrowed against the pain. "He would have ended up with a sprained ankle at worst."

I couldn't believe these people. "Unless he landed wrong. In which case you'd be whining that it wasn't supposed to happen."

"She's just saying that to get us thrown out of the competition because she knows she can't beat us," Zoe shouted.

I turned to give her a glare, watching her aura pulse as she tried to use her power on all of us. Luckily, it was hard to influence a group this large. "You programmed your boyfriend to try to kill me."

"I did no such thing." She turned to Tish. "All you've got is her word against mine, and she's got a million reasons to lie."

"You've got one better one," I returned. "Do the words 'felony magic' mean anything to you? You could get ten years for that. Twenty if he'd killed me."

"I didn't commit felony magic." But she looked pale.

"I'll tell you one thing," I told her softly. "If I catch you doing this shit one more time, you're going to have worse to worry about than Dave. Because I do not fuck around."

Zoe whirled toward Tish. "Did you hear that? She threatened me. She is *insane*. That magic syndrome of hers is eating her brain. She's not safe to be around people."

"I'm not the only one with a million reasons," I

said in a flat voice.

"I do not like this at all," Valeria announced. "There is too much money at stake, and too many stupid people competing for it." The cold yellow look she gave Zoe made it clear who she was talking about. She turned to Tisha. "I'm entitled to safe working conditions. You assured me that this production wouldn't make my situation worse. I'm beginning to think you lied."

"This is a reality show," Sharp told her. "You signed a waiver and an NDA, so don't think you can go to the media and run your mouth."

"That is entirely dependent on whether you kill or injure someone." Valeria gave her a haughty look -- and nobody does haughty better than a cat. "Anyway, what can you do to me, put me in a cage?" She curled her lip, revealing her fangs. "I'm used to it." She turned with a flick of her tail and walked away.

Dave watched her pass. "You really need to consider BFS."

She didn't acknowledge him by so much as cocking an ear.

* * *

Considering the way I'd just laid out two of the Sorcerers -- and hadn't done myself a lot of good either -- the producers decided to delay the final two dance challenges to the next night. We all headed back to our respective bungalows, where we ate dinner under the watchful gaze of our camera crew.

By the time we'd finished, the adrenaline crash from my run-in with the Sorcerers had imploded my aura into spikes.

Raven and Kordell were in better shape than I was, so they decided to get in some more practice. They headed to the beach to work, followed by our shooters and audio team.

I'd told them I was planning to head to bed, since my skull was throbbing to my heartbeat. Dave and Smilodon stayed with me, saying he wanted to make sure I didn't relapse.

"I could use a little aura help," I told him after they'd all trooped off. "Or I could work a spell to block off my magic if you don't feel like doing it."

"Oh, I don't mind." Smiley settled on the floor as Dave's manifestation stepped clear of him. "In fact, I think I can do you one better. Especially since Zoe the Bard bitch just proved she's going to be a problem."

I snorted. "Ya think?"

He laughed and dropped a hand on my knee. "Come on, it's time I teach you that trick of Genevieve's I've been talking about."

I grimaced as my head gave a warning pulse. "I'm not sure I'm up to it. Besides, I hate to point this out, but you're not an Arc. Not sure how much Arcanist magic you can teach me."

"The force, you must have faith in," Dave said in a dead-on Yoda. In his normal voice, he added, "But in the meantime, I can give you a treatment so you can concentrate." He sat beside me, and I turned toward him. He took my face between his golden palms. Power rolled from his fingers, cool and soothing, and I groaned in relief.

By the time he released me, my headache was gone. He stood, catching my wrists to pull me to my feet. "Come. Work on that spell, we must."

"Okay, but if an asthmatic with a light saber shows up, I'm outta here."

"Speaking of glowing weapons, we're going to need your magic pastels -- or whatever it is you use to work spells."

"Okay." Curiosity engaged, I went to retrieve my tackle box of mystical supplies from my bedroom.

Smiley ranging ahead of us, we left the bungalow to Raven's voice soaring through the night with that impossible clarity that made the hair rise on the back of my neck. We both paused, caught by her magic. "She really is hella good."

Dave snorted. "When she's not fleeing in terror from me. Speaking of, I'd better quit doing my lightning bug impression if we don't want to attract more cams than the Super Bowl." He sank back into Smiley, and I followed the cat off into the palms.

"Where do we want to do this?" I asked. "The beach is out if we don't want to end up providing B roll."

"How about the pool where we had..." He broke off, smiling slightly. "... The picnic?"

"Works for me." That was putting it mildly. An evening at the pool sounded like a perfect setting for a seduction. Now that my headache was gone, I craved another mind-blowing taste of sex with Dave. The Humanists could kiss my Arc-y ass. "Hope nobody's already there." It would really suck to have our sexy time torpedoed by someone's evening swim.

A ten-minute walk later, we emerged at the pool. Moonlight painted the palms, edging their fronds in silver filigree. Nobody was in sight. I felt my lingering tension drain as I listened to the pounding splash of the waterfall. The pool's surface danced and rippled under the tumbling water, moonlight scattering like diamonds over its face.

Dave manifested again, leaving Smiley to make a happy cat rumble and wade into the water. That tiger loved to swim more than a dolphin.

"I figured I could demonstrate the general idea

on this rock," Dave told me, pointing out the outcropping of smooth black stone where we'd eaten our picnic. He stepped onto it and knelt. "Got that chalk?"

Joining him, I knelt and flipped open my artist's tackle box, then handed him a stick of luminescent yellow.

"This is the key bit you need." He started sketching four intricate sigils -- circles, as many mystical symbols were, marked with curved lines that intersected at different points.

My brows rose. I'd memorized a lot of glyphs, but I didn't recognize those at all. "What do they do?"

"Allow whatever spell you cast to use the Earth's magical field as a power source."

I gaped. "Wait, what now?" I couldn't have heard that right. What he'd just said was the magical equivalent of *"They let you draw on the power of a nuclear bomb."*

What the hell was he getting me into?

I studied the shapes, trying to analyze their structure. Sigils have a kind of visual grammar that gives significance to every curve, every line, every flourish. "Where the fuck did you learn something like that?"

"Indigo Ford."

"The *terrorist?* She was drawing on the Earth's magic?" It was common knowledge that the Earth had a magical field -- one generated by all the people, plants and animals living on the planet -- but I hadn't known anybody had figured out how to tap into it.

Because the nuke thing? *Not* a good idea.

Dave met my appalled gaze. "How do you think she managed to maintain that death spell of hers over the months it took her to work it? Indigo and her husband cast a different part of that spell for each of the seven people they stalked and sacrificed. Then they allowed each section to go dormant. The whole spell would have eroded away to nothing without Earth's magic sustaining it. Fred Briggs's sacrifice was supposed to trigger the spell. If Genevieve hadn't disrupted Fred's section right after he died, it would have gone off and killed every member of the House and Senate, as well as the president and vice president. Just like a magical time bomb."

"Sweet God." I sounded stunned even to myself. "I wondered how that spell had survived that long. Some experts swore it wouldn't have worked even if Gen hadn't disabled it. But if Indigo used the Earth as a power source…" I stared down at the sigils. There was no sense of active magic coming from them, much less that level of power. But then, Dave didn't have the Arcanist magic to use them. "And it all hinged on these four sigils?"

He tapped a symbol with one finger. "Yeah. They used the deaths to establish each section, but ultimately the Earth would have powered it."

I gave him an uneasy look. "Are you supposed to be sharing this around?"

He shrugged. "No, though I was never told not to."

"Probably didn't occur to them because you're not an Arc."

Dave snorted. "Probably didn't occur to them because I have four legs and a tail."

"Yeah, people do seem to both fear you and underestimate the *hell* out of you."

"Basically. Anyway, you were CIA, right? I doubt this is the only top-secret thing you know."

"Some of which still give me nightmares." I

looked at the sigil. "Now they'll have company."

"I'm sorry about that. It's just that... I think you need to know this. You may have to use it."

"Against Zoe?" I snorted. "I don't need a magical suitcase nuke to take care of that little twit. I could knock her on her skinny ass with a tap on the head." Hell, I could do a lot worse, not that I'd tell Dave that.

"It's not just her. There's something going on here..." He shrugged, rolling his lean shoulders. "You ever had that feeling a mission is about to go in the shitter? I've got it now, and I don't know why."

I gave him an uneasy look, knowing a bit too well what he meant. I'd been feeling the same. "Well, this *is* the ultimate weird situation. All these Talents we never worked with in the Corps. Bards, Primos... We don't really know what they could do if they got pissed enough to cut loose. Like that bitch Zoe."

"Yeah, but this is a fucking reality TV show, for God's sake. None of these people are exactly Caliphate sorcerers. Yeah, Zoe does shit with her magic she shouldn't be doing, but she ain't building MEEDs."

"So why does the hair on the back of my neck keep doing that thing?"

"Sheer paranoia?"

"That, or a combat-trained instinct for self-preservation."

"There's a difference?"

"Not that I've noticed."

I looked at the sigils. "Maybe I *had* better learn these sigils. Just in case. Are you sure these are correct? Because if all four aren't exactly right... I could end up leaving a crater, and that would suck." Which was a serious understatement. It hadn't been unusual for either Caliphate sorcerers or Corps Arcs to point the tail of a stroke the wrong way and blow themselves to hell.

"I've been watching Genevieve draw them for particularly tricky healing spells for the past four years. And my memory is good."

I looked at the sigils. "Draw them again."

I made him draw the sigils ten more times, erasing the chalk with a wet rag in between, until I was confident I had the design memorized. I'd spent years studying sigil work, first with my ruthless psycho of a grandmother, then with the Corps, and ultimately with CIA sorcerers. I used that experience now to dissect how the shapes worked to collect and channel the Earth's vast energies.

Taking the chalk from Dave, I started drawing the sequence, feeding my magic into them as I went. At first, they felt no different than any other sigils I'd ever drawn, drinking my magic, making my aura reverberate with delicate silver sensations.

But as I swooped the chalk into the third sigil, I began to feel resistance, as if I was trying to force the positive poles of two magnets together. The chalk jerked in my hand, and I had to fight to keep it on track. Power began to buzz through my fingers. "Oh, holy God," I breathed.

Deep down I hadn't really believed this would work. Yet never, in all the years I'd been an Arc, had my own materials fought me. I had to put real muscle into it as I started drawing the final sigil. As I drew the last sweeping curve, power jolted through me, surging up my arm like a burning wind.

I looked up at Dave, every hair on my body rising as magic rolled through me, intoxicating as a shot of aged Scotch.

His golden face broke into a smile. "I knew you could do it."

My mind flashed through all the possibilities inherent in the sigils as the magic continued to build, accompanied by a full-body rush of terror and excitement. I looked down at the sigils. They'd lifted from the stone to begin orbiting me like tiny, glowing planets. Their energy seemed to vibrate the roots of my teeth.

This is dangerous as fuck.

I stared down at my own aura, checking for tangles. Normally, working magic triggered my Kimora's.

I found the exact opposite. Instead of the tangles that had been the bane of my existence for years, color pulsed and rolled in my field, smooth and brilliant. Flowing more evenly than it had in years. "Wow." I looked up, meeting Dave's gaze.

He closed his eyes, and I knew he was checking my aura. "That looks a lot better." Opening his eyes, he gave me a smile that looked a little forced. "Maybe you won't need me anymore."

"Bullshit." Suddenly all that loose energy exploded into desire. I leaned forward, grabbed his face in my hands, and took his mouth, hungry, kissing him with all the raw craving I felt.

His magic sparked hot against my aura, but his body felt stiff. Resistant. I had the feeling he was fighting his need. Or maybe he just didn't trust mine.

"Make love to me," I whispered against his mouth, my voice ragged. Pleading. "I need you."

He pulled back a fraction, golden eyes staring into mine. "You sure about that?"

"Yes, damn it, I am." I pushed into him, sliding up onto his lap as he knelt there, all but climbing his magical body. Hungry to taste him, to feel his power, his magic. His need. *Him.*

Chapter Eight
Dave

I had a lap full of woman. Ariel felt solid and real against me, her breasts mashed against my chest, her soft mound pressing against my erection through our pants.

I didn't feel anything like a ghost.

This shouldn't work. Not any of it. And I didn't care. She kissed me hungrily, her aura surging against mine. "You feel amazing," she breathed.

I reached up and cupped her face, and what I was thinking came out of my mouth without stopping at my brain. "I wish I could see you naked."

She pulled away from me, and for moment I thought I had pissed her off. I had to arrest a dive at her, the instinct to pull her back.

Instead she rose off my lap, her big eyes gleaming at me, and reached down to grab the hem of her T-shirt.

I sat frozen as she jerked the tee off over her head and sent it flying, apparently not caring about the possibility of being seen.

"What if someone comes?"

Ariel shrugged. "What the fuck. People have built entire careers around sex tapes." She twisted to unfasten her bra in one of those impossibly flexible moves women do. She shrugged off the lace cups with an elegant little roll of her shoulders while I sat there like an idiot. Her breasts looked full and round and beautiful in the moonlight. Sweet handfuls no surgeon had ever been anywhere near, tipped with hard, dark little nipples.

Her mouth curved slowly, feline and hot, eyes on mine as she reached down to the zipper of her shorts.

A small voice told me the least I could do is help her get undressed, but I couldn't seem to move. Yeah, we'd had sex before, but it had seemed more like a kinky little fantasy than anything real. Hell, she'd never even taken off her swimsuit, assuming you could call that collection of tiny scraps a "suit."

Wriggling her lush hips, she stripped down her shorts and panties and kicked them aside with her narrow, slender feet. Then she stood looking at me, gaze challenging, as I sat staring up at her.

Impossibly long legs, sweet breasts, a neat triangle of pussy hair. Her body was lean, as Talents tended to be from burning magic, and her hair lay over her shoulders in a tumble of shining curls that looked dark in the moonlight. So beautiful she took my breath.

As I stared at her in dazed need, I realized sigils rotated around us, still orbiting, trailing sparks. "You never took down that spell." It seemed to be my night for staying saying stupid shit. So much for the vaunted Dave Frost wit.

"Don't care." She moved forward, stepping right into the path of one of the sigils, which sailed in one hip and out the other. Her eyes went wide. "Damn. That was different." She glanced around with a frown as the glyphs kept right on circling. She flicked me a wicked little smile. "But I think I'll worry about that later. Just now I'm not in the mood."

Then she stepped astride my bent knees and settled, naked and lovely, across my lap. "You're looking a little stunned there, big guy." Ariel ran her fingers over the angles of my mani's jaw.

"You don't think I have too many legs?" I tried to say like a joke, but it didn't come out that way.

"We've already established I don't much care how many legs you've got." She slid one long, slender hand down the length of my abdomen and rested it over the bulge in my magical cammies. "Though I am deeply curious about this particular part of your anatomy." Biting her lip, she looked up at me, eyes bright. "Think you could get rid of the uniform and satisfy my curiosity? It's only fair."

"Yeah, but I doubt your view would be anywhere near as good as mine." With a thought, I made my uniform vanish, leaving me sitting naked under her. I looked down and frowned. I'd played basketball in high school, and I was built accordingly -- tall and elongated, less beefy than lean. I thought of Kurt, Jake -- even dumbass Bobby -- all of whom had pumped iron every chance they got. Oh, I'd done some of that. You had to be strong to hump a hundred pounds of Corps gear. But I'd never been a bodybuilder.

Suddenly it occurred to me that my manifestation could look however the hell I wanted it to. Hell, if I wanted to turn into a Chris Hemsworth clone, I could pull it off as easily as one of my Yoda imitations. "I'm not exactly a stud, but if you give me a minute, I'm pretty good with my manife --"

"Don't you fucking dare." She surged against me. Before I quite knew what was going on, my shoulders hit the stone with her riding me down. Sigils revolved slowly around us as she stretched out on top of me and lowered her head for a leisurely, very thorough kiss. Silken breasts pressed against my chest, as her soft little belly rolled against my cock.

Which is when I finally remembered I hadn't been a virgin in a very long time. My hands found her ass, stroked the sleek curves, drifted across the dip of her waist, and traced the sides of breasts soft as rabbit fur.

She made a low, approving sound and kissed me, her pointed little tongue sliding into my mouth. It didn't feel exactly the way it had when I was flesh and blood.

It was more.

Our magic swirled and surged together, rolling back and forth like water. Merging. With my eyes closed, I could see it. I couldn't tell where her aura ended and mine began. It felt amazing.

This was hardly the first time I'd been touched by a Talent. Genevieve and Erica constantly scratched me behind the ears or rubbed a hand through my fur. This wasn't like that. I wasn't a pet to Ariel, not even unconsciously.

She pulled away from me, her eyes glittering and wild. "Suck me," she said in a hoarse, hot demand.

I gave her a cocky grin and rolled over with her, bracing weight on my elbows as I gazed down at her in the moonlight. Her mane of curls foamed around her head, and her eyes shown up at me, bright as gemstones. I shouldn't have been able to see the color, but some trick of our auras made rainbows seem to swirl in them. I leaned down and took her nipple in my mouth. Taking my time, I began to suck softly, gradually increasing the strength of my pull.

"Yeah," she said raggedly. "Like that. Just like that." I cupped her other breast as I raked my teeth gently over the peak, flicking it with my tongue. She made a rough sound of desire and rolled her hips, pumping up at me, urging me on.

Her aura was burning even brighter now. It seemed to tug on mine, dancing over my skin, currents pulling my dick, my balls, my nipples. I wondered if I could do the same to her, so I concentrated, all my attention focused on those marvelously sensitive breasts, swirling my aura around them.

"Oh, God!" she gasped. "Are you doing that? That's... that's amazing..."

Mmm. It's working. I suckled one nipple as I tightened my aura around the other, teasing it. With my eyes closed, I watched her magic pulse brighter, spilling into shades of violet. It was rare for me to see auras in any other color than gold, though I knew she was more sensitive.

Inspired, I sent my aura probing between those long, lovely legs. Slipped deep, and felt her arch upward against my mouth, gasping. "Dave! Dave, what are you doing... ?"

Looking up through my closed eyes, I watched rainbow patterns playing over her skin, and it was the most beautiful thing I'd ever seen.

"How are you... ? Oh," she breathed. "I see." Ariel gripped me, her fingers digging into my skin, making color blaze over my skin. I felt her aura tug at mine, playing with it as I'd played with hers. Wave after wave of color spilled and swirled, until I could feel my scalp tingling, my balls pulsing, the skin of my cock tight as a drumhead.

We touched and teased and played, experimenting with our auras, savoring the colors, the sensations. It was all so fucking intense.

And not just because I was having sex for only the second time in five years. That I would have understood. But this... It had *never* been anything like this. This wasn't just two bodies having a good time. It felt as if the core of me was touching the core of her.

All the while I could see the sigils circling us, brighter than I'd ever seen magic glow. Cycling through every color in the spectrum, spilling light across the black stone, across the pale, perfect skin of her lean body. I'd worked with a lot of Arcanists over the years, seen a lot of spells -- some of them deadly -- but I had never seen sigils do that. They'd always glowed in one shade of blue or red or green, depending on the spell being cast and the Arc who cast them.

Just then a sigil plowed right through my head, and a pulse of hot white lust shot down my spine. "Let me eat you," I gasped, a moment before it occurred to me that could be taken the wrong way, coming from a tiger. My eyes flew open. "I mean..."

Before I could reword the sentence, she grinned up at me wickedly. Her eyes were glowing like Smiley's did when headlights hit them in the dark. "I thought you'd never ask. Sixty-nine? Because I've been wondering how glow-in-the-dark dick tastes."

Ariel flipped me onto my back so fast, she took me off guard. The next heartbeat she was on top of me, her ass in my face, and I felt her mouth close around the head of my cock. Then she was working her way lower, engulfing me, inch by inch. I shuddered and lifted my head to her pussy. Grabbing her soft lips, I parted her, took a long, wet lick.

Oh my God, that taste! Astringent and delicious and smelling like pure sex. I groaned in joy and began to eat her greedily. Licking and stroking, circling her clit with my tongue, pressing in. Loving every lap like a cat drinking cream.

All the while, Ariel was sucking me, one long-fingered hand wrapped around my cock, the other stroking my balls while she did things to my aura that made pleasure dance over every nerve ending I had.

Each and every lick, stroke and suckle either of us gave the other sent my lust burning higher. I forgot about the fact that I was technically dead. I forgot my soul was bound in the body of a tiger. I forgot about absolutely everything but Ariel. Her sweet pussy, her soft mouth, her gentle, skillful hands. Sigils flashed past my head, and I dimly realized they were orbiting faster than before. With every circuit, it seemed the pleasure spiraled higher...

But that realization whipped away like a leaf in a tornado, lost in the intensifying storm of lust I could feel building as our bodies climbed toward orgasm.

With a growl that sounded a hell of a lot less human than it should, I rolled her over to her back, parted her legs wide...

And hesitated, years of training kicking in. "Condom... Oh, hell, I don't need one now. Dead."

"Not dead!" She growled through her teeth, and I realized I'd spoken aloud. "You're the most *alive* man I've ever known."

I grinned like a maniac and drove my cock into her in one deep, hard stroke. She lifted her legs and wrapped them around my ass, grinding up at me as I started shafting her as hard as I could, until her breasts danced and our auras flared, cycling through colors I didn't even know the name of. Shouldn't even be able to see, with my partially colorblind tiger eyes.

"Beautiful," she gasped. "You're so fucking beautiful!"

She meant it. I could see it in those dazzled eyes. I could feel it in liquid grip of her cunt as we ground together. "More!" she demanded, hunching hard, her fingers digging into my glowing shoulders.

Writhing together, sigils whipping through us like comets, we came, screaming, our auras blazing through all the shades of the spectrum. Smiley roared in a shattering blast of sound that would have made me jump if he hadn't been making the sound I wanted, *needed* to make.

We collapsed together at last, panting, clinging, covered in sweat. The light of our auras dimmed, no longer so blinding or colorful. The furious rotation of the sigils slowed with the beat of our hearts, dimmed, took on a steady, muted golden glow.

We lay side-by-side, trying to get our breath back. "Damn," I panted. "That was even better than the first time. And the first time almost blew my head off."

"Yeah." Ariel was breathing just as hard as she stared blindly at the sky, blinking. Idly, she reached into the path of one of the sigils, which passed through her hand. Her eyes widened with sudden realization, her mouth going a little slack. "Oh man, we just made love in a circle. Talk about a missed opportunity. I'll bet I could have cast a hell of a spell."

I lifted my brows at her. "What do you mean?"

"Blood sacrifices aren't the only way to juice up a spell. Sex is the other biggie."

I snorted. "This was a hell of a lot more fun." Remembering Fred Briggs's murder -- and the spell it had been intended to power -- I winced.

She gestured at the orbiting sigils. "Seriously, this isn't the kind of spell you want spread around." Something hard and bleak crossed her face. "I can think of a lot of Arcs who definitely shouldn't be trusted with it. My dear old granny leaps to mind. She did enough damage with the spells she *did* know. Especially to me -- she's the reason I developed Kimura's to begin with."

My brows lifted, and I studied her cautiously. It sounded like she might be willing to open up. For once. "I don't really know very much about Kimura's, beyond it making your life hell. It is something you've always had?"

"No. I only developed it recently. Some doctors think the cause is more psychological than anything else. Then again, some doctors say *every* problem women have is all in our heads. But this time they may have a point."

Without thinking, I reached out with my Feral magic. An image flashed through my mind. A graying woman loomed over me -- her wrinkled face twisted in a cruel smile. The shape of her eyes reminded me of Ariel's, except the color was more a watery gray rather than vivid blue. "Who the fuck is that?"

"Who's who?" Ariel frowned. "What are you talking about?"

I shook my head. "Must've been my imagination. I got this... image? Memory? A woman, though I don't remember seeing her before. She has really long white hair -- hip length -- and there's this *look* on her..." I broke off, feeling Smilodon's hackles rise as he growled.

Ariel stared at me, her eyes enormous. "That... sounds like my grandmother. I was just thinking about her. I didn't know Ferals are telepathic."

I shook my head. "We're not. Yeah, we can form psychic bonds with animals, even Normie animals, but there are usually too many psychic barriers to manage it with another human." Yet I was still seeing that face. There was a viciousness in those old eyes that chilled me. "Right now I'm praying you had only minimal contact with that bitch, because she looks like she makes Dalmatian puppies into coats."

Ariel snorted. "I wish. She wanted to make *me* into a coat."

"That... didn't sound like a joke."

"It wasn't. My grandmother was an incredibly

powerful witch. She had this little trick she did. You know that thing I did to Oz? She taught me that... by doing it to me. But she didn't just knock people cold -- she could kill with it. She could... torture with it." Her voice dropped to a ragged whisper that told me more than I wanted to know. "And since it didn't leave any marks, it was the perfect thing to do to a kid."

Ice rolled over me. I felt sick.

Smilodon padded right into the circle, ignoring the orbiting sigils, and curled up on the other side of her like a big furry wall. She jerked and gave him a wild look, as if she expected to see something other than him.

"He's not going to hurt you," I told her. "He just knows you're in pain and wants to comfort you."

He wasn't the only one.

Ariel relaxed back against the stone. Hesitantly, she lifted a hand to stroke it along Smiley's side, running her fingers through his fur. "She killed my grandfather. She told me about it. He was another Arcanist, a healer. He was so good at it, he could even treat adults -- and you know how hard that is." Children responded well to magical healing, but adults were resistant to anything except minor cosmetic magic like facelifts.

"She *murdered* your grandfather? Why? What happened?"

Ariel shrugged. "It was when my mom turned fourteen. Arcs usually develop their power around thirteen or so, but Mom was a Normie." Her delicate jaw hardened. "Grandma decided she'd be more useful as a human sacrifice, so Granddad grabbed Mom and ran."

"They go to the cops?"

"Nope. Small town, and the local police weren't

about to take on Grandma. She had a well-deserved reputation for killing people in ways you couldn't prove. Eventually she tracked Granddad down, but by then he'd dropped Mom off at a church and kept going. He knew Grandma could track him, so he lured her away. Dodged her for three years before she finally caught up and killed him."

"And she got away with it?"

Ariel lifted one shoulder. "An autopsy said his cause of death was stroke. There was no proof whatsoever that she'd killed him."

"So how'd she get her hands on you?"

"Mom met and married this guy who belonged to this... Well, it was a cult. The kind where the preacher was God's anointed and has a right to thirty percent of the cult members' wages. They also took the 'Thou shalt not suffer a witch to live' thing literally."

"Given your grandmother, I can see why your mom would like that idea." I studied Ariel's bleak expression. "But it must have been problematic when you hit thirteen."

She snorted. "You could say that. I had this cousin on my Dad's side. Laurie was my best friend -- we'd grown up together. When we were twelve, she started having migraines. Turned out to be neuroblastoma -- brain cancer -- which was stage four when they found it. The doctor gave her six months at most. I'd spend time with her to keep her company, and we'd draw."

I frowned. I could see where this was going, but I had questions. "Where'd you get the supplies?" I'd helped Genevieve make her pastels often enough to know their creation involved a complex magical process that took days. Gen often ended up flat on her ass for a couple of days afterward.

Ariel shook her head. "I didn't have any magical supplies -- just colored pencils. I drew several portraits of her based on photos from before she got sick -- I wanted to give them to her parents. She started looking better."

"And when she went to the doctor, he said she was cured."

"He actually asked them the name of the healer they'd used, because he had another child he wanted the Arc to look at."

"Oooh, boy."

"Yep. Mom and Dad figured she'd been healed by prayer, but Preacher Rice suspected I had to be an Arc because I'd done those drawings. And they were..." She made finger quotes. "...*too good*. He told my folks no ordinary kid could have done drawings like that. There had to be something demonic at work. They didn't believe him -- didn't want to believe him -- but Rice finally convinced my father. Which left him with the question of who the powers had come from."

I winced. This couldn't be going anywhere good. "Well, shit."

"They had this massive fight. I will never forget the expression of rage and repugnance on Dad's face when he looked at me. He accused my mother of cheating on him. Since neither of them had power, she must have slept with a 'sorcerer.' She finally admitted she came from a family of Arcs. Told him all about my grandmother. He and Rice decided Grandma had passed her evil on to me."

"You'd just saved your cousin's *life*."

"But I'd used magic to do it. Rice swore I'd put Laurie's immortal soul in danger -- she'd have been better off to just die."

I cursed as only ex-military can. "Rice was a

piece of work."

"Yep. So he convinced my folks I needed to be exorcised. The whole church gathered to pray for me, but Rice..." She shook her head. "There was something off about him."

"Well, he was a cult leader. Which meant he was also a con artist."

"And worse. Rice said God had told him they could beat the evil into leaving. So he took a belt to me with my parents watching, but afterward he said it hadn't worked. They tried starving me, but I got so dangerously thin, Dad convinced Rice he'd be charged if I died. Next they tried holding me underwater in the baptismal font. If Mom hadn't known CPR, I'd have died."

I felt like the top of my head was about to blow off from sheer rage. "Where in the hell were the state officials? Your teachers?"

"I was homeschooled."

"That was convenient," I snarled.

"Yeah. Somewhere in there, I started seeing auras, and what I saw in Rice's... It didn't look like other people's, not even the other cultists. It was... really dark and red, and sometimes when he got worked up, it would blow white. I've since learned you see that kind of aura in serial sex predators."

"Is this asshole still alive?" I asked in a carefully controlled voice.

"Died a few years later. And no, I wasn't involved."

"Never occurred to me you would be."

She snorted. "Don't think I wouldn't have been tempted."

"Why didn't your mother do something? Especially considering what she'd endured at your grandmother's hands."

"She cooperated *because* of Grandma. When I begged her to help me, she told me Grandma was a monster. If we didn't drive the demon out, I'd be a monster too."

The thought of what she'd endured filled me with a furious, helpless rage that made me want to kill somebody. Her grandma. The pedo preacher. Her frightened, gullible parents. Each and every one of them deserved a close encounter with Smilodon.

But if she'd had to endure this hell, the least I could do is listen. Maybe talking about it would help her find peace. If that was all I could do for her, I was willing.

"One night my folks held me down while Rice burned me with a cigarette. They'd stopped bringing in the rest of the congregation by then, because a lot of them couldn't stomach Rice's 'treatment.' People were talking about calling the cops. I was so scared, so angry. And one night I just... cracked open. All of pain I was feeling, the exhaustion, the terror... I drove it into them all, and all three of them just went down. Out cold." She shook her head. "I told a Corps Arc trainer about it once, and she accused me of lying. Said I would have had to work a spell to do something like that -- people can't just knock other folks out."

"Should have used it on her."

Ariel rolled her eyes. "Somehow I thought that wouldn't be very good for my military career."

"You were probably right."

"Anyway, that's when I ran. I was staggering down the street, barefoot, dressed in a T-shirt and jeans, half-starved, cigarette burns, bruised to hell. A deputy rolls up, takes one look and drives me straight to the hospital. Mom and Dad tried to come get me, but by then Social Services and detectives were involved."

"I hope you reported them."

"Honey, I sang like the cast of *Hamilton*. They arrested my parents and Rice, and a bunch of the congregation found themselves either witnesses or accessories to child abuse and neglect charges. Instant scandal."

"I'll bet."

"My folks lost custody, but Mom got her revenge. She told them about Grandma, since she was my only other living relative at that point."

My jaw dropped. "Shit. Knowingly?"

"Yep. I'd dragged the family name through the mud, and anyway, I was a witch. I deserved what I got."

"Christ," I said. "Did the bitch at least go to jail?"

"She and Dad got five years. Rice got ten and died in prison. Turns out I wasn't the only teenage parishioner who'd brought out the worst in him, though at least he hadn't actually tortured them."

"But *you* ended up with the Wicked Bitch of the South." By far the worst sentence.

"Yeah. At first it wasn't that bad. Unlike Mom, I had power, and Grandma thought I could be useful. So she taught me all about magic -- the sigils, the spells, the history. She put me to work amplifying the power of her workings. You can make good money as an Arcanist, and we worked for some very powerful people, though some of what they had us do could have resulted in felony magic charges."

"Jesus." No wonder she didn't talk about this stuff.

"I was fourteen or so when this millionaire's wife hired Granny to take care of hubby. Evidently he was cheating. Anyway, Granny Dearest took me with her when she visited this guy who gave her a glowing vial. She'd been working at Starbucks…"

"Wait, what now?"

"Wait for it. Seems the millionaire's bodyguard stopped at Starbucks every morning for a latte for himself and an Americano for the boss. Granny took his order like she always did, but this time she added the vial's contents to the latte. That morning at a board meeting, he shot the boss, two fellow bodyguards, the secretary, and three board members before the fourth bodyguard managed to kill him. The potion was called Berserker, and it lived up to its billing. Because it was a mass shooting, the cops never suspected the wife."

"How did you grow up sane?"

"Mom and Dad did love me when I was little." Her slight smile was wistful. "At least for a while."

"What happened then?" I wasn't sure I wanted to hear more, but I had to know.

Ariel shrugged. "I started fighting her on the worst stuff, but it never ended well. Turns out she could do things with her magic that made what Rice had done look like paper cuts. Just by touching me, she could make my aura feel like barbed wire. Without leaving so much as a bruise."

"So that's where the Kimura's comes from?"

"That or guilt. I finally had enough when she got a contract to assassinate this millionaire's business rival. She wanted me to do it, since that's the kind of spell that gets you the death penalty. I was eighteen by then, and she said no jury would vote to kill a pretty little teenage girl."

"God, she was a piece of work."

"Yep. Except I said no, because I'd had it. Grandma was basically the whole reason my mom had

let me get tortured and almost killed. Plus, I had no
interest in killing anybody, especially not so some
sociopath could get a multimillion-dollar highway
construction contract. Who *does* that? So I told her I
wasn't doing it, and if she tried to force me, I was
going to the Feds. I knew enough about what she'd
been up to, they'd be able to make any charges stick."

"Bet that refusal didn't go over well."

"Not exactly, no. She grabbed me. I could feel her
power building. Suddenly I couldn't breathe, and it felt
like my heart was about to explode. This wasn't just
one of her nasty little punishments, either. She told me
if I wouldn't do what she told me to do, I was useless.
She might as well kill me. I felt her driving magic into
my brain like a red-hot ice pick. Everything was going
dark and I just… unloaded on her. Like I had when I
was thirteen, but this time with all the power and skill I
hadn't had then. There was this thud. The light came
back, and she was lying there dead. I'd killed her. I'd
deflected the stroke she'd tried to give me right back at
her."

"Good," I growled. Smiley chuffed, fully in
agreement.

"I called the police. Didn't confess. Quite. I didn't
want to die, and I didn't think I'd had a choice anyway.
It should have been self-defense."

"It *was* self-defense."

"Maybe. Maybe not. At any rate, it was a moot
point because the coroner said it was a massive stroke.
Given she was in her seventies, he wasn't surprised. I
kept my fucking mouth shut."

"I repeat, *you're allowed to defend your life*."

"But how could I prove I'd been abused? She
didn't leave any marks. And I already had a history of
claiming child abuse. Without physical evidence, who

was to say I didn't just murder her and make up a story I figured the court would buy?" Ariel gave me a long look before she added, "Quite frankly, I'm amazed you believe me."

"Lies have a smell. And I'm not smelling any lies on you."

Her tight smile held no humor at all. "Anyway, I had to do something with my life, so I enlisted in the Arcane Corps, figuring I could finally do some good with my magic. I hunted sorcerers and disarmed MEEDs. Then this sorcerer in a burqa came out wearing enough explosives to level the surrounding block, and I used Grandma's little trick on him."

"Which put you on the CIA's radar."

"Right. So I ended up killing people after all. Sorcerers or terrorist commanders, but still. When the war ended, they had me doing things a little less questionable with my magic. Until Roth was elected, and Indigo and Virgil Ford tried to decapitate the federal government."

"Those idiots," I growled. "We'd told them that was what was going to happen, but nooo. They just had to hand the Humanists the perfect excuse for the Final Solution. So what did you do then?"

"I'd developed Kimura's Syndrome. My therapist thought it was probably a combo of guilt and PTSD." She fell silent, staring into the distance. "My doc at the CIA put me on Aurarest, which helped me control it. Until Roth decided to purge all the Talents from government service, and I lost my health insurance."

"Why didn't the VA pay for your meds? You're a combat vet."

"It did, up until Roth and his buddies in Congress carved out an exception to deny Talents benefits. 'Cause, you know, we just fought for the country because we enjoy killing people, not because we're patriots." She sighed. "I tried getting a job as a healer, but turns out I couldn't do it anymore. The one girl I was hired to treat ended up dying. She was twenty-eight."

I lifted a brow at her. "If she was an adult, it was a long shot anyway." Magical healing worked well for kids, but the efficacy faded the older you were.

"Maybe. She still died. And I found after that I couldn't seem to heal. I didn't want to try corporate magic after what happened with Grandma. I just... I guess I started sliding into a depression. And the Kimura's keeps getting worse. Hell, it's been getting worse just since we've been here." She fell silent for a long moment, watching the sigils revolve over our heads. "When I heard about the show, I applied, and they cast me at once. There's this Bronze Star I got..."

"Tish loves herself a war hero."

"It *is* good marketing. Anyway, I really need to win this thing. I'm thinking of going to Europe. I just can't take it here anymore. The Humanists are going to win both the White House and Congress again sooner or later. I don't see how we can avoid it. What makes it worse is that some Talents genuinely are psychotic."

"I've said it once, I'll say it again. The existence of assholes does not prove the entire human race puckers."

She laughed. "Anybody can pucker, Dave."

I had always been the bracing voice of sanity for my friends. But now I had no idea what to say that would make any of this better. So I said the only thing I could. "Ariel, we're going to win this. I'm going to get you that money."

And I meant it. I might only have five more years

to live, but I was somehow going to help make life better for her. She was entitled to a little peace, damn it.

No matter what I had to do to get it for her.

Chapter Nine

Ariel

The next night, the audience filled the seats under the spotlights as the other teams gathered beneath their banners. Jackson's guards watched for hopefully imaginary keyboard terrorists. The whole enchilada was surrounded by cameras, some on tripods, some shoulder-mounted. A drone looped, buzzing, overhead.

Our team took our places. Every last one of us had something to prove.

After the little stunt the Sorcerers' Arcanist had pulled, Dave and Kordell had added even more flourishes to the act. I'd carefully walked the entire area before the shoot, looking for any more Arc booby traps, but I didn't find any. Evidently Zoe and Kieran weren't as stupid as I'd feared.

They were still going to wish they hadn't fucked with us.

It took a lot to make Kordell mad, but he'd had time to think about what they'd tried to do to him. Whatever stage fright he'd suffered from was gone, burned away by his anger.

He waited for his cue concealed in the trees, wearing only a pair of black Speedos. A misting of baby oil called attention to the lean, rolling muscle of his body, accentuated by the tiger stripes I'd applied in magical paint.

I knelt on the sand in the center of a circle designed to help me generate the act's magical effects. The four sigils Dave taught me rotated among the rest, forcing my aura to flow in fast, even currents. I was dressed in a black spandex body suit provided by the costume department. Black makeup covered my face and hands, so I looked like a shadow surrounded by rotating light.

Raven took her place out on the darkened beach, her guitar in her hands. The Bard wore a thigh-length black silk dress covered in appliqués of swirling gold that made her look as lithe as a reed. Long strands of metallic black and gold fringe shimmered and swayed around her legs as she moved. She'd dyed her pixie-cut hair in metallic gold and black streaks that made her eyes look enormous.

Dave's drums sounded first, softly at first, slowly, establishing the rhythm. Raven's fingers danced over the guitar strings as I sent sigils streaming through the night to spiral around her body. Their soft glow illuminated her ageless face as she began to sing, starting low and soft, the volume gradually increasing as her voice soared toward the higher reaches of her impressive range.

> *Deep in my Feral heart*
> *Where all my passions start,*
> *I feel your magic's call.*
> *I want to give you all,*
> *All my Feral heart.*

Kordell raced toward her out of the darkness. Every time his long, bare feet hit the sand, his painted stripes pulsed with magic, shedding comet trails of sparks that drifted behind him.

Smilodon roared and exploded from the palms in a surge of muscular power. Even the judges gasped as the huge Amur tiger bounded toward him.

Kordell threw himself into the air, flying right over the tiger's head. He hit the ground rolling and sprang to his feet to dance around Raven in time to the pounding beat of Dave's drums.

Raven's voice deepened into a rasping growl as she hit the chorus. Even I felt the hair on the back of my neck rise, though I'd heard her perform the song dozens of times now.

> *You make my hunger roar,*
> *All I want is more.*
> *See the gold of my eyes?*
> *I tell you no lies --*
> *I'm the cat you're looking for.*

Despite all the practices we'd done, I'd never seen Kordell dance like this -- nothing held back, power pumped into every gesture he made. Though the audience couldn't see his magic the way I did, they looked entranced by his grace and power. I sent my own magic whirling around him and Smilodon, illuminating their bodies with sigils and whirling sparks, making Kordell's eyes glow as bright as Smiley's.

They stalked one another, the Primo in a half crouch as feline and graceful as the cat's. Smilodon charged him again and again. Massive paws just missed gleaming dark skin in blurring attacks as the two whirled and leaped around Raven.

> *I taste your Arcane kiss*
> *and feel your fire hiss*
> *As your magic heats my skin,*
> *You make me want to sin*
> *Deep in my Feral Heart.*

Raven never so much as flinched, even when Smiley passed so close his fur brushed her thigh. All her concentration was focused on the magic she pumped into the air with her blurring fingertips and soaring mezzo-soprano. The song showcased the three-octave vocal range that had made her one of the greatest singers of her generation.

I took a quick glance at the audience -- the writers, editors, production assistants, and off-duty camera crew who'd been drafted to provide audience reactions. They all wore rapt, awed expressions, firmly in the grip of our magic.

Smilodon leaped directly at Kordell's face, his claws flashing. The dancer ducked, one hand reaching up to brush across the tiger's belly as the enormous Familiar passed overhead. The crowd gasped.

You make my hunger roar,
All I want is more.
See the gold of my eyes?
I tell you no lies --
I'm the cat you're looking for.

Kordell whirled to Raven, his arms outstretched as if begging, but she turned away, lifting one delicate shoulder. Refusing to be denied, he danced around her, spinning, muscular shoulders rolling, streaming comet tails of magic from his painted stripes.

One of Smilodon's massive forepaws whipped out, appearing to hit Kordell across the head. He somersaulted backward to crumple at Raven's feet. Roaring, the tiger charged. She looked up into his snarling face.

And fear exploded across her aura, an explosion of lemon yellow as her PTSD ignited...

Oh God, don't lose it. Don't lose it. Don't lose it!

But Raven didn't break, didn't run. She just went right on playing furiously over the pound of Dave's drums.

See me stalk you in the dark,
Listen to my passion growl,
'Cause I wanna hear you yowl.
Feel your power spark

Deep in your Feral Heart.

Kordell threw himself to his feet, meeting Smiley's pounce, his hands slamming against the tiger's forepaws as he braced as if catching the cat in mid-lunge.

My cue to conjure.

A golden tiger appeared around him -- a perfect copy of a Feral mani, though illusion rather than bulletproof shell.

Dave caught himself, balancing on his hind legs as though Kordell was really arresting his charge, holding him away from Raven as she sang the chorus.

> *You make my hunger roar,*
> *All I want is more.*
> *See the gold of my eyes?*
> *I tell you no lies,*
> *I'm the cat you're looking for.*

The last words rang over the beach in a voice so high and pure, I felt tears sting my eyes as gooseflesh rose on my arms. Kordell wrenched forward, surrounded by my tiger illusion. Dave threw himself into an impossible backward leap as if the dancer had knocked him flying. He landed hard on the sand, rolled, and fell limp.

Kordell wheeled back to Raven, his body still surrounded by the illusionary tiger manifestation. She threw herself into his arms.

I cut all the magic, and the beach went dark.

The audience erupted into applause and roars of approval.

I ran to join my team as the surrounding banks of LEDs flashed on, revealing Raven on her knees with her arms thrown around Smilodon's furry neck. "You kicked ass," Dave told her, manifesting to return the hug before turning to haul Kordell into another. "You were amazing!"

"That was incredible!" I agreed, joining the group hug. Raven trembled in my arms. "I did it," she whispered raggedly. "I thought for a minute I was going to lose it, but I didn't. I held it together."

"Yes, you did," Dave said. "And I know how hard it must have been, because I've felt the same."

She gave him a glowing grin that made her look about fifteen.

* * *

Twenty minutes later, we assembled at the judges' table to learn our score.

"Well, you redeemed yourself," Valeria told Raven. "That took real courage. Perhaps you're more than a spoiled Bard after all."

There were several things I badly wanted to say to the furry bitch, but I kept my mouth carefully shut.

Next the lioness turned to Dave. "You have impressive control over that cat. It would've been easy for him to get carried away, chasing the Primo like that, given our hunting instincts." Running from any predator -- even a Familiar -- is a good way to trigger their drive to chase and kill.

Dave gave her a long flat look. "Smilodon doesn't get carried away." He said it so coolly I suspected I wasn't the only one who was pissed by her dismissal of Raven's victory over her phobia.

The Bard judge, Lilly Gardner, was almost effusive in her praise of Raven's performance and vocal range, while Arcanist Jaylen Payne complimented the realism of my Feral illusion. "But what's really impressive is the way you avoided upstaging the other performers. The line between 'just enough' and 'too much' is really fine when it comes to special effects."

The high point, though, was Evan Hall, the Primo Judge, who was glowing in his critique of Kordell's performance, discussing technical details that largely flew over my head. Then he added. "You've got a lot more guts than me. I'm not sure I could have stood there with that thing bearing down on me." To Dave, he added, "No offense."

"None taken," Dave drawled, more than a hint of sarcasm in his voice.

We got perfect tens from all four judges.

Grinning, we turned to saunter off the beach and out of the spotlight, passing the Sorcerers on the way.

"Nice job," Oz told Dave. "Valeria's right about your control." The big man gave him a broad smile, evidently not seeing the dirty look Zoe shot him. That, or he didn't care.

But that glare was mild compared to the one she gave me. I returned it with a beatific smile, one hand resting on Smilodon's broad furry back.

Turned out fury wasn't as good a fuel for the Sorcerers as it had been for us. Zoe's voice cracked on her song's climactic line. That would've been bad enough, but her anger bled into her voice, giving the song an unpleasant edge. It seemed to distract their Prima, because the ballerina lost her balance while landing a leap and fell. She rolled to her feet immediately, wincing as Zoe hit a note that sounded like the aural equivalent of my Kimura's.

Raven leaned close to me and whispered, "That's the thing about being a Bard. Emotions you feel can warp your magic into effects you don't intend. You have to be careful to keep it under control -- and she wasn't." Raven's eyes glittered as she added a last deadly insult. "Amateur."

The judges' reactions were equally withering --
and the score they awarded was 23. Most of the points
they did receive were a result of Oz's performance as
the dancer's nightmare bear. I had to work to keep my
face expressionless as the cameras scanned us. A smirk
would have made me look petty. Besides, I did feel bad
for the Prima. It wasn't Nichole's fault she'd been
teamed with a flaming bitch.

Besides, tonight's score notwithstanding, there
were four other challenges to get through. We might
fuck up just as badly.

* * *

Two weeks later

Seething in frustration, Zoe balled up the sheet of
paper with its shitty lyrics, crushed it as small as
possible, and fired it across the room at the wastepaper
basket. And missed.

Cursing, she threw herself back against the
pillows she'd piled against the bed's bamboo
headboard. *If I can't come up with a better song than that,
we're finished.*

She'd had hopes they'd pull it out after their
decent performance on the third challenge. It had
involved Nicole teaching the team a dance they'd had
to perform while working their respective magic. It
had been a nerve-wracking pain in the ass, but they'd
come in second. Zoe had managed to contain her
nerves with some magical help from Keiran, and she'd
won kudos from the judges.

But a week later, it had all gone to hell. The team
had hit a booby trap in the timed maze challenge that
had stunned them all for a crucial fifty-four seconds.
They hadn't been able to make up the lost time. Worse,
the Bard judge cited Zoe's performance as a

contributing factor in the poor score *again*. Adding insult to injury, Gardner had said the song Zoe wrote was banal. Like the has-been cunt had a third of Zoe's talent.

To put the cherry on the shit sundae, Zoe's tension and frustration had bled into her voice, and it threw the team off. She should have let Keiran cast another spell on her, but she was afraid the little weasel would plant some command in the spell to keep her from using her magic to control the team. That bitch Ariel had done a very good job of making them all distrust her.

She hated to think what they were saying about her in the confessionals.

At this rate, no record producer will let me in the lobby once the show airs. I'll lose what followers I do have, which means no more sponsors -- and no more money.

She had one last chance to turn it around. Later in the week, the Ferals were supposed to have a mock battle -- one of those highly visual scenarios the show's producers loved. Then after that, they'd have another group performance with some surprise element they'd learn about at the last minute.

At least she'd managed to mend fences with Oz. Her usual combination of sex appeal, Bard talent, and ruthlessness had allowed her to reassert her influence on the big Feral. Men were a lot easier to handle when she got their dicks involved. Still, she'd been forced to work at it much harder than she usually did. She...

"Zoe?"

Oh, shit, Oz. She wiped the frustrated anger off her face and purred, "Come on in."

He stepped into the bedroom and swept a hard glance over her. She noticed his gaze lingered on the curve of her breasts.

Best money she'd ever spent.

"Jackson's here," he said. "He wants to see you." Breasts notwithstanding, his gaze was hard. "What the hell's going on with him, anyway? I don't like the way he smells."

Shit. Sweat dribbled down her spine. Lying to Oz was tricky. Bears had better noses than bloodhounds, and he could literally smell lies. Worse, that was just one of the abilities his beast gave him. She'd had a lot of nightmares over the past three weeks about what he might do to her if he found out what she was up to.

Zoe thrust the fear away and gave him a dazzling smile. And laughed even as his eyes narrowed, pumping power into the sound. His eyes dilated slightly, his body reacting to her magic.

"No, I don't trust Jackson either." Which, God knew, was the truth. The next bit wasn't. "But he's got this business opportunity -- a variety show." She was going to have to tell Jackson to play along. It wouldn't do to have him out her to the bear. That could blow up in both their faces.

To her relief, a frown of worry crossed Oz's hard, handsome face. "I'm not so sure getting involved with him is a good idea. He smells like he's up to something."

"Maybe, but he's got a whole lot of money." She gave another laugh, the sexy little magical chuckle she'd perfected when she was sixteen.

His eyes narrowed in jealousy, and Zoe silently cursed herself, realizing that was the wrong play. "Just what has he got you doing?"

"Nothing against the rules. He just really dislikes Ariel Piper. No idea why." The trick of lying to a Feral was to immediately follow the lie with some portion of the truth. They couldn't parse which was which and weren't even sure you were lying at all.

She rolled off the bed to slide her arms around his neck, pressing against his tall, delicious body. If not for the fear of what Oz and his bear might do when the shit hit the fan, she'd be enjoying this a lot more. Standing up on her tiptoes, Zoe managed to reach the big Feral's mouth. Humming softly under her breath, she kissed him. For moment he stood rigid against her, resisting her attempts at influence. But as she kept humming and purring power at him with every kiss, that muscled body began to relax. To her immense satisfaction, she felt him begin to harden.

Satisfied that she had him back under control, Zoe took a step back and gave him a slow, lazy smile. "Don't you worry about Jackson. Believe me, he's no competition where you're concerned."

His eyes were a bit unfocused, and his smile looked dreamy. "Go see what he wants and come back up. I have a couple things I want to discuss with you myself."

She gave him a wicked smile and turned with a roll of one hip. As she closed the door behind her, the smile drained from her face, and she strode toward the door.

As she feared, when she opened it, Jackson wore a deeply pissed-off expression. "I do not care to be kept waiting, witch."

There were times Jackson scared her more than Oz's bear. Mostly because of his Arc bodyguard, who was standing there with his eyes closed, making sure she didn't try to use her power on his boss. Knowing he was deaf made her nervous as hell -- if he went for her, she'd have no way to stop him.

Pulling the door closed behind her, she ducked past Jackson and his men. "Not here. Oz could hear a gnat fart."

"You should be more worried about me." But Jackson followed, bodyguards trailing like lethal shadows.

When they were a sufficient distance away, she said, "Oz is getting suspicious. I had to calm him down."

"I don't see why. I can always buy him off."

"Might not be as easy as you think. That man is all honor and duty."

Jackson curled his lip. "It's been my experience that no one's honor is that important if enough money is involved." He smirked. "Assuming they have any to begin with."

Zoe eyed him, wondering if that was a dig. She shot a glance at the bodyguard, whose eyes were still closed. "Do you really want to risk pissing off a Kodiak?"

Jackson's grin turned ugly. "I've hunted bears. They're not that hard to kill." He gave her an icy look. "And you'd die even easier."

Zoe broke step as her heart began to pound. "Was that a threat?"

"Now that you mention it, it was." He bared his teeth. "I am disappointed with the way you're keeping our bargain. The Mystics took the last three challenges. They're well ahead on points. I want them to go down in the next challenge, and I want them to go down hard."

"The next challenge is between the Ferals," she said, frowning. "The rest of us aren't even involved." Tish had said so in the briefing that morning.

"Don't worry about that part. I've made some arrangements. Your job is to make sure Frost's head isn't in the game."

"How the hell am I supposed to do that?" Zoe demanded. "Ariel can see my magic, and Frost is not going to let me get close enough to work him. He's not an idiot."

"Actually, I have an idea about that." Jackson started describing what he wanted her to do.

Yeah, Zoe thought, listening in appalled fascination. *Not a guy you want to piss off.*

* * *

Ariel

I stared at the ceiling, listening to Smilodon rumble in his sleep in the next room. Tigers didn't purr, but he was coming damn close. I didn't blame him. I was all but purring too.

Dave and I had spent a couple of stolen hours at the pool, where we swam under the stars -- among other things. My body was still buzzing from the magical high that seemed to get more intense every time we made love. And we'd managed to do that a *lot* over the past two weeks, despite all the cameras. The trick was to know where the shooters were -- and go somewhere else. That, or go so damn late nobody was on duty.

Which meant my bed was out, since the bungalow was wall-to-wall cams. Luckily we'd found a couple of nice, private spots in the palms, hidden by fallen trees or big rocks. Our favorite was still the pool, though there'd been a couple of times we'd had to go elsewhere because another couple had beaten us to the punch.

Even my Kimora's Syndrome was better. I hadn't had any attacks since Dave and I had gotten involved. That was even more striking considering how rare it was for me to have days completely free from pain.

Aurarest had done a good job of blunting the misery, but my power wasn't the only cost I paid for it. It also made me feel dull and slow. I'd been willing to put up with the side effects, but I'd never liked them.

Sex with Dave, on the other hand, made me feel sharp and energized rather than drugged. I'd had other Talent lovers, but none of them had affected me like he did -- and not just when it came to pain. His intelligence and humor made just being with him a delight.

I'd forgotten what it was like not being lonely. Assuming I'd ever known. Between my Humanist parents and my sociopath grandmother, my relationships had always been problematic.

No wonder Dave dazzled me.

Contributing to my good mood, the team had been cleaning up in the challenges. It wasn't all due to Dave and me, either. When it came to the performance elements, Raven and Kordell played off one another's creativity to kick all kinds of artistic ass. I'd even wondered for a while there if they were going to get romantically involved, until I realized her feelings for him were more maternal than anything else. Seemed she had a son about his age.

I suspected Kordell had a crush on her, though. Raven might be sixty, but she looked forty and moved like she was twenty-five. I wanted to meet the Arc who did her facelifts.

I was beginning to think we were actually going to win this thing.

I grinned happily into the dark. For the first time since my powers had kicked in at thirteen, I felt happy. Oh, the Arcane Corps had given me a sense of purpose that felt good -- I was protecting the people who protected our country. But the flip side of that was the knowledge that if I made the wrong decision or cast the wrong spell, people who depended on me could die. Plus, I'd had to kill. I'd done it because it was necessary, but I'd sure as hell never enjoyed it.

This, on the other hand, was pure, uncut happiness. I might even walk away with the million bucks, unless things went very, very wrong.

Either way, I was moving to Laurel County, SC, where I could be close to Dave at Briggs Feral Sanctuary. I wanted to be with him as long as possible.

At that thought, some of my joy fizzled. If he was right, he had only a few years to live. But maybe I could do something about that. I'd never felt more powerful than I did in Dave's arms. And those sigils of his had all kinds of possibilities. I'd been working on a spell...

I heard his cat shift on his tiger bed in the next room. Too bad I couldn't join him. I'd love to curl up next to that big, furry body, but Dave wasn't having it. "I have too many nightmares," he'd told me, sounding grim. "And I don't want to wake up to find you bleeding because I raked you with my claws."

Maybe he wouldn't have nightmares at all if I were with him. But that was an argument for another day.

With a contented sigh, I rolled over and let myself drift off...

* * *

Sigils radiating deep crimson light floated inches from my eyes. A woman screamed, "Dave! Shit! Dave!"

It was my voice.

Terror swamped me with an intensity I'd never felt before, not even the day my grandmother almost killed me.

An ear-shattering roar blasted through the air, echoed by horrified screams.

Oz!

The Kodiak bear reared, towering over Dave. Smilodon's answering roar vibrated through my skull as he lunged at the shining monster. His own body glowed too, as if Dave had manifested a tiger shell around himself. The Kodiak crashed down on him, but Smiley braced and caught him. A living bear would probably have knocked him off his feet with its greater weight, but Oz weighed a third what Dave did despite his magical bear strength.

But before Dave could do more than rake the bear's shell with his claws, the liger and the lion charged at him from behind, forcing him to release Oz and leap away.

The Ferals had him surrounded. I could see Chris, Oz and Tyrone inside their manifestations, faces twisted in fury. The auras of all three men had blown white. They weren't just pissed -- they were insane with murderous rage.

"But this is just a game!" I screamed. This wasn't right. None of it. They were supposed to fight one-on-one. They sure weren't supposed to rip into Dave en masse.

Somebody had cast a fucking berserker spell on them.

Smilodon dropped to all fours and backed away, head whipping from side to side as he tried to keep track of them all. He roared, lips peeled back off his scimitar fangs.

Chris charged, ramming him. The tiger retreated, half-rearing as he raked at the liger's manifestation. It wasn't much smaller than the Kodiak. In life, Kaiju would have outweighed Smiley by four hundred pounds.

The bear slammed into Dave's right side, bowling him over. Flat on his back, Smilodon raked at the bear with all four limbs, trying furiously to penetrate his mani. On either side of him, the liger and the lion darted in. One of them clamped his teeth into Smilodon's rear leg. Dave screamed in agony.

They're going to tear him apart! I've got to get through the ward! I gathered all my strength, all my power, and threw it against the magical barrier around the arena, fighting to blow it apart like I had the one at the cage.

It was like trying to punch through a bank vault door with your bare fist. The rebound magic made my skull ring.

Dave's manifestation was growing dimmer. If it crashed, they'd rip him apart.

The liger raked his claws over any part of Dave he could reach… And the manifestation winked out.

"Dave!" I screamed.

Through my closed lids, I saw glowing arms encircle me. I shrieked, instinctively drawing power for a psychic jolt…

"Ariel, it's me!" Dave said in my ear, voice tight and controlled. "You're all right! You're just having a nightmare."

My eyes opened to see his glowing face looming over me on the bed. Anxiety chased over his aura in shades of lemon yellow. Beside my bed, Smilodon rumbled, moaning in distress.

"She okay?" Raven asked from the doorway, eyes wide, hair in spikes, a robe open over her floral silk pajamas.

Kordell gave me a worried frown from over her shoulder. "Is there anything we can do?"

Still only half-awake, I shuddered in terror. The Bard hurried over, bending to stroke a maternal hand through my hair. Her touch felt cool and soothing. "It's okay," Raven said, though her smile looked tight. "Night terrors are a bitch, I know." She shook her head. "God knows I've had my share."

Dave rubbed my back. "What did you dream?"

"You were in the arena. All the Ferals were trying to kill you. I couldn't get to you through the wards. They got you down -- they were going to rip you apart..." Tears of remembered pain and helplessness rolled cold down my face.

"Shhhh," Dave's voice was low, as soothing and calm as his smile. "It didn't happen. It's not going to happen. The contest is strictly one-on-one, remember?"

"I've been having nightmares too," Kordell told me. "The stress has been pretty bad."

Raven grimaced. "I had a doozy when we got here. About Roger." She shuddered.

"This wasn't a nightmare," I told them raggedly. "Or not just a nightmare. Sometimes I have precognitive dreams. I think this was one of them."

"There's absolutely no way any of those guys would try to kill me," Dave told me patiently. "They're all friends of mine. I served with them."

"I think they were under some kind of spell."

Dave frowned. "You mean like what happened to Bobby? A magical booby trap?"

"Yeah, that's exactly what I mean. Maybe in the wards I couldn't get through."

"If someone did sabotage the wards," Kordell asked, "would you be able to spot it like you did with that spell they laid for me?"

I shrugged. "Yeah. From what Tish said in the morning briefing, the ward's only there as a safety measure." Because getting hit by an airborne tiger would hurt. "I should be able to spot any sigil that does something else."

Raven gave me a smile. "Then there you go. You can just check out the arena and make sure no one's planted anything. If they have, we raise hell. You did before and it worked."

"You did save me a broken leg." Kordell grimaced. "Or worse."

"Yeah, but I really think this was a nightmare." Dave rubbed calming circles over my back. "It's one thing to trip Kordell, it's another to get me torn apart by crazed Ferals. It would be a huge scandal. Not even Zoe would risk that."

He had a damn good point there, and I felt myself begin to relax. "Maybe you're right," I said. "Sometimes it can be tough to tell the difference between nightmares and precog dreams."

Dave looked over at Raven and Kordell. "Why don't you all go back to bed? I'm just going to sit with her for a while until she calms down."

"I do sing one hell of a lullaby," Raven offered.

I forced a grin. "Nah. We'll just talk a while."

She gave us a long look before nodding and turning to Kordell. "Let's leave them to it. We've got to get up early tomorrow. I still want to nail down the choreography for that third stanza."

After the door closed behind them, Dave lay down in the bed with me, wrapping his arms around me. With a little chuff, Smilodon flopped down on the floor. "Let's just cuddle for a while, shall we?" He held me, stroking my hair, not saying anything more.

After a moment, I felt the tension and lingering terror drain away as I began to feel a little silly. He was right. Not even Zoe would try anything that crazy. I settled down, surrounded in the soothing magic of his arms. The tension drained away, and I slid into sleep.

Barely an hour later, I jerked awake again, Dream Dave's agonized screams ringing in my ears as Real Dave called my name. "It's okay, baby! You're okay."

Raven, looking frazzled, walked in and offered to sing me to sleep again. This time I didn't turn her down.

But I also knew I was going to have to come up with a plan to protect Dave if I wanted to sleep again. I was still searching for a solution as I drifted off, Raven's throaty voice purring a spell, Dave stroking my back.

I woke up the next morning with the plan that had come to me as I slept.

* * *

I sat in the bungalow's kitchen a day later, my materials arranged neatly on the table in front of me -- fifteen sigils made of air-dried clay, a neat coil of smooth white cord, a bottle of Gorilla Glue and another of Elmer's.

I'd kicked my teammates out of the house that morning so I could work on my project without anyone else's magic disturbing the spell. Raven and Kordell had gone to the beach to refine their act for the final challenge, while Dave headed to the pool to fish. I intended to join him once I finished the collar so we could cast the spell to activate it.

I'd worked my own blood into the clay before molding it into three-dimensional sigils, let them dry overnight, then painted them for an extra layer of power. The magical paint was dry now, and all that was left was to braid them onto the cord I intended to tie around Smilodon's neck.

I wished I could ignore the dreams I'd had as nothing more than a recurring nightmare. Unfortunately, two Mideast tours in the Arcane Corps, plus another five years with the CIA had taught me it wasn't a good idea to ignore my precognition.

Unfortunately, I had a nagging feeling the collar design was missing something. I'd need a deeper connection between me and Dave once he was inside that ward. I bit my lip as I leaned an elbow on the table, twisting a lock of my hair around my fingers.

Which was when my eyes focused on the copper curl.

Chapter Ten

Dave

This was the kind of day that demonstrated why Amur tigers live in Siberia. There's nothing like a fur coat to make a hot day even more miserable.

Smilodon and I stood on the stone outcrop's edge, looking down the length of the man-made waterfall. "Cannonball!" I yelled, and we launched ourselves off the rock outcrop, sailed through the air, and hit the pool with a gigantic splash.

And sank like a rock into instant cool.

Sighing in relief, we swam back to the surface to find our assigned shooter grinning at us happily from behind her camera's eyepiece. Tamika Brannon, who'd replaced FerretCam Dick, wanted to grab some useful B-roll for editing purposes. Me playing in the water like a giant house cat fit the bill nicely. Besides, we had time to kill before Ariel planned to come out and finish the spell. I needed to blow off steam over the past couple of painfully restless nights.

As Smiley tiger-paddled, something silver darted past beneath the water. Jackson had stocked the lake with freshwater fish for his millionaire B&B guests.

Smilodon dove, big paws lashing out to scoop the carp into our open jaws. The fish went nuts, its scaled body whipping back and forth. Our jaws clamped. *Crunch.* Fishie went limp as we surfaced and swam toward the picnic rock to clamber out and flop down. As Smiley tore into the snack with happy greed, I shot a glance up at the sun. Ariel was supposed to join us soon with the new collar.

Jesus. The woman weighed a buck twenty, tops, yet she wanted to protect the Tooth Tank.

I told myself it was ridiculous to feel so happy

about that. Her concern didn't really mean our relationship was going anywhere. First, I still had too many legs. Second, the show would be wrapping next week after the final challenge. We'd both be going home, me to BFS, her to New York.

The thought made my chest ache.

We'd spent the past two weeks making love and working together as a team. It had made me imagine life if we could somehow make our relationship permanent. Yeah, sex with Ariel was literally magical, but it was more than that. I was fascinated by her intelligence, her sheer guts.

And the fact that someone so utterly female could project stone killer when she got pissed. I'd known plenty of stone killers and plenty of pretty women, but the combo pack was…

"Hey, Dave?" Tamika said. Camera still balanced on one shoulder, she lifted her walkie-talkie as if she'd just received new orders. "I've gotta go. Jackson's called a meeting."

"Is the cast supposed to attend?"

"Nope. Just the production crew." She walked off with her camera.

Huh. Most of the time Smiley couldn't lick his balls without somebody catching it for posterity, but now they were all voluntarily leaving us to our own devices? I wasn't sure I liked the sound of that. Smiley rumbled -- he didn't either. We waited, tense, but when nothing exploded, he went back to his sushi.

"Dave?"

I snapped my head up to see Valeria Sanz gazing at me from the trees.

"Shit, I knew it." I jerked off the stone as if spring loaded. "What's going on? Is there a problem?"

She manifested a hand and waved off my

concern. "Oh, nothing like that. I just wanted to have a word with you."

I stared. "Why? I mean, I thought fraternization isn't allowed."

"Well, no," she said, padding closer. "I just decided to make an exception."

Uh-*huh*. I backed up a step and closed my eyes, but there was no sign of magical interference in her aura. "What led to this sudden turnabout?"

She hopped up on the stone next to me and lay down on her belly, her ears tilted toward me. "I heard something today that disturbed me. Zoe informs me that you and Ariel Piper are involved."

I shook my head. "Now there's somebody you definitely don't want to fraternize with. Zoe never uses her power for anything but evil."

She chuffed, her tufted tail tip twitching. "Oh, believe me, I'm aware. And I won't deny she had ulterior motives. That's why I wanted to see if it was true." She gave me an unnerving predator stare. "*Are* you and Ariel involved? I knew there was some sort of showmance thing going on, but I assumed it was an act."

Irritation stung me. "I don't see how that's any of your business."

Her golden eyes narrowed. "So it *is* true. Are you in love with her?"

Her tone was so incredulous that I felt my hackles rise. "Again, I don't see how that's any concern of yours."

"You're right, of course." Valeria's gaze went a little sad, a little distant. "But I've been down that road, and trust me, you won't find the scenery very pleasant."

I closed my eyes again for another look. I still

didn't see any sign of a spell, but that didn't mean she wasn't under the Bard's influence. I was nowhere near as sensitive when it came to detecting magic as Ariel. Too bad she wasn't here to check. "Are you sure Zoe hasn't gotten to you?"

Valeria chuffed, the big cat version of a laugh. "Oh, she gave it her best shot. But I was married to a Bard for ten years. He didn't often try to influence me deliberately, but sometimes his subconscious had other ideas. I grew some rather thick mental shields. And that silly twit has nowhere near his power."

"Okay. But again, I don't understand why you'd care about my love life."

"Gerry and I were still married when I died."

"Oh, shit. I'm... I'm sorry," I said, knowing how lame that must sound.

"I'll give him this, he tried. He really did love me, you know." She looked off over the lake, her expression distant. "We both loved each other a great deal. I only wish I hadn't been overwhelmed by stupid patriotism. It's one thing to go fight for your country and lose your life. People have been doing that for centuries -- leaving their families behind. But this... The body was gone, but the soul survived. Enough of me that he thought..." She sighed heavily. "He said that if I'd come back as a quadriplegic, he wouldn't have left me. So how could he leave me like this? In sickness and in health, right?"

"That does sound like love."

"Yes. But the reaction of the people around us -- his family..." She shook her head, the human action looking odd in a lioness. "His mother said that I was an animal and that I might kill him. That I wasn't safe around his brother's children. After all, everyone has heard of tragic situations when a Meld loses control...

It makes it hard to argue otherwise, doesn't?"

"Yeah," I said. My voice sounded a little rough. I wasn't controlling my vocal magic as well as I should have been.

"And when he tried to bring me home, the neighbors lost their collective minds." She curled a lip, revealing one three-inch fang. "They were all terrified I was going to eat their children."

I sighed. "Yeah, the same thing happened to me when I went home to my parents. They've got this farm in Texas where we raise horse Familiars. You can't use them for combat, but they've been bred to work cattle for centuries. Unfortunately, this Human Heritage asshole whipped up the neighbors. My father started getting death threats. They swore they were going to kill me -- send me back to hell where I supposedly come from." I curled my own lip. "Being a demon and all."

Her tail whipped. "That sounds even worse than what happened to me."

"And it went downhill from there. They firebombed one of the horse barns. We lost ten Familiar horses to those fuckers. We were lucky the fire didn't spread to the house and kill everybody in it. The story went national -- 'Combat vet targeted by neighbors.' Kurt's dad called and asked if I wanted to come to BFS, so I went. I was too worried they'd go after my parents next."

"And they might have."

"Yeah. BFS gets picketed, but it's been a tourist draw in Laurel County since the 1990s, and people have grown up going there on school tours. Plus, Talents have lived in Laurelton since right after the Civil War. Even with that, we have to deal with the fucking Humanists."

"Yes, one of the local preachers accused Gerry and me of bestiality," she said sadly. "He demanded the county sheriff charge him, since the law's still on the books. I knew they'd never understand about my manifestation. Anyway, they'd have found something to charge Gerry with. Necrophilia or something. So I left him -- I didn't want him to go to prison over their bullshit. We didn't even need a divorce since I'm legally dead. I was trying to decide whether to go to the VA facility for Melds when Tisha offered me this gig." She paused, studying me. "I have been thinking about what you said about BFS. Do you think your friend Kurt would be able to take me in?"

"Of course. Fred founded BFS years ago because of situations like this." It was odd. Three weeks ago, I would have been over the moon if she'd asked that question. Now my reaction was no different than if any other Arcane Corps vet had asked the question. "You'll like it there. It's a beautiful facility." I grimaced. "Though Human Heritage can be a pain in the ass. Kurt's filed a lawsuit against them for interfering in his business. He may even manage to collect damages if we get the right judge."

She studied me, her eyes bright gold. "That is the question, isn't it? The situation in the country is so delicate right now. That's one of the reasons why I decided to come talk to you. You're right, this conversation is not exactly kosher. But I don't want to see you try to go down this road with Ariel. I'm sure she's a perfectly nice girl but..." The lioness shook her head. "She doesn't understand how many barriers there will be to this relationship." Valeria hesitated a moment. "And then there's the Kimura Syndrome. Zoe believes Ariel is simply using you to control her pain -- that she's going to dump you in short order."

I eyed her, not happy that she'd been gossiping about me with Zoe Fucking Maddox. "Again…"

"None of my business, I know. But when I had to leave Gerry…" Valeria broke off, staring at one of the mounds of flowers beside the waterfall. "… I was crushed. I'd lost my life. My humanity. The man I loved. Everything." She looked at me. "Even if Ariel isn't using you -- and I'm fully willing to grant that she's not -- neither of you understand what you're getting into."

"That isn't your problem, Valeria." And yet, she'd just put into words a feeling I'd been trying to ignore for the past two weeks.

* * *

Ariel

I strode up the path toward the pool, the new collar in my hand. Zoe stepped from the palms into my path, a nasty little smirk on her face. "Why, look -- it's *the Little Mermaid.*"

I lifted a brow. "Does that make you Ursula?"

But the insult didn't land because she'd just gotten a good look at me. Her eyes widened. "What the hell did you do to your hair?"

I controlled the impulse to reach for what was left of it. "What are you, the hair police?"

She gave me a malicious little smirk. "The producers are going to be pissed. You just screwed the hell out of continuity when they try to edit this thing."

Oh, fuck, she had a point. They wouldn't be able to use footage of me with long hair as cutaways in scenes with my new cut. I hadn't thought of that. I forced myself to give a careless shrug. "That's why they pay editors the big bucks."

I started to shoulder past her, when she said,

"You should be worried about what your furry fuckbuddy will think. Not that it matters -- I'd say that relationship is doomed anyway."

I stopped dead and studied her, suspecting she was trying something. But no, there was no sign of magical activity in her aura. Nothing but the green glow of smug satisfaction and malice. "What do you mean by that?"

Zoe laughed. "You'll find out," she said and sauntered off, ass swinging like a pendulum of a grandfather clock.

The buzz in the back of my head grew even louder. I was strongly tempted to follow her and give her a punch in that surgically perfect nose. Or maybe a nasty little jolt, grandma-style.

Reluctantly, I discarded the idea. Testing Tisha's patience was probably not a good idea. Besides, I had the feeling I needed to check on Dave, so I turned and headed toward the pool, my strides just short of running.

As I approached the clearing, I heard voices and broke step, frowning. It sounded like Valeria Sanz. What the hell did Ms. *No Fraternization* want with Dave? Every muscle I had coiled as an ugly little spike of jealousy took root in my chest, burning and nasty.

"I realize a new love can be very seductive, especially when there's so much magic involved," the judge was saying. "But like it or not, you and Ariel are going to have to deal with the real world. I'm very much afraid you'll find it as painful for you as it was for Gerry and me."

"Every relationship runs into rough water," Dave told her. "That doesn't mean it's doomed."

Temper streamed through me, and I stalked into the clearing. "What happened to 'I can't even talk to you, Dave'?" I demanded.

Remembering the cameras, I paused and glanced around, imagining just how humiliating it would be to have this conversation appear on the show. Oddly, there were no cams around. Come to think of it, Elaine, my own shooter, had ducked out on me earlier. *What's with that?*

Valeria stared at me, her ears rotating forward. "What on earth did you do to your hair? It looks as if you cut it with hedge clippers." Her gaze dropped to the bundle in my hand, spotting the red strands knotted among the braided cords. "You used it to make that." Her eyes closed and her tail lashed at what she saw. "That's a really strong spell. What is it?"

"It's a collar," Dave told her.

"She's making you wear a spelled collar?"

Before I could tell the Meld where she could go, Dave sighed. "It's not like that. Ariel's convinced something's off about tomorrow's challenge. She wants to make sure she can punch through the wards if she needs to."

"Why do you think there would be a problem with the wards? They're just designed to keep someone from getting knocked into the audience."

"I'm pretty sure they're more than that," I told her, mentally bracing myself for her reaction.

"Again, on the basis of what?"

Damn it. "I had a dream. The other Ferals were trying to kill Dave inside that circle, and I couldn't get to him."

Sure enough, amusement swirled through the cat's aura. "You butchered your hair because you had a nightmare?" Golden eyes narrowed. "You must be in love with him. No woman would do *that* to her hair otherwise."

I could feel my cheeks going hot, and it pissed me off. "Stereotype much?"

Her voice went dust-dry. "Yes, I ended up in the body of a lioness because I'm such a traditional girl." She stalked toward me, and I had to repress the instinct to step back. "*Are* you in love with him?"

My fists clenched. "I've always had precognitive dreams. If I did see the future, everyone in that circle will be in danger. So yes, I'd do worse than hack off my hair to keep that vision from coming true."

She paused, her head tilting. "Just exactly what did you dream?"

"Like I said, they were attacking Dave. Not one by one, the way the challenge is supposed to run. All at once."

"Have you told Tish?"

"I intend to. But there's something weird going on here. They're ignoring safety protocols they shouldn't be ignoring. Look at what happened when Kieran set that booby trap for Kordell. Tish said the day before anybody who cast that kind of spell would be off the island, yet they didn't do shit to either him or Zoe."

Valeria's tail lashed. "I overheard that discussion. Tish wanted to take action, but Jackson overruled her. He said replacing them would put the shoot too far behind."

I shrugged. "There you go."

"Tish still needs to know."

"And I'm going to tell her after Dave and I finish this spell, but I'm not expecting much."

Valeria eyed me. "I think you should know Dave has invited me to move to BFS. I decided to accept his kind offer."

Anger stabbed through me, sharp as a blade and

spiked with hurt and betrayal. "Good for you."

She turned her regal head and looked at Dave. "You see? You'd better handle this." Without another word, she padded past me into the trees, tail tip twitching.

I grappled for self-control only to feel it skid out of reach. "'Handle' what?"

His manifestation emerged from Smilodon, raking his hands through his short-cropped hair. "She was married when she was killed in combat. When she came home to her husband, the neighbors lost their minds." Shaking his head, Dave sighed. "They tried to get him charged with bestiality, so Valeria left him to keep him out of jail. She'd been trying to decide whether to go the VA Familiar facility when Tish offered her a role on the show."

I winced at that. "That snake pit?"

"Supposedly, it's better than it was. After that *60 Minutes* investigation, the Corps started trying to clean it up, though I gather the cages are still pretty cramped. They're renovating but..." He shook his head. "BFS would be a huge improvement. We've got three more Melds, plus four Familiars whose Ferals live in the county. Our enclosures are much larger, and we've built treehouses that are pretty comfortable." He looked down at the ground and asked softly, "Is she right? Are you in love with me?"

I was suddenly royally sick of this discussion. No matter what I said, it was going to bite me on the ass. "Look, I need to cast this. Can we table this discussion?" I strode past him to the stone where we'd worked the first spell.

And made love.

I crouched and started drawing sigils, then had to stop and erase one so badly drawn it would have blown both of us to hell. Tried again. Fucked up again.

"Shit, this isn't going to work." I sat down on the stone, folded in my legs in a lotus, closed my eyes, and started doing tactical breathing to calm myself down.

Damn that furry bitch anyway.

I was far too conscious of Dave watching me. Finally, as if realizing he wasn't helping my concentration, he sank back into Smiley. *Probably trying to put more distance between us.* The thought sent a combination of frustrated anger and despair rolling through me.

Oh, fuck, she's right. I was in love with Dave.

This wasn't just about the money, the reality show, or the magic. It wasn't even about the Kimura's or new and interesting sex. Dave had sunk his claws right into my soul.

And I knew him well enough to realize he was *not* going to want a public romance with me. Under his dirty mouth and Arcane Corps swagger, Dave was a southern boy with a deeply religious upbringing.

I'm never going to get this thing cast if I don't get my head out of my ass. Strong emotions interfered with concentration and control, as that idiot Zoe had proved repeatedly over the last month. You needed discipline to work magic.

Luckily, I'd learned how to cast under worse conditions, so I concentrated on blanking my mind. Breathing deeply, eyes closed, I fought to ignore the golden glow of Dave's spirit occupying the space where his cat stood. Even unmanifested, he blazed to my senses.

It took longer than it should have, but I finally managed to sink into a meditative trance. Opening my eyes and keeping my mind ruthlessly blank, I spread the collar out on the stone and began carefully copying the sigils. With every stroke, I sent my power rolling down my arm and into the pastel stick. As I completed each sigil, the matching glyph on the collar took on a soft glow.

Pain began to throb behind my eyes. My aura was kinking again, though I'd stopped having problems with that a couple of weeks ago. Probably because any time it had shown sign of tangling, Dave had insisted on smoothing it out.

Acting like he *cared*.

Finally, the spell was done. I looked up at him, keeping my voice exquisitely polite. "Step inside the spell, please."

To my surprise, I saw that his aura swirled with deep shades of red -- markers of pain. Almost like this hurt him as much as it did me. "Ariel..."

"Look, we need to get this done." I thought of several other things I'd like to add, but they'd only start the fight I was trying to put off.

Smilodon stepped into the circle, placing his big paws carefully to avoid smudging the sigils. He sat down and curled his long tail around his forepaws, looking for all the world like the world's biggest house cat.

The tiger moaned, the sound plaintive and sad. I suspected some of the red in Dave's aura came from him. He really was remarkably sweet for a Tooth Tank. He dropped his head, looking down at the spell circle. "Wait, you used the earth sigils for this?" Dave sounded uneasy. "Don't you think that's overkill?"

"Better overkill than *get* killed. Besides, if it was just a nightmare, we won't need it." I grimaced. "And I'll have sacrificed all that hair for nothing."

"Ariel, I..."

"I don't want to hear it." I reached out a finger

and sent magic pouring into the sigils. Pain rammed into the center of my skull like a spear, but the sigils lifted off the stone as the spell activated and began to rotate slowly around us. In my hands, the collar's clay sigils began to luminesce, responding to the rise of magic.

I turned to Smilodon and wrapped the collar around his throat. I'd measured his neck the day before, so it fit precisely. I could feel its magic humming between my hands, resonating with my aura as I tied it off.

I poured power into it and the spell flared to life, amplified by the circle rotating around us. Magic blazed around us, and Smilodon's eyes widened.

And I *felt* him -- felt both Dave and Smiley in a link that seemed to reach all the way to the soul. The decency and strength that contained the ferocious predator underneath. Emotion roared through me so intense it took my breath. The headache that had been building since I'd found Valeria with him disappeared, swept away by the intensity of the magical bond I'd just created.

"I can... I can *feel* you," Dave said, his voice soft with wonder. "She's right. You are in love with me."

I stared back, crazy joy blazing through me as I saw the truth he'd tried to hide from both of us. "And you love me." I could feel it there in his mind -- the emotion that had been slowly growing ever since I kissed him.

But before my happiness could take root, I heard his voice in my mind. *This is going to end in pain. It can't go any other way.*

Following so hard on the joyous realization, his rejection felt like a knife in the chest. I surged to my feet in helpless fury. "So you're not even going to try?"

"It doesn't matter whether I try or not, because this relationship has clusterfuck written all over it." He manifested, stepping out of Smilodon, who groaned at our distress. The tiger rose and moved to press against my hip as if trying to comfort me.

I dropped my hand to his head as I glared at Dave. "I'm willing to take the chance. Why aren't you?"

"Because I'm not a fucking masochist! You know how the humanists are going to react when this hits the air. They're going to lose their fucking minds over this. Just like Valeria's neighbors. Just like mine!"

"It's none of their God damn business!" I yelled. "Not any of them."

"Do you have any idea what kind of jokes they're going to tell about you?" He cursed, low and vicious, but I could feel that most of his anger was for himself. "Kurt warned me this reality TV thing was going to blow up in my face. I should have listened to him."

Whirling away, he started to sink into Smilodon, but I grabbed his arm. It felt solid under my fingers. "I'm tired of being alone, Dave. I've been alone all my life. Been a fucking target all my God damn life. All I want is what we have right now. Don't take it away from me."

He shot me a glittering look. "Don't you get it? I have only five more years to live. You're better off forgetting me instead of destroying your life for a relationship which is doomed to begin with. That's what Valeria was telling me, and she was right."

I blinked furiously. I was *not* going to cry. "So you won't even try?"

"I don't want to spend what's left of my life in the eye of a shitstorm!" he shouted. "And I won't leave you with the fallout." He paused, glaring at me, breathing hard. "What's going to happen to Kurt's cats if we can't raise donations because there's a mob with guns outside the sanctuary?"

"Sue the fuckers! They do not have the right to disrupt Kurt's business because they're bigoted asshats."

"We *are* suing them. There's no guarantee we'll win, especially if we get a Humanist judge. Do you really want me to plunge my best friend into that kind of PR hell just because you like sex with me? There's a lot of dicks out there, sweetheart. Why don't you go find one that's socially acceptable?" With that, his manifestation swirled back into his cat.

Feeling as if he'd slapped me, I stared at him. "You son of a bitch."

He roared at me in sheer, raw frustration, the sound so loud I jumped, my ears ringing.

Dave whirled, only to stop at the sight of the sigils that still surrounded us. The spell wasn't warded, so he could easily break it just by stepping out of the circle. But the backlash would knock me on my ass, and he obviously didn't want to do that. "*Let me out.*"

I jerked my hand in a gesture that snapped the spell. The sigils sank back into the ground as those on his collar vanished back into the clay. As if released from a trap, Dave sprang off the stone and ran.

My knees gave as the pain took my strength. I didn't even feel the impact as my ass hit the stone. Wrapping my arms around my shins, I begin to cry.

* * *

Dave

I lay in my tiger bed, agonizingly aware of the waves of pain that seemed to radiate through my collar. Ariel had fallen asleep, but even so, her mind still reverberated with misery.

The bond she'd created was one hell of a spell. I'd never heard of anyone trying anything remotely similar. It was built on my own magic -- the ability all Ferals had to build psychic connections with animals, though it didn't generally work with humans.

Ariel had changed that. Hell, we were a little *too* connected now, because I knew exactly how badly I'd hurt her. And how little she deserved it.

I was such an asshole.

And yet, I also wasn't wrong. This relationship was not something that was going to work for either of us.

But God, I wanted it to.

Ironically the one relationship that would work, the whole reason I was here to begin with -- a relationship with Valeria -- held absolutely no appeal for me anymore. She might make a decent companion, but I wouldn't love her, not the way I did Ariel. Making love to her wouldn't be the same. Yeah, at least Smilodon would get his share of the physical passion, something that wouldn't happen with Ariel, but still...

A spike of terror made me convulse, my head snapping off the bed's thick rubber padding. Images flooded my mind: rotating sigils, myself down on my back as Chris, Oz and Tyrone simultaneously attacked me, fangs and claws ripping into my tiger manifestation's protective shell.

Ariel was having another nightmare.

We rolled to our feet to bolt out of our room and down the hall to hers. Manifesting an arm, I shoved the door open, and we charged inside.

I poured out of Smiley to kneel beside Ariel on the mattress as she writhed in a nightmare. Her face was contorted with the same terror and despair I could feel vibrating through our bond. "Ariel! It's okay, you're having a nightmare!"

"Dave!" she shrieked, bolting upright into my arms, eyes flying wide.

"You're dreaming!" I told her, fighting to keep my voice under control and soothing. "You're okay, you're safe…"

She clung to me, gasping, her eyes wild as she shivered against me. Waves of fear rolled through the collar, and I tightened my hold on her shoulders.

"Ariel? Dave?" Raven called through the door.

"It's fine, Rave. Go back to bed. I've got her."

"I could sing…"

"No, I'm… I'm fine," Ariel lied, trembling as I held her.

Out in the hall, I heard Raven talking to Kordell, then the sound of their respective doors closing.

I saw the moment when Ariel's waking mind finally came back online. "That was definitely no nightmare," she gasped, sagging against me. "I can feel it. *It's going to happen.*"

I sighed and rubbed her back, trying to settle her. "It still doesn't make any sense."

Her mouth tightened as she looked up at me, her devastated expression taking on a weary rebellion. "I don't care. There's something going on we don't know about. I'm telling Tish what I saw in the morning. And I'm going to go over that arena with a fine-tooth comb."

The slim muscles of her back felt like knotted ropes under my hands. "Why don't you lie down? I'll give you a back rub." And it would distract her from the storm of emotion I could feel through the collar.

She drew back and planted one hand on my chest as if to push me away. "That's not necessary. I'm awake now. I'll be fine."

The rejection stung, and I glowered. "You're not fine. You're terrified, and we both know it."

"Well, that's my problem, isn't it?" Ariel slid off the bed as if unable to bear being that close to me any longer. She gave me a cool, regal glance, though I could feel how much a lie it was. "Thanks for waking me up. You need to get some sleep. We've got a busy day tomorrow."

My hands flexed helplessly, but I couldn't really blame her. Not after what I'd said. The way I'd hurt her.

I rose from the bed and flowed back into Smilodon. "We'll sleep on the floor."

Ariel didn't throw me out, but only because she didn't really want to be alone. I could feel that much through the collar. I lay down. After a pause, she got back in bed. It took here a long time to fall asleep.

I stayed awake despite the pull of Smilodon's exhaustion. He didn't complain. We both wanted to be available in case she needed us again.

Chapter Eleven

Ariel

Blood streamed down Smilodon's furred throat as the glowing bear charged in to sink his manifested fangs into the tiger's haunch. Dave whirled, a huge paw flashing out. Even as he raked his claws over the Kodiak's manifestation, Chris slammed into him, bowling him over onto his back...

I came awake screaming for the second time that night. Dave was already there, glowing arms around me. "It's all right, it's all right, I've got you. It was just a dream."

I grabbed him and held on as if I could protect him from what I'd seen. Tears rolled down my face as I shook, sobbing. "It's not enough! What I've done, it's not enough..."

I could hear the near hysteria in my own voice, and I distantly realized I'd done it again -- freaked out everyone in the house.

Thanks to our new bond, I could feel him trying to be the voice of reason. "You've done everything anyone could ask you to do. This spell on my collar..."

"... Is not enough." I raised my shaking hands and wiped away the tears. "I need to strengthen the spell somehow. I haven't done enough, or I wouldn't still be having this dream."

I rolled off the bed, almost stepping on Smilodon, who lay curled on the floor, watching us with his whiskers drooping sadly. I hopped over him and snatched up the backpack of magical gear I'd left on a chair.

As I headed toward the kitchen with it, Dave and Smiley followed. "What are you going to do?"

I ignored the question, mind churning over the

plan that had popped into my head.

"Dave?" Raven called from her bedroom.

"I've got her."

I ignored him, heading to the kitchen island, where I started digging through my pack until I found a clean squirt bottle, the kind I sometimes used for paint. I took the cap off and filled the bottle from the tap, then capped it again. After making sure the tip was still closed, I tucked it back in my bag.

I started opening drawers until I found the one that held the knives. When I reached to pluck one of them out, glowing fingers clamped around my wrist. "What the fuck are you doing?" Dave demanded. "All the collar's telling me is you're planning something, and I don't like the way you feel."

"I need some blood for my spell. It's no big -- I know you've seen Genevieve do this."

"You've got a jar of powdered blood. What the hell do you need fresh for?" His eyes narrowed. "And how many times have you bled yourself on this trip?"

"Not that often. Don't worry, I'm not going to slit my wrists."

"I'm relieved to hear it," he said icily. "Because Smiley and I will knock you down and sit on you."

That actually made me smile. "Knowing how much you weigh, I wouldn't want that." I made a shooing gesture at him. "Look, I'm fine. I'm going to be up working for a while."

"Yeah, I gathered that." He eyed me. "Considering the last time you hacked off all your hair, I'm worried about what you'll cut next."

"Hey, Raven said the new 'do is cute." It should be. It had taken the stylist an hour of swearing to repair the damage I'd done in my Arcanist fog.

Dave gave me a grim look. "Why are you *doing*

this? What part of 'Valeria is coming to BFS' did you not get?"

I stared at him, feeling as if he'd slapped me.

He flinched, both at my reaction and his resulting wave of guilt. "Ariel…"

"You're wasting your time. You can't piss me off so bad I'll say, 'Fuck you,' and quit fighting to save your furry ass."

He swore. Yeah, I'd known I was right about his motivation for the cheap shot. I snorted and knelt to look for a cookie sheet. When I found one, I tucked it under my arm, then grabbed the knife and the backpack and headed for the door. Dave and Smiley followed.

"Go to bed," I told them as I stepped out into the moonlight. "You're going to need the sleep."

"I could say the same to you." He and the cat pushed through the door before I could close it.

"I'm not fighting three melded Ferals in a few hours." *Possibly to the death.* I headed for the trees. I needed the rock at the waterfall again.

"We're not shooting until the evening. I'll have plenty of time to take a nap. And if you think I'm going to leave you alone to do God knows what with that knife, you're out of your fucking mind."

"Don't be so melodramatic. I have no intention of hurting myself. For one thing, you're going to need me to keep your ass alive."

"Assuming that dream is precognitive."

"Oh, it's precog." I glared at him over my shoulder as we headed down the path. "Every time -- and I do mean *every* time -- I have a recurring dream like this, it happens. And I'm going to God damn well make sure you come out of this alive. You and the other Ferals."

"I have absolutely no intention of killing any of those men. First, they're friends of mine. And second, if they're under the influence of some shithead's spell, they're not responsible for what they're doing."

"Unlike, say, Zoe."

"Unless we've got an enemy we don't even know about."

I snorted. "That little bitch is in this up to her lip plumpers."

We fell grimly silent the rest of the way to the waterfall.

I made a beeline for the black stone I'd been using for spells, put down my pack and the kitchen knife, and dug out my tackle box. I flipped it open and promptly spotted an X-Acto knife. Which was what I usually used for a blood draw, since it was basically a scalpel. I picked it up, got a fresh blade out of the box, and changed them out.

Dave frowned. "Why did you need a butcher knife when you had that?"

I shrugged. "Wasn't thinking very clearly."

"I noticed." He and Smiley watched as I sketched the spell circle I'd designed earlier. Just as I started to feed it power, the pair stepped into it with me. I ignored them, feeding power into the sigils, which rose off the stone and began to rotate, glowing softly red in the darkness.

I opened the squeeze bottle and positioned it in front of my knees. Picking up the X-Acto, I slashed a quick, shallow stroke across my left hand. Blood welled up.

A rumble of disapproval sounded in stereo -- coming from both Dave's manifestation and Smiley.

As the sigils rotated around me, I squeezed my fist over the mouth of the bottle to collect a stream of blood. Once I had enough for the spell, I started to reach for my pack. I needed to bandage the cut before I screwed up the working.

"Looking for this?" Dave held up a pack of gauze and a roll of bandage wrap. He must have dug them out of the pack while I was busy. I started to reach for them, but he said, "Give me your hand, you twit."

When I obeyed, he produced a clean cloth and applied it to my palm, holding pressure on it until the cut stopped bleeding. Next he cleaned the wound with a few wet wipes, put a gauze pad over my palm, and looped bandage wrap around my wrist, palm and thumb to secure it in place. Arcane Corps training in action.

"How often do you do blood draws?" he asked. "You didn't even flinch."

I snorted. "My grandmother started bleeding me when I was thirteen."

"Your grandmother needed someone to bleed *her*. With a baseball bat."

"I considered it more than once." With my hand properly bandaged, I dug in the pack for the roll of parchment paper, then put it down over the cookie sheet. Next, I dug out the last of my Air-Dry clay and began shaping the same sigils I'd used for Dave's collar, laying them out on the cookie sheet.

"I've already got one collar," Dave said, as I felt his irritation radiating through it.

"This isn't for you. It's for me. I'm making a choker, a couple of bracelets, and two anklets."

I looked up to see him watching me, his expression odd. I frowned. "What?"

"I hurt you today," he said, his voice low. "Why are you doing all this for me?"

"What part of 'I don't want you to die' do you

not get?" I deliberately used the same phrasing he had earlier.

He winced, recognizing it. "Okay, now I definitely feel like an asshole."

"That may be because you've been an asshole." Sitting in the circle with him in the collar, I didn't even have to concentrate to feel his guilt.

But there was affection there too. No, it was more than affection -- it felt a lot like love. That should have made me feel a little better about his attitude, but it didn't.

"See, now, that's what pisses me off. You love me as much as I do you. But you're such a stubborn jerk you're not going let it go anywhere. Because you don't have the balls."

There's absolutely nothing that will piss off a combat vet any faster than accusing him of cowardice. Dave's eyes narrowed as his anger spiked. "My balls are not the issue. I just don't want you to get hurt."

"You know what's gonna hurt a lot more? Never seeing your ass again -- assuming we survive tomorrow -- because you're so worried about what a bunch of brainless bigots think."

He glowered. "I'm worried about what they'll *do*, Ariel. To *you*. And Kurt and Gen and the BFS cats, but mostly you."

"I can take care of myself. And judging by what Kurt and Gen did to the polar bear, the witch, *and* the magical assassin, they can too."

He shook his head. "Christ, you're stubborn."

"Yeah, I get that a lot. Look, you…"

He leaned in, moving with that weightless speed that came with being a manifestation. Then his mouth was on mine, and I could feel the heat of his magic burning through me. I froze at the hot taste of him, the heat of his manifested hands. My entire body seemed to burst into flame.

I made a little growling sound and reached up, grabbing the back of his neck to drag him closer, kissing him back. Hard.

Suddenly I wanted nothing more than to fuck his brains out. And why not? There were two ways to cast a powerful spell: blood and sex. And sex was always more fun.

He pulled away from me, his gaze so fierce and intent, I shivered. I started to reach for him again, but he vanished, swirling back into Smilodon.

The cat made a rumbling, disgusted sound somewhere between a moan and a growl. Swear to God, the tiger shook his head. And it was definitely Smiley doing it -- I could feel his frustration through the collar.

The tiger whirled. I broke the circle the instant before he leaped out of it and raced off into the dark palms. "Coward!" I yelled after him, so frustrated and pissed I wanted to scream.

"Idiot!" he shouted back as his big body crashed through the night.

I felt his anger through the collar, but I could also feel that he had absolutely no intention of coming back. The asshole was still determined to protect me.

Completely ignoring the fact that he was the one that needed the protection.

* * *

Tisha stared at me as if I'd grown an extra head. "Let me get this straight," she said slowly. "You think that someone, presumably Zoe, is going to try to murder Dave Frost by driving all the other Ferals insane with a spell."

I could feel my cheeks getting hot, but I wasn't

going to back down. "I know it sounds insane, but I also know what I saw. I had that nightmare multiple times, and it always ends the same way: with him dead. The only time that happens is when it's a precognitive vision."

The showrunner's mouth worked. When I checked her aura I saw a chaotic storm of neon green disbelief shot with fear-yellow streaks and anger-red sparks. "You do realize there's a big difference between planting a spell to trip somebody and committing felony magical murder in front of twenty cameras? Zoe isn't exactly a brain trust, but even she's not that stupid."

"I'm telling you, we need to check it out. If I'm right, it could cost Dave his life." Inspiration hit and I added, "Not to mention blowing the show completely out of the water. Everybody involved with this thing would find themselves ass-deep in scandal, maybe even charged by the Bahamian authorities." Private island or not, Hammerhead Cay was in the Bahamas, so the Royal Bahamas Police Force would have to investigate any crimes committed there.

Tish raked both hands through her hair in a gesture of frustration and turned to look out over the arena, where preparations were underway for the evening's shoot. I could hear Candice Green, the director, arguing with somebody about camera angles and F-stops.

"Don't you think it's a lot more likely you've just been having a nightmare? I've had some God-awful dreams myself since we've been here. They didn't mean jack, other than that I'm under a lot of stress."

Yeah, I'd been afraid that would be her reaction. "Look, ask Chris. He can tell you how often my dreams have been accurate."

Tish sighed. "All right, I'll talk to him. I'll also make damn sure Zoe realizes she better not try it, assuming she even intends to. I mean, what the hell would it get her? All she'd accomplish is shutting down the show, and then nobody wins any money. Think about it -- breaking the kid's leg at least made some degree of sense. And it wouldn't have shut down production. This would. The girl may have more breast than brains, but she's not that stupid."

"Or she figures if she doesn't win the money, she wants to make sure we don't either."

Tish pursed her lips, considering the idea. "I'd believe that if there was any way she could avoid getting caught. But Zoe has to know she's the first one we'd suspect." She studied me. "Ask the doc for a sleeping pill. You look like shit. And what the fuck did you do to your hair? I could kick your ass for that. Do you have any idea what kind of continuity problems we're going to have?"

"Sorry," I said, meaning it. "I needed it for a spell."

"What, the 'Give Tish a migraine' spell? Because I gotta say, it worked. All right, I'm going to talk to Chris, then have a word with The Queen of Tits and Ass." She stomped off.

* * *

Jackson kept his face expressionless as Tish told him and Candice Green about Ariel's visions.

"Shit," Candice said, blowing out a breath. She was a tall, thin woman with the good bone structure of a former actress, steel gray hair and intense blue eyes. "This could really blow us out of the fucking water."

For a moment, Jackson considered abandoning the whole plan. Zoe had to know he was involved in whatever the witch had foreseen. She'd roll over on him once the shit hit the fan. *Maybe I need to have her taken care of.*

On second thought, no. Unless he missed his guess, she'd keep quiet after it all went down, at least initially. That would give him time enough to have Andre take care of her. Since the big Arcanist was deaf, he was probably the only one who could do the job without her talking him out of it.

When Tish finally ran down, Jackson gave her the incredulous stare that had been making underlings sweat for thirty years. "You don't seriously mean to pull the plug on that challenge because an Arc had a nightmare?"

"Chris served with Ariel in the Arcane Corps. He said she had dreams similar to this about some girl's school in an Afghan village. So the team got the kids out. Five minutes later, a truck plowed into the building and exploded. Suicide bomber. Nobody was hurt, though the school burned down. And the driver ended up juicy confetti, but fuck him. Another time, Ariel stopped Chris just before he stepped on a MEED she'd dreamed about the night before."

"That doesn't mean she's right about this."

"Chris thinks she is." Tish sighed, scrubbing her hands through her short cap of curls. "The guy turns into a thousand-pound cross between a tiger and a lion, and he went *pale* when I told him about her Dave dream. Another thing, if we continue as planned and she's right, not only could Dave end up dead, the survivors would sue the living shit out of Hammerhead Productions. And they'd probably win."

Jackson waved a negligent hand. "Good point." He paused, imagining what he'd say if it wasn't *his* plan the Arc bitch was trying to sabotage. "Let Ariel check the wards before the shoot. Presumably she'd be able to spot a booby trap, assuming someone plants one. Oh, and talk to Zoe and the ward Arcanist..."

"That's Jimmy Pope."

Who cares? "Take Valeria with you and let her sniff everybody when you question them. If there's problem, we can nip it quietly in the bud."

Tish paused, then nodded slowly. "Yeah, that should do it."

He watched in satisfaction as she walked off. That should cover his tracks nicely. She would testify they'd taken precautions -- assuming she lived to testify.

For all the good it would do Dave Frost or Ariel Piper.

* * *

Zoe stared at Tish as the showrunner detailed Ariel's allegations, feeling her eyes going wide with horror.

She was intensely aware of Valeria sitting at the woman's side. She had a pretty good idea why the lioness was there -- to sniff for lies.

Logically, Oz was far more dangerous than Valeria, who was only a fourth the size of his Kodiak manifestation. But there was a big difference between the physical presence of a big predator and the magical manifestation of a man she knew she could control.

Valeria's flat gold gaze suggested Zoe had better damn well not try anything on *her*.

Meanwhile, Kieran and Oz were both staring at her, eyes narrow with suspicion. They obviously believed she was capable of this insanity too.

It pissed her off.

"Oh, come on," Zoe snapped. "Do you really think I'd try to kill Dave Frost, national hero? I'm on this show to *help* my career. Being involved in a scandal this bad would blow it right out of the water."

As she spoke, Valeria's eyes closed, lioness nostrils flaring as she breathed deep of Zoe's scent.

Oz was doing the same. Definitely sniffing for lies.

A bead of sweat rolled down her spine. "I don't know what that bitch saw," she continued, knowing she'd better tell the utter truth. "But I'm not involved."

Tish turned to look down at Valeria. The lioness flicked her tail tip. "She's telling the truth... as far as I can tell."

The showrunner glowered at Zoe. "You'd better be. Because I can assure you, if *anything* happens tomorrow, I'm going to hang your skinny little ass out to dry." She turned the glare on Kieran and Oz. "And that includes you two."

Oz spread his hands. "Look, Dave is a friend of mine. I've known him for years. There's no way in hell I'd try to hurt him. Plus, like she said -- he's a fucking hero."

"That's the problem," Valeria told him softly. "You might not *want* to do anything to him, but neither did his Corps teammate. Dave still ended up dead. Cat or not, he's out of extra lives. And so are the rest of you." She paused a moment, studying him intently. "If you sense anything weird tomorrow, if you start feeling magic that shouldn't be there, you need to call a halt right then. Because you may not be able to later."

"Yeah, I know the drill," Oz said, glowering at Zoe. "And If I catch *anybody* trying to cast a spell on me or anybody else, they'll regret it."

Well, shit, Zoe thought, disgusted. It was going to take her hours to get her teammates calmed down now. And she'd have to do it delicately, because Kieran was going to be watching for it.

Come to think of it, she should probably keep her magic to herself, judging from the icy look in both men's eyes.

It was lucky nobody knew about Jackson.

Should I warn Tish? If something goes sideways tomorrow, I could be charged an accessory.

But remembering the ice in the billionaire's eyes, she knew if she ratted out Jackson, he would *not* take it well. Besides, she had no proof he intended to do whatever Ariel had seen -- assuming the bitch hadn't made the whole thing up. For one thing, look at the money he'd lose. And that's assuming he wasn't charged in connection with the crime. Jackson hadn't gotten that rich by being that stupid.

The silly little cunt was just freaking herself out. That was all.

Please, God.

* * *

Ariel

As the blood-red sun sank into the ocean, I walked the perimeter of the ward circle, looking for the spell that could cost Dave his life.

The assembled crowd watched in silence from chairs around the combat circle. The four team banners flapped heavily in the ocean wind just outside the wards. Each team's Bard, Arcanist and Primo/Prima sat in the front row just beyond their flag, ready to cheer on their Feral teammate.

And they all seemed to be glaring at me.

Once again, the plan was to shoot after night fell, so that the magical glow of the Ferals' manifestations would be even more dramatic.

The twilight made it easier to see the sigils, drawn on the two-hundred-foot portable ring.

Assembled from sections of matte black plastic only a few inches wide, the ring had just enough tooth to take the luminous magical pastel the Arcanist had used.

He'd done a professional job. Each symbol was cleanly drawn, not a stroke out of place. I'd walked around the circle twice, checking and rechecking, but there was absolutely no sign of any sigil that shouldn't be there.

Whatever spell I'd seen in my dream, it hadn't been cast among the wards' sigils.

Jesus, have I done all this over a nightmare? I was acutely aware of the camera crews panning to follow me. *This is going to end up on the show.*

So were my night terrors. The bedroom cams had probably captured footage of my panicked screams. I wasn't looking forward to watching *that* when the show aired in a few months. *Everyone in the country is going to think I'm a moron.*

I lifted my gaze to eye the sand of the combat ring. If the spell hadn't been planted among the wards, it had to be somewhere in there.

Assuming it was anywhere at all.

I stepped into the ring and began to walk a spiral search pattern, magical senses scanning for the spell I feared. Yet I didn't see so much as a faint shimmer of magical energies. *There's nothing here. Or at least, I hope to hell there's nothing here, because if there is, I can't find it. And then Dave's going to end up dead.*

My hands curled into frustrated fists as I finally turned to stalk back the show's management.

Tish, Jackson, director Candice Green, Valeria, and the four Ferals watched my approach, all of them looking either tense, anxious or impatient. And maybe a little pissed at the delay. Just beyond them, Zoe glared at me from beneath her team's flag, radiating hostility.

My cheeks burned, and I hoped it was too dark to see my humiliated flush. "There's no sign of anything among the ward sigils that shouldn't be there,"

"I fucking told you there wouldn't be." Jimmy Pope growled. Tall and graying, the Arcanist's aura burned red with outrage. He was the show's head ward specialist, and he'd taken my suspicions as an enormous insult. Not that I could blame him.

"So it was just a bad dream after all," Jackson said, a faint smile in the curve of his lips.

I frowned at him. I knew why Pope was pissed, but Jackson's aura was even uglier -- all angry reds, shot with swirls of violet satisfaction and hints of smug green. There was a lot of hostility there. Evidently I'd really pissed the billionaire off.

I've probably made a bad enemy.

"However," he continued, giving me a charming smile at distinct odds with his aura, "I appreciate your letting us know about the possible problem. We wouldn't want to take chances with something like that. It would torpedo the entire show." Deceptive orange flared through his aura.

The fuck? Was he involved in this thing?

But that made absolutely no sense. Why would he torpedo his own show? More likely he was telling a polite lie to disguise his irritation over the shooting delay. Reading auras was like reading expressions in the sense that you couldn't always be sure what inspired them.

Dave spoke up. "Or maybe somebody thought twice. They realized you were going to catch them and aborted the plot."

"Makes sense to me," Chris said. "The Corps

rated her precog as ninety-three percent accurate."

Tyrone looked troubled. "How likely is it that there's a spell you missed?"

I paused a long moment before shaking my head. "There's definitely not anything in the wards. Every sigil is exactly what it should be, and there's no sign of anything below that." My head had begun throbbing sometime during the search, and when I looked down I could see my aura beginning to kink from magical exertion and stress. I ignored it. "I even went over the arena itself, but again, no sign of anything. And I'm sensitive enough that I would've picked it up if there had been. Maybe Dave's right and our would-be attacker chickened out." I slid a look at Zoe, who glared back. There was a lot of yellow in her aura, mixed with all that angry red. What the hell was she so scared of? *Had* she done something? Maybe I should have followed my first inclination and interrogated her myself. I'd have been able to spot her lies better than Tish. But the showrunner had pointed out that was likely to do nothing but start a screaming row, and I'd known she was right.

Maybe Zoe was scared because she did have something planned and was afraid I'd catch her at it. Then again, maybe she was afraid of being accused of something she hadn't done.

Then there was the really ugly possibility that she knew something but hadn't been directly involved. Something that might end up with Dave dead.

"We -- the Ferals, I mean -- we've all discussed this," Oz said, as if reading my anxiety. Then again, maybe he could smell it, given his bear's senses. "If there's any problem at all, if we feel anything off, we'll call a halt."

Assuming you have time. Once a booby trap went

off, there was fuck-all you could do about it.

I turned to Pope, who was still glaring. "Look, I'm sorry about this. I just couldn't take the chance."

"You should be sorry," he snarled. "I don't appreciate accusations that I'm dirty just because you had a fucking nightmare. I worked for thirty years establishing a rep for being competent and honest, and you just kicked shit all over it."

My cheeks blazed even hotter, but I knew the man was entitled to his rage. "I can't blame you for being angry. I'd be pissed too."

At that, the furious churn of his aura dimmed. He sighed and said reluctantly, "Look, if some kind of problem arises, I'll drop the ward so you can help your friend." The words sounded grudging, but there was no deception in his aura. He meant it.

"Oh, hell no!" Dave shot me a tight look. "If the shit hits the fan, the last thing you need to do is walk into that circle. I don't care how many terrorists you've killed, when it comes to a bunch of maddened Ferals, you'd be kibble."

"Man's got a point," Oz drawled. "You were able to take me out the last time because I hadn't manifested. My bear shell has held under Caliphate AK-47 fire. You wouldn't be able to punch through it."

Which was why Dave and I were wearing six different sets of magical spells. But they didn't need to know that, so I kept my mouth shut. Besides, for all I knew, he was right.

"That's assuming she had anything more than a nightmare," Jackson interrupted. "Obviously, she's been under a great deal of stress."

His smile was so condescending, I ground my teeth. My instinct was to clap back at him, but I'd made enough of an idiot out of myself for one night. Besides, my skull was aching so viciously, all I wanted was to sit down.

Too bad I couldn't cast a pain-blocker spell, but doing anything to blunt my magical senses was a really dumb idea just now.

Dave moved over beside me and lowered his head. "Your aura looks like hell. And I can feel how much pain you're in."

I snorted. "Hadn't noticed."

He slid a glowing arm around my shoulder in a gesture that looked more friendly than romantic. At his touch, my aura began to smooth, and the sigh slid from my lips, despite my best intentions. Aware of the cameras, I fought not to collapse against him. To my surprise, he tilted my chin up and took my mouth. Magic seemed to explode through me, a wave of heat and strength.

My eyes widened in shock. After everything he'd said about the scandal we were courting, I hadn't expected him to kiss me in front of God and our future television audience.

And this was no ordinary kiss either. His mouth felt hot on mine, and I sensed the leap of his passion. Could see it swirling in shades of deep, rich violet.

For a moment, my pride insisted I stay rigid, but then I remembered those fucking dreams. What if he was hurt? What if he died?

As if my body had a will of its own, I turned into him, my arms sliding up to encircle his neck as I pressed against him. His magic rolled through my roiling aura, so sensual and rich, the churn instantly quieted. As the pain faded, I felt Smilodon's big shoulder press against my leg, heard his rumble as he rubbed his jaw against my hip, scent marking me. When we reluctantly pulled apart, Dave whispered,

"I'm going to be all right. But regardless of what happens, I don't want you in that circle. I'll find a way to win this without endangering you." He pressed his lips against my forehead, pulled away and swirled back into Smilodon.

Chapter Twelve

Ariel

"So if all that's settled," Green said, sounding long-suffering, "let's get this challenge wrapped. Places, everybody."

The Ferals stepped into the arena and walked toward their individual banners. Chris shot me an encouraging smile as he went, but they all looked anxious and uncertain.

I turned and headed for the Mystics banner where Raven and Kordell sat wearing tight expressions of sympathy and concern. I had work to do. "Have you got that squirt bottle?" I'd bled myself again before the shoot, much to Dave's irritation.

The Bard handed it over. "You didn't find anything?"

"There was no sign whatsoever of any spell that shouldn't be there, either in the wards or on the arena sand."

"So it was just an ordinary dream?" Kordell asked, looking hopeful.

"I doubt it. Of course, the entire production crew now think I'm crazy. I hope they're right." Better half the country laugh at me than Dave bleed out on the sand. I wasn't sure there was any way in hell I'd be able to save him. Healing magic is tricky, and when I'd tried it after leaving the CIA, my patient had died.

Grimacing, I tried not to remember the cancer patient I'd failed to save, emaciated and pale as bone, deep shadows under her eyes.

I moved a couple of feet away to get enough room for what I had in mind, then dropped to my knees. "Hey, give me a hand," I told my friends. "Kneel between me and the beach, would you? I need a wind break."

The pair exchanged a look, then moved to do as I asked, blocking the breeze enough for my purposes. I held out the squeeze bottle, arm straight, and pivoted in place, letting a stream of water fall to create a dark circle in the sand. When I finished, it was close enough to a circle to serve my purposes.

Kneeling with my back to the breeze, I carefully began drawing the sigils for my spell with the bottle. This really would be much easier with my pastels, but they wouldn't work at all on sand.

Raven leaned in and asked softly, "What are you doing? Is the Kimora's bothering you again?"

"No, this is an amplification spell."

She looked a little closer. "Are those sigils on your bracelets? Like Dave's collar?"

"Exactly like Dave's collar. Got them on my anklets and choker too."

Kordell looked intrigued. "What do you have in mind?"

"See?" Zoe demanded, triumph and malice in her voice. "She *is* working a spell."

I looked up to tell her to fuck off, but swallowed the words when I saw Jaylen Payne beside her.

The Arcanist judge stood just outside the circle, his hands on his hips. "What is that working supposed to do?"

Zoe smirked, as malicious as a mean girl in a teen romcom. As usual, she wore one of her collection of skimpy bathing suits -- this one bright red -- a lace coverup, and fuck-me-red heels. Freaking *heels*. In the sand. "Like I told you, she's cheating."

"We're allowed to use our power to help our teammates," I told her, enunciating with great precision. "Which is why Tish didn't kick your ass off the island for trying to break Kordell's leg."

Jaylen frowned. "So what does the spell do?"

"Amplifies my power," I said flatly. "Other than that, not a damn thing. Unlike some people, I don't plant booby traps."

"Yeah, right," Zoe drawled. "Maybe the real reason she was walking around the arena is to plant spells of her own. Maybe the whole nightmare thing was just a ruse."

Jaylen gave Zoe a cool look. "I watched her. She didn't do a damn thing except examine the wards. If she had, I'd have seen her."

Zoe's face twisted in frustration, and she drew back a foot. Before she could kick sand over my working, Kordell was up and sweeping an arm around her waist to lift her right off her feet.

"Let go of me, you bastard!" Cursing, she kicked furiously as he carried her a safe distance from the spell.

"Haven't you made enough of an idiot out of yourself," Kordell snapped as he dropped her on the sand.

One high-heeled foot rolled under her as she landed, dumping her on her lush ass. "Owww! Asshole!"

"Bitch," he returned coolly. She started to jump up and come at him again, but he thrust out a finger. "You are not my favorite person. You need to go back to your team and quit trying to make trouble for mine."

She opened her mouth and drew breath. I saw the magic gathering in her throat, but before she could start singing, Raven's voice cut over hers in the chorus of "Hit the road, Jack."

Zoe tried to fight the compulsion, but a heartbeat

later, she spun and stalked away, heading right back to her seat. She plopped down next to her teammates, face bright red with embarrassment.

"Nicely done," Jaylen told Raven.

"It certainly was," Lilly put in, grinning. The Bard judge had walked up while I was distracted. "It's hard to use your power on another Bard." She gave Raven an approving look before turning her attention to me. "Good luck today. I hope like hell your dreams were wrong."

"So do I," I said quietly, as the two judges headed back to their seats.

Breathing a sigh of relief, I went back to my working. We were going to need all the magic I could muster.

* * *

Dave

When Candice called, "Action," Pope activated his spell. As the sigils rose from the circle and began to rotate, I looked around at my teammates seated on the other side of the magical barrier. Ariel knelt in the circle she'd cast, looking tense, her hands clenching and unclenching.

Raven's face was dead white, eyes wide. Shit, she must be having a flashback to that damn video. Next to her, Kordell followed my gaze, saw her expression, and took her hand. Her fingers clamped so tightly around his, her knuckles went white. Yeah, her phobia was hitting her hard.

Since there was nothing I could do to help, I turned to study my competition. The other Ferals looked as wired as I felt, obviously worried about Ariel's vision -- assuming it *was* a vision and not a simple nightmare.

I remembered the flashes of her dream through my collar. The three Ferals, faces twisted in madness, all attacking me simultaneously, ripping into me in a wild, bloodthirsty frenzy...

Bobby had worn that same insane expression as he'd whirled on me. I remembered the heavy impact of his lioness's paw slamming into my head, the crack of my neck breaking, the world spinning as I hit the ground. Unable to feel, unable to breathe as death dragged me into ice and terror. Smilodon, fighting desperately to hold on to me, to pull me to the safety of his body.

This time there'd be no new body waiting. If Ariel was right, Smilodon would die with me.

I'd be sweating like a pig if I were still human.

Someone was growling, and I realized it was Smiley, reacting to the wave of remembered terror and pain, so vivid in the PTSD flashback it felt as real as it had the day I'd died.

"Dave?" Ariel's voice whispered from the collar, accompanied by a wave of calming magic. *"You need to chill. You're scaring everybody."*

I glanced around the arena and realized she was right. My fellow Ferals were looking at each other, growing alarm on their faces.

No wonder. I could see my tiger self through Ariel's eyes: crouched, tail lashing, ears flattened as we reacted to the flashback pumping adrenaline, terror and rage through us.

My friends' Feral magic gathered in the air like a storm as they prepared to defend themselves.

Oh my God, I'm about to make Ariel's vision come true. It wasn't a spell, it was me losing my shit.

"No, because you're not *going to lose your shit."* Ariel's determination and belief in me poured from the

collar. *Your control is better than this.* But I could feel her fear.

I could also feel the love driving the fear, pure and bright and deep. I seized that love, dragging it closer, using it to fight the panic. Smilodon helped, flooding our shared mind with images -- memories -- of watching me make love to Ariel at the waterfall, our magic glowing around us. We looked... beautiful. As if we belonged together. Smiley had shared that moment of pleasure, of being one with her. He'd shared my love.

Those images combined with Ariel's belief knocked me out of the death spiral of fear and rage. My Arcane Corps training kicked in and I began tactical breathing. The technique -- breathing in through the nose for a count of four, holding the breath for a count of four, then exhaling through the mouth for a count of four, then repeating the process -- lowered the heartrate and made it possible to think. Since you lost higher brain function in an adrenaline dump, tactical breathing could be a life saver.

As my fear decreased, Ariel began to relax a little, though her determination to make sure I survived reverberated through the collar. Even if I decided I didn't want her, she wanted to know I lived.

Of course, I want you. How could I do anything else?

With that thought, I felt my desperation drain. I straightened out of my crouch, rolled my ears forward, and said aloud, "It's okay. I just had a little bit of a flashback, but I'm okay now."

"You sure about that?" Oz gave me a long, narrow look. "Because, frankly, I'm not interested in acting out Ariel's nightmare. I don't think that shit ends well for anybody."

"He's fine," Chris said firmly. "He's going to be

fine." I wasn't sure whether he was trying to convince me or himself.

"Do you need a break?" Tish asked, moving around to the Mystics side of the ring to study me.

"You need me to sing?" Raven stepped up beside the showrunner. She looked completely calm, as if she hadn't been having her own panic attack minutes earlier. The thought that I needed her had helped her regain control.

Before I could answer, she began to sing "Feral Heart." The last dregs of anxiety drained away, soothed by her magic.

I blew out a long breath. "Thanks. I've got it now."

"Can we get this on the road?" Jackson demanded. He was lounging in a director's chair looking impatient. "We need to get the shot sometime before the next Ice Age." God, the man was an asshole. He must drive his PR team nuts.

Deliberately, Smiley and I sank down on our belly and controlled the restless lash of our tail.

"Amelia," director Candice Green called. "Let's do that opening again. Ready?"

When Sharp nodded, everyone else fell silent.

"Action."

Despite my best intentions, I felt myself start to tense again. If the shit was going to hit the fan, it would be soon.

* * *

Ariel

I blew out a breath and sagged. I'd damned near managed to trigger the very scenario I'd wanted to prevent. That was the problem with precognition. Misinterpreting a vision could bite you on the ass.

But maybe the danger was over now. Maybe Dave was right, and the stink I'd raised had convinced Zoe -- or whomever -- to drop the idea.

I wanted desperately to believe that. Unfortunately, that damn little voice in the back of my head didn't buy it for a second. I sat coiled and tense as the shoot began, ready to feed power to Dave through my sigil accessories if things went south.

Dressed in peach slacks and a flowing silk shirt, Amelia Sharp planted her sandaled feet on her mark just outside the ward circle and went into her intro. "In today's challenge, you Ferals will demonstrate your combat skills using your animal manifestations. You'll fight until one of you can no longer maintain your mani. Fortunately, damage to the shell doesn't hurt the man inside it..."

"I wouldn't go that far," Dave muttered through his collar.

"... but enough damage will make your manifestation collapse." Which the Ferals knew, of course. Our future Normie audience wouldn't, though, which was the point of the spiel. "When you sense you're about to lose your magical shell, tap out. If you don't, Valeria Sanz, our Feral judge, will do it for you -- she can see when your mani is about to drop. By the same token, if you see your opponent's manifestation about to collapse, back off. Otherwise somebody could get seriously injured, and we don't want that."

"Ya think?" I muttered. Normally I wouldn't be worried, since this kind of mock battle was part of routine training in the Corps. The Caliphate's Ferals had gone after any civilian crowd they could find, and it had been up to our guys to stop them. When it came to terrorism, not even a bomb could inflict more sheer panic than a tiger in a girl's school.

There was a reason we'd all hated the Caliphukers.

But the upshot of all that training was the guys knew how to fight each other without inflicting serious injuries. It would look dangerous and exciting to a Normie television audience, but it was actually pretty safe.

As long as nobody's planted a booby trap I didn't spot.

"We'll start with six bouts," Sharp continued, "which will give each of you a chance to fight the others. The two who amass the most points in the preliminary bouts will face each other in the final challenge."

That little voice of mine? Screaming again. I started tactical breathing.

"Points will be awarded based on the blows landed, similar to MMA or boxing. Losing your manifestation will be considered a knockout.

"So show America what you can do, Ferals. Our first contestants will be Oz and Chris."

Both men rose from their seats and walked to the center of the ring. Studying their auras, I saw matching cool green shades of anticipation, spiked with swirls of an uneasy shade closer to yellow. Not quite fear, but they were a little nervous. Probably worried about my vision.

Sharp let the tension build. Both Ferals were big guys, though Oz was three inches taller. They stared at each other, intent. As determined as you'd expect for a couple of guys with a million bucks on the line.

"Begin," Sharp called. The arena lights went down.

And they manifested, flooding the darkness with a dramatic blaze of golden light. Oz's bear seemed to explode around him, its field picking him up and surrounding him like an enormous Kodiak cocoon.

Kaiju was scarcely smaller. Chris barely had to duck to sink into the magical beast, since the cat's head was level with his ribcage. With a chorus of earsplitting roars that made the audience yelp, the two Ferals charged.

I'd seen manifested Ferals fight before, both in training and in actual combat, but most of the audience hadn't. There were amazed gasps when Chris leaped, clearing twenty feet in a bound to slam into Oz, grabbing the rearing bear with huge, clawed paws and trying to chomp down on the Kodiak's muzzle. The impact bowled Oz right off his feet.

The two men rolled across the sand to slam into the ward in an explosion of magical sparks. I heard Chris yelp as his back hit it. The ward had been good thinking.

The next ten minutes were a furious blur as the bear and the liger tore at each other with teeth and claws.

Their acrobatic bounds would have been impossible for real animals. When you're moving two hundred pounds of human with magical muscle designed for five times that, the usual laws of physics no longer apply. That gave them more magical force to throw into speed and impact, even without the sheer mass of flesh and blood animals behind the blows. I'm sure the audience thought they were ripping each other to shreds.

Nope. Though the marks of fangs and claws showed on their manifestations as dim slashes, I could tell their manis weren't in danger of collapse. What's more, nether one was angry, though I watched their auras closely. In fact, they seemed to be having a good time.

Not surprising. Ferals enjoyed using their manifestations, and they often got in these sorts of fights for the sheer joy of it. Now that they were no longer in the service, they probably got few chances to play with other big predators.

Still, using so much magic is exhausting, which makes it hard to keep up for long. Ten minutes later, Oz's bear managed to clamp his jaws around the liger's throat. Chris wrapped all four paws around the bear and began ripping at him, overbalancing the bigger Feral. Oz fell onto his back, but he didn't let go, no matter how Chris writhed and fought. The liger's manifestation was going dimmer, and I could see it beginning to crack under the pressure of the bear's jaws.

"If you don't tap out," Valeria called, "I'm doing it for you."

Chris growled, but he threw out a paw and slapped it on the ground. Oz let him go and they disentangled themselves, the glow of their animals winking out. They shook hands. "Good bout," Chris told him, his smile only a little tight.

"Yes, that was a very nice bout," Valeria agreed. "I make it twenty points for Chris and twenty-four for Oz." Chris's team groaned as Oz's cheered lustily.

I managed to ignore the smirk Zoe threw in my direction and the smug swirl of her aura. *Yeah, well, we're still in the lead.*

Both men headed back to their respective flags to collapse into chairs and guzzle three or four bottles of PowerUp in succession. I'd always hated the taste, but the gently glowing drink was a sure way to recharge.

It was Dave and Tyrone's turn now. I felt the muscles in my shoulders begin to tense. After Sharp's introduction of the pair, Tyrone's lion appeared in that dramatic golden explosion. Dave summoned his own version, covering his cat in a golden glow that was visibly dimmer than Tyrone's. He needed the mani's protection against his opponent's fangs and claws. Without it, the lion Feral would have ripped him apart while he was still struggling to break Tyrone's shell.

The trouble was Dave's tiger manifestation wasn't as strong as the other Ferals' -- or even his purely human one. As he'd explained, he had to use a lot of magic to keep his human mind functioning. That left less for his shell. And when he expanded the field to cover Smilodon...

Which was the whole point of the collar. I could reinforce his magic with mine. Which ordinarily wouldn't be enough -- except I'd added those Earth sigils to my spell. If push came to shove, I'd use it.

"Begin!" Sharp barked.

Tyrone leaped, clearing the distance between them in one of those impossible weightless bounds. Dave reared to meet him, his great paws spread, mouth gaped wide.

You had to admire Tyrone's sheer guts. Manifestation or no manifestation, Dave was a real tiger.

The lion manifestation slammed into him, but Dave braced and caught him, wrapping his forelegs around Tyrone even as the lion ripped at him. The shell grew brighter where the claws bit. Dave was reinforcing it where he needed it most, letting it thin elsewhere. The two surged against each other until the tiger wrenched sideways and sent Tyrone flying.

The lion Feral hit the ground and rolled to all fours in time to meet Dave's charge.

Ty leaped up to rip at him, trying to wear his manifestation down. It was a good strategy -- because the tiger massed more, he'd tire faster.

But when Tyrone slammed into him for the third time in two minutes, Dave fell onto his back, dragging the lion with him. He rolled, flipping Tyrone onto his back, then going for the Feral's throat. Locking his jaws tight, he ripped at Ty's manifestation with his claws.

The lion went wild, roaring as he raked at Dave's belly with his hind legs, forelegs clawing his ribs. Dave didn't release him as the two cats writhed together in a snarling, roaring knot.

The tiger's full weight crushed down on Tyrone, who was having to use most of his magic to support it. Which meant Ty couldn't use as much of his strength on his claw attacks.

As I watched, the lion's shell dimmed under the jaws clamped around his throat. "Tap out," Dave said, though his mouth was full of lion. "Manifestation's weakening."

Finally, with a disgusted curse, Tyrone tapped out. Dave rolled off and let him up, and he rose, glaring in frustration.

Valeria awarded Dave thirty points to Tyrone's fifteen.

"This isn't exactly a fair fight," Ty snapped. "He outweighs me by four hundred pounds."

Dave shrugged. "Yeah, but your manifestation's stronger than mine."

"Which means jack if you end up on top," Tyrone growled, his lion in his voice. "You're going to walk away with this whole damn contest."

I frowned. Over the past weeks, Tyrone had proven that he was a cool, disciplined man keenly aware of his responsibility to control his cat. Yet fury surged through his aura in shades of dark red that made me worry he might explode into real violence.

Maybe it was just natural frustration, but it seemed... more than that.

Sharp announced that Tyrone would be fighting Chris next, so they gave him a half-hour break to rest.

I watched, frowning, as Ty spent the time guzzling PowerUp and getting increasingly pissed. The Wizards were in fourth place. Judging from his aura, he was obviously frustrated that he wasn't racking up enough points to change that.

When the break was over, Tyrone went after Chris in a frenzy of fangs and claws. Chris bulled into him, knocking him to the ground. It was the second time Tyrone had been pinned, and he was in no mood for it. He attacked Chris so savagely, his claws punched through the liger manifestation. It was obvious he wasn't holding back at all --if they'd been flesh and blood, he'd have disemboweled Chris.

Chris's mani almost fell, but he was every bit as angry as Tyrone, and he refused to tap out even as Tyrone's claws dug dark furrows through his shell. It suddenly brightened, and I tensed, recognizing the effort to strengthen a falling manifestation.

"All right," Valeria roared, her voice cutting across the furious snarls of the two Ferals, "That's it, fight's over. Separate now, boys!"

They ignored her. "Shit," Dave growled, and I could feel his worry that he was going to have to wade in and try to separate them -- and it might not go well. I swallowed and got ready to feed him power.

"SEPARATE!" Valeria roared, her voice magically amplified until my ears rang and my chest vibrated.

Tyrone let go and jumped back. Yet instead of dropping their manifestations, the two huge cats crouched, snarling at each other.

A deep male voice bellowed, "Drop your manifestations and go to your corners!"

Now *I* jumped. *Jesus fuck, that sounds like Master Sergeant Adley!* And I knew for a fact that deadly old bastard was thousands of miles away.

But the sound of the Corps' most feared drill sergeant did what Valeria couldn't. Both men stopped, glaring, then reluctantly dropped their manifestations and stalked back to their flags.

Just as he reached his seat, Chris whirled, eyes widening, then going narrow with realization. "Damn it, Dave!"

"Hey, it worked," Dave said cheerfully, and I realized he'd been the source of the voice. "I saw Adley make a Corps general snap to attention once. Sheer spinal reflex. That general was *so* pissed."

I could believe it. In a Corps full of scary sons of bitches, Master Sergeant Glenn Adley, a Polar Bear Feral, was one of the scariest.

Laughter spread over the crowd -- at least among Corps vets. To my relief, the two men's auras cooled.

Just then, one of the LED studio lights suddenly blew, raining sparks over the audience to shouts of surprise and alarm. Candice called a break to replace it and check the fuses. Those of us playing audience stood up to stretch. I glanced toward the arena, expecting to see the Ferals clustered together, giving each other shit.

Instead, all four still sat under their respective flags, drinking PowerUp and glaring at each other. Anger swirled through their auras. Even Dave had poured himself a bowlful and was lapping it up.

Realization hit. *Oh, shit, what if it's the PowerUp?*

I'd noticed the bottles glowed during my search, but PowerUp always glowed. Besides, I'd been convinced the danger was an Arc spell. The idea that the Alchemist was involved had never even occurred to me, though the barista had served my stupid ass. Had the Humanists hired the bastard? *Fuckety fuck with a side order of fuck.*

I hurried toward Tish, who was standing with Jackson and the director in a little huddle. I didn't even apologize for butting in. "I need to get into the arena and check the PowerUp. I think there's something wrong with it."

"This again?" Jackson wheeled on me, his face going red with irritation. "Look, I've indulged your paranoia all I intend to. *There's nothing wrong.* You had a fucking nightmare. Get over it, you stupid little…"

Tish's eyes narrowed. "Jackson." Just the one word, low with warning.

He glanced at her and clamped his mouth shut. Jackson Gilbert might be filthy rich, but Tish was a legend, both for the shows she'd turned into hits and the progress she'd made in getting Talents roles and power. If there was a row between Jackson and Tish and it hit social media… Well, Jackson would get the worst of it. There were a lot of millionaire producers, but only one Tisha Jennings.

Tish studied him, her expression icy. "It wouldn't hurt to check."

"Forget it," Jackson snapped. "We're down to the wire on this damn show. If I pull the plug now, we'll miss our deadline to complete shooting. There won't be time to get it all edited before the fall release."

"Only if there's something in those bottles," I growled back. "It'll take me five minutes to check. And the Ferals aren't acting right. They're all too pissed."

"What part of 'losing a million dollars' do you not understand? That would piss anyone off."

"If she's right about her vision and people are injured, everyone on this shoot will sue the living fuck out of Hammerhead Productions," Tish observed, her voice mild. Her eyes weren't. "We can take five to let her check the bottles."

Jackson glared at her, but she didn't back down.

A muscle rolling in his jaw, the producer turned to me and snapped, "Fine. Check the fucking bottles. But after this, too, turns out to be nothing, I don't want to hear a God damn word out of you for the rest of the shoot."

I gave him a frigid nod. He turned and bellowed, "Hey, Jimmy! Let Ms. Piper through your ward. She wants to make sure the damn PowerUp hasn't been spiked with another figment of her imagination."

Prick.

The Ward Arc walked over to join me. "So you decided I'm not the bad guy, huh?" Pope asked tartly.

"I apologized for that already," I said, having to work to keep my tone polite. "Could you open the ward for me, please?"

"Considering the heart attack you gave the last Arcanist when you broke his ward, I'd be delighted," he replied, curling a lip. "Where do you want to go in?"

"At the Mystics flag." I trusted Dave, but I wasn't sure about the other three. The last thing I wanted to do was trigger one of them. If someone had done anything to the PowerUp, it might be in Dave's bottles of the drink too.

Of course, if it wasn't, I was going to have to go check the others' stashes too. That could get diccy.

As we approached the section of the ward, Raven and Kordell rose from their seats and hurried over. "What are you doing?" Raven demanded.

"I'm going into the arena," I told her. "They're all acting off. It finally hit me that the only thing in that circle that's glowing is the PowerUp. If I was going to make those Ferals crazy, a potion in those bottles would do the job."

Raven stared at me. "Let me get this straight. You think they're under the influence of something that's making them murderous, and you want to go *in* there?"

Kordell frowned. "Ariel, that doesn't sound like a good idea."

"She's nuts," Jimmy agreed. "But if she wants to die as cat chow, it's her funeral." He shrugged, and I had the impression he wouldn't much care.

My stomach gave a sickening roll, but I ignored it. "Dave's not going to let anything happen to me. And if they've been drugged, we can't afford to let those Ferals out. If there is a spell on them, I may be able to break it, or at least knock them cold long enough for us to sedate them until it wears off."

Raven shook her head. "Still risky as hell."

"Not as risky as doing nothing if I'm right."

Jimmy frowned, studying me. "You really do believe those Ferals are going to try to kill you." Scoffing, the Arc turned toward his creation. "You're batshit crazy -- both for believing it and being willing to go in there anyway."

"Would you quit psychoanalyzing me and open the damn ward?" Though he was probably right. "And be ready to bring it back up the minute I'm through."

He walked up to the ward and the brightly glowing wall of rotating sigils that delineated it. Stretching out a hand, he touched a finger to the nearest glyph as it floated by. I saw his aura pulse once, and the sigils froze. "Go."

I ducked beneath the ward ring, feeling sweat trickle down my spine. *What if I'm wrong? None of my dreams were anything like this.*

Of course, part of what made precognition so tricky is that knowledge of the future can cause people to make different decisions, which in turn changes the outcome.

But that screaming little voice in my head was absolutely convinced. If I was making a fucking idiot out of myself, so be it. I'd rather feel stupid than watch Dave die.

Chapter Thirteen

Ariel

Dave sprawled on a blanket on the sand, a crate of PowerUp next to him. He turned that golden Feral gaze on me as I approached, and his eyes widened as he surged to his feet. "What the hell are you doing in here?"

"Following a hunch," I told him, and knelt to examine the contents of the wooden crate. It held a couple of dozen bottles. A number looked empty. "How many of these things have you drunk?"

"I don't know -- ten?"

I looked up at him, startled. "Ten? I didn't think you even *liked* PowerUp."

His tail flicked. "I'm really thirsty. Besides, I needed the magical boost. You think the drinks are the problem? I thought it was supposed to be the ward."

"I thought so too, but other than you guys, the drinks are only magical things in this circle." I plucked out a bottle and tested the top. The cap appeared firmly sealed, but that didn't necessarily mean anything.

Only one way to find out.

I still had enough blood infused water in my squirt bottle to get in one more circle, so I went to work. As I drew, I told him, "When I was in the Corps, I learned how to run magical analyses on potions. I'm going to see if there's anything in this bottle that shouldn't be there."

"You think someone's spiked the PowerUp?" He sounded incredulous. "*Why?*"

"The mood's gotten increasingly ugly in here, and I don't think it's natural."

"They're getting bitchy because they're *losing.*

They know they can't beat me."

I glanced up at him, frowning. Dave was always flirting, joking and producing embarrassing sound effects. I'd never heard him sound conceited, not even when he'd had reason to be. *And he's drunk ten bottles of this shit. If it was spiked, how much has he taken? Another thing -- given his size and weight, how much would it take to affect him?*

"The hell is she doing now?" Oz demanded.

"Back. Off."

I glanced up from my spell. Dave had panted himself in the path of the other three Ferals, who'd walked over to investigate.

"She trying to give you some other advantage beside the ones you've already got?" Tyrone growled.

Dave's tail flicked in agitation. "She thinks somebody's spiked the PowerUp."

Oz rolled his eyes. "*This* again?"

"You ignored Valeria when she ordered you to break it off," I told him, finishing the last sigil. Good thing this was a simple spell. Judging from their growing anger, I was running out of time. Plus, any drug would affect them a lot sooner than it would a tiger. "If Dave hadn't imitated the master sergeant to calm you down, somebody would've gotten hurt."

I touched the nearest sigil and sent a wave of power flowing into it. The glyphs began to glow as they rose from the ground and started revolving. I took the PowerUp bottle and pressed the base into the sand until it would stand upright. Then I sat back to watch.

The softly glowing liquid began to bubble and swirl as the spell started separating the potion into its components. The non-magical ingredients -- the water, sugar, dextrose, salt, chemicals and flavoring -- sank to the bottom, filling up the lower four fifths. As I watched, a layer of bright cobalt blue swirled up to fill most of the remaining space -- the Surge potion, with its assorted magical ingredients designed to help the body recover the energies it burned using magic.

I heard Oz snort. "Looks like regular old PowerUp to me. You need to start taking sleeping pills, Piper. You're losing it."

"Maybe," I told him, watching something pink beginning to swirl through the glowing blue. "Maybe not."

More time ticked past as I watched the bubble and swirl, painfully aware of the four Ferals shifting and growling around me.

"Was she always this crazy?" Oz said. "How the fuck did you stand it?"

"She was never like this," Chris growled, a subsonic rumble in his voice that made me swallow.

Definitely running out of time. I concentrated on the thin swirling currents as my head began to throb. My Kimura's was acting up again, but I ignored it. Didn't have time. "Something else is floating to the top," I said, sweat breaking out on my forehead. "Not much. But there's a thin layer of glow that's the wrong color for Surge. I'm betting on Frenzy."

"Frenzy?" Chris demanded, startled. "The shit they gave the suicide bombers?"

"Yep."

Dave swore.

"Can't be," Tyrone said. "I've drunk eight bottles of that shit. I'd have eaten somebody by now."

"I think whoever spiked this didn't put much in any individual bottle. They didn't want you to go off right away." *Except...* I frowned. "That's not the right color for Frenzy." I'd analyzed samples of the Caliphate's favorite suicide potion often enough to recognize it. Frenzy was a neon green that reminded me of antifreeze. Caliphate leaders gave it to Normie suicide volunteers because it made them fearless and aggressive -- willing to blow up a wedding even if they died too.

This, though, was a strange pinkish orange that floated on the surface like an oil slick. It wasn't any of the potions I'd been trained to recognize fighting overseas, or even when I'd worked for the CIA. Yet something about it looked vaguely familiar. Like I'd seen it before. *But where?*

A bubble of the liquid rose to the surface and popped, spraying the inside of the bottle with oily pink. I felt my face go cold as I realized what it was.

I bolted to my feet and whirled toward the ward. "Jimmy!" I shouted, hearing my voice crack in fear. "Do not open that ward! I don't give a fuck what happens, don't you dare open it!"

Jimmy Pope was standing there just beyond the ward, his arms crossed, an expression of faint amusement on his face. Probably thinking I was making myself look like a fool again.

At my tone, he straightened, eyes widening. "What? What did you... ?"

I raised the bottle with its thin, glowing layer of oily pink. "It's Berserker! That's a Schedule Four Illegal Potion. It's like Frenzy with a meth chaser, followed by snorting a line of coke. It doesn't hit Talents as hard as norms -- our natural magic provides some resistance. But over time..."

"The fuck are you talking about?" Tish demanded. "What the hell is Berserker?"

"Illegal as shit. You get life in prison just for possessing it."

"Isn't that the stuff your psycho granny gave the

bodyguard to make him kill his boss?" Dave demanded.

"Yeah." My heart was pounding so hard, it hurt. I could feel my aura kinking tighter, pain pulsing over my skin. *There's no way in hell all five of us are getting out of here alive. And I don't have a prayer.*

"Bullshit," Oz snarled, his big shoulders tensing. His aura was a deep, furious red, brightening into white as his anger grew. "Never heard of it. This is some backstabbing bullshit people are always pulling on these God damn reality shows. You're trying to make us all look like fools!"

"Sounds like it to me too," Tyrone agreed. He turned to Dave as magic began to churn through his aura. "You in on this, Frost?"

"I don't need her help to kick your ass," Dave snarled.

"Then what's with the collar?" Chris spat. "Those sigils match the ones she's wearing. You expect us to believe she hasn't been helping you?"

"I'd never have thought you'd be the type to pull this kind of fuckery," Oz growled, the red of his aura lightening. Burning toward the lethal white of suicidal rage.

"You're one to talk, considering what Zoe's had you doing," Dave retorted.

Shut up, Dave, I told him through the collar, but I could tell he wasn't paying attention.

"Zoe hasn't done shit!" Oz insisted, taking a step toward him with rage pumping through his aura.

"Dave's right." Ty's Feral gold eyes glittered. "Zoe's a manipulative bitch who's been leading you around by the dick for the past month."

"Fuck you!"

Slowly, I began to back away, knowing I needed

some distance between me and them in case they manifested. I'd learned in the Corps that the last thing you wanted to do with a triggered Feral was to run. He'd chase you, and that was a great way to get dead.

"Bitch!" Oz said, glaring murder at me, the word rumbling at a register no human vocal cords could produce. "You did this! *Somehow you did this.*"

"I wouldn't." Dave moved in front of me, his head down, ears laid back.

I shot a glance over my shoulder. My gaze fell on Jackson and the ten guys who provided security for the island, all of them with their rifles at the ready. Even Jackson held an AR-15.

The billionaire's gaze met mine through the ward, and his lips curled into a faint, icy smile. I could see the smug green in his aura, the pleasure in cruelty that my grandmother had shown so many times right before she hurt me.

Motherfucker. It's Jackson. It's been Jackson all along.

* * *

Dave

Every time I breathed in, I scented Ariel's fear. What's more, I could feel it through the collar -- her conviction that whatever happened, she wouldn't leave the circle alive. She might be right. The other Ferals' magic seemed to rake over my skin like claws, all simmering bloodlust as they stared at her with murderous yellow eyes.

Fury blazed up in me, made me want to kill them before they could so much as touch her.

"No," Ariel told me. *"You'll give Jackson an excuse to shoot us all."*

"Jackson?"

"He's behind this. Look at the bastards. If it wasn't for

Pope's ward, they'd have already opened fire."

I followed her gaze and saw Jackson standing there, an AR-15 in his hands and a smug, nasty grin on his face. *Wait, Gilbert's doing this? Why?*

I have no idea. Maybe the son of a bitch has turned Humanist.

Suddenly Tisha's demand that we stage a Showmance -- regardless of the political backlash -- seemed a lot more sinister. I'd thought she was just being tone deaf, but if Ariel was right, Gilbert was trying to make us look like perverts. Another manipulative shit playing games. Trying to kill us.

Trying to kill Ariel.

Before I could roar out my rage, Oz's savage growl dragged my head around as he moved toward us, gaze fixed on Ariel as if he meant to rip her apart. "If you think I'm going to let you get away with this," he said, his eyes nowhere near sane, "You're in for a fucking shock."

Magic exploded around him, surging into the massive glowing shape of his Kodiak. I felt Ariel's terror spike as the enormous creature loomed over us, well over ten feet tall. He made her looked like a toddler as she stared up at him. But even worse was the icy frenzy on his face. The decent man I'd known since Basic had been replaced by a psychotic killer.

The thought of what he might do to her added a spike of terror to my rage. "Don't start anything I'm going to have to finish," I said over Smilodon's basso snarl.

"You think we didn't notice you've been cheating?" Oz's upper lip curled. "That fucking collar..."

"The collar isn't what you need to worry about," I spat. "All this muscle is real, not magic. So are these teeth. Are you sure you want to pick a fight with me?"

It was the wrong thing to say. The stink of his rage intensified. "I'm not afraid of you!"

Chris took a step toward me. "And there are three of us."

"You cheating motherfucker." Tyrone bared his teeth as they both manifested in an explosion of power that beat against my senses and filled the air with the smell of ozone and aggression. "We'll kill you *and* your bitch!"

"Do you hear yourselves?" Ariel demanded. Through the collar, I could feel her mind working furiously, looking for a way to calm us all down. "*This isn't you!* Dave's your friend, and each of you has a hundred pounds on me even without the magic. It's the PowerUp doing this. Jackson spiked it. He's trying to make you all look like monsters!"

Oz stared at her through the shell of his bear. "Jackson? You said it was Zoe. Get your fucking story straight."

"*Think!*" Ariel shouted as I tensed, trying to decide who to go after first. "There are twenty cameras pointing at us. If you kill me, that's felony magical murder. And you know what the Humanists will do with that."

"Which is why you're full of shit." Tyrone laughed, the sound ugly with derision. "Jackson Gilbert has *never* been anything but a friend to Talents. Why in the hell would he do something like that?"

"I have no fucking idea, but I saw the look on his face," Ariel snapped. "He smirked at me when I said the bottles were drugged."

"Because he thinks you're crazy. I'm not listening to this shit any longer." Tyrone slunk toward her, lips pulled off his teeth. His manifestation echoed the expression, showing glowing fangs. To the others, he added, "You get him, I'll take care of her. He won't be so tough without her magic."

"If you touch her, you're dead." I told him, coiling to leap. "I'll rip your heart out and eat it."

"You won't get the chance." Chris and Oz separated, and I realized they intended to flank me and tear me apart.

Good thing there were two of me. *Protect her*, I told Smiley.

"No," Ariel protested, the collar telling her what I intended. *"You're going to need all your power. I can take Tyrone down with a spell blast."*

"You'd be kibble in thirty seconds. Smiley can protect you long enough for you to knock Ty out, then you both can give me a hand."

Smilodon's spirit surged out of our body and streamed around hers. Kurt had tried something similar when he'd channeled his power through Genevieve, but he'd almost fried her in the process. We couldn't risk that, so we just created a manifestation *around* her. This tiger mani was only a little bigger than my human one, but it would provide Ariel with some protection.

Just hang on and be ready to hit him, I told her. She had no idea how to fight as a tiger, so Smiley would have to handle it.

"Oh, you've got to be fucking kidding me!" With a roar of fury, Tyrone charged her.

Shit. I'd have to trust Smiley to protect her. I was going to have my paws full with Chris and Oz.

I circled to the side, backpedaling to keep the liger between me and the bear. That was how we'd been taught to fight multiple attackers in the Arcane Corps. Force your opponents to come at you one at a time -- make them get in each other's way. It's the only way to survive when you're outnumbered.

Chris leaped, sailing ten feet through the air like something out of a Marvel movie. I ducked, but his right paw raked claws over my shoulder as he flew over my head.

Ariel's voice rang through the collar, shrill with alarm. *"Dave!"*

"Don't worry about me. Focus on Ty!" Chris landed and wheeled on me. I lashed out, slashing the liger's glowing muzzle with my claws. He punched out with one forepaw, then the other. Blood and sparks flew as I snarled at the pain.

"You're a dumbass," Oz sneered, trying to corner me as I whirled aside, keeping the liger between us. "Are you really giving your manifestation to that little cunt witch?"

"We're going to rip you open like a piñata," Chris taunted, spinning to face me, still rearing weightlessly. "It won't even be a challenge."

"We'll see, won't we?" I growled.

But over the next ten minutes, Chris and Oz harried me like a wolf pack on a bull, using all their magical muscle in darting attacks and pounces. And since they weighed a fraction of what their animals would have, it was like fighting Spider-Man. Whenever I went for one, the other would jump ten feet and land on my head to take a big bite. When I reared to grab him, his partner would rake my haunches with his claws. It wasn't long before I bled from a dozen wounds. And I still hadn't managed to punch a tooth through either manifestation.

Maybe I could have defended myself if I'd kept Smilodon and his magic, but if I had, Ariel would already be dead. And that just wasn't an option.

Oz had reared on his hind legs, threatening to land on my head, when I glimpsed something glowing shooting toward me out of the corner of one eye. I leaped, twisting, and batted Chris out of the air like a tennis ball. He went flying, and I raced grimly after him. Before he could regain his feet, I pounced, pinning him with my full weight. Dim slashes over his mani's throat marked where I'd hit him, and I bit down. If I could just get a good grip, I could punch through and collapse his manifestation. Magic zapped my jaws and tongue like a live wire, but I ignored the vibrating pain and bit harder, wrapping my forelegs around his liger's chest and raking my claws over his ribs. He howled in fury and wrenched, rolling me beneath him.

For an unarmed human, the ground wasn't a good place to be. But for a big cat, it was pretty much ideal, since it freed all four legs, plus teeth. I clawed his ribs as I kicked my back legs down his mani's belly. If he'd been flesh and blood, I'd have disemboweled him.

Unfortunately, a Feral's manifestation could withstand machine gun fire. Though I raked furrows along his mani's stomach, I knew it would take more than that to collapse it. Neither of us would be tapping out this time.

Trouble was, I *wasn't* bulletproof. Even as I dug at him, I felt his claws tearing at my sides in whiplashes of pain.

Oz roared, one paw slamming into my side hard enough to knock the breath out of me. I ground my teeth into the liger's shining throat even as his magic stung my mouth, my tongue, even the roots of my teeth.

The bear charged and rammed me, knocking me off Chris so hard we went airborne. We hit the ground in a rolling tumble that clipped my tongue with my fangs. I tasted blood. Then I was sliding across the circle on my left side with the bear blazing and raging on top of me. Oz dove, fangs tearing into my side just below my ribs on the right. The pain was like something out of hell -- vicious, burning, the tearing wrench of his teeth punching into my flesh, biting and pulling away.

Roaring, I tore free and leaped away. When my paws hit the ground, the explosion of pain almost buckled my legs. Both Ferals hit me then, tumbling me onto my back.

I went after Oz with all four sets of claws, maddened by the pain. Staring through their manifestations, I barely recognized either man, their faces were so contorted with sheer, screaming insanity.

They were going to kill me. And then Ariel was next.

* * *

Ariel

The lion dove for my mani's throat, slamming into Smilodon and bowling us right over onto our back. Peering through Smiley's shell, I stared directly into Ty's open jaws as his teeth clamped down on my tiger's throat. We were less than half his size -- Dave hadn't had the magic to create anything larger.

Smiley roared at the pain of his magical attack, clawing and kicking.

I'd never realized how terrifying it was to be inside a manifestation in combat. Unlike Dave or the Ferals, I had no control over what was going on. I could only watch as Smilodon fought Ty amid flying sparks and jolts of magic that blazed through my body like electricity.

Even worse impressions flooded my mind from the collar. Oz and Chris had pinned Dave the same way, both of them savaging him as he fought back desperately.

Just like my nightmare. After all I'd done, I still hadn't managed to save him. I'd only insured I'd die with him.

Damn it, every time I'd thought I had a chance, that I'd finally found peace, love… *It was snatched away!* My parents had betrayed me, my grandmother had betrayed me. Even the military and the government had used and abandoned me. Now I was losing Dave, the one person who'd actually given a shit about me in my entire life. He'd loved me enough to use Smiley's mani to protect me, even knowing he needed it himself. I was getting him killed.

Damn it, no! Not this time.

I stared down Ty's throat as he clamped down in the grip big cats used to suffocate their prey. He couldn't suffocate me this way, not so long as I had the manifestation, but the minute it failed, I was dead. I could see my fate in the frenzied burn of his fury, white hot with madness.

I can't just watch! I've got to do something! But there were both our manifestations between me and Tyrone, and if I tried to drop mine, he'd just kill me.

There was no way I could punch through his shell -- the only way to do that was to inflict such a pounding on it, the Feral ran out of magic. Judging by the way my tiger was beginning to dim, I was in more danger of that than he was…

"I'm going to fucking kill you!" Tyrone snarled at me through his manifestation's teeth and the thin gold glow of its palate.

My eyes widened as the idea burst into my mind.

I grabbed for the choker around my throat, my forefinger finding the first of the four earth sigils. I'd spaced them just so, both on the front of the necklace, my bracelets, and the anklets. I spread my fingers, seeking the clay sigils, recognizing the ones I wanted by the furious burn of the Earth.

Power lanced through my body, so fierce and hot it was all I could do not to scream as it arched through my aura. I made no effort to control it -- just let it rage into my aura until it blazed.

Tyrone's eyes widened.

"Drop it, Smiley!" The tiger saw the image in my mind and obeyed, a chunk of his throat mani vanishing the instant before my free hand stabbed through the space it had been, shooting between the lion's fangs to punch into the thin glow of its palate. My palm slapped Tyrone's forehead. I sent my power punching into his skull.

His eyes rolled back, and the golden lion vanished as he fell against me, out cold. I rolled him off me. But even as I lunged to my feet, a bolt of fire blasted from the collar into my belly. The explosion of red-hot agony was worse than anything I'd ever felt -- and I was a pro at pain.

Oh fuck, it's Dave!

Smilodon roared in rage and terror, and we raced across the sand toward the three battling Ferals. An image flashed through my mind, layered over my vision: Oz rearing over me, eyes insane from the Berserker. *No, not me. Dave. I was seeing what Dave saw through Smilodon.*

Furry paws lashed out as Dave raked Oz's glowing muzzle, trying to punch through his manifestation. Sparks exploded around me with the painful jolt of hitting someone else's manifestation.

Dave didn't have the strength to break through. He'd given me too much of his magic, and Oz had ripped a vicious gut wound in his right side.

He was bleeding to death.

As I ran toward them, I saw Chris drive in, fangs slicing across Dave's rib cage in another scarlet explosion of pain.

Gotta get them the fuck off him! I clawed for the magic I'd pulled from the Earth, pouring it into my hand. *Hope I've got enough... Please, God, let it be enough...*

I saw in a flash that he'd reinforced the part of his mani facing Dave -- but that left the top of it thinner. *There!* I told Smiley.

And we leaped.

When we landed on Chris's back, he stiffened with a roar of shock. Before he could reinforce his thinned head mani, I drove the spell blade through the weakness and into his skull.

Chris managed a choked scream as I poured power into him. Not enough to kill him -- quite. He wasn't the one who needed killing.

He collapsed, his liger manifestation winking out as he lost consciousness. I leaped clear...

The roar was so loud, it actually hurt my ears. I looked up to see Oz whirl toward me, leaving Dave lying in a bloody heap on the sand. "Oh no, you *don't*, you fucking witch!" the bear Feral bellowed. And charged.

Oh, shit.

* * *

God damn it, Jackson thought. *How the hell did it all go to shit so fast?*

For this to work without raising a lot of questions he didn't want to answer, the Ferals had to go berserk and kill people -- preferably Dave.

Instead, that damn witch had somehow manifested a freaking *tiger*, something she shouldn't have been able to do.

Jackson wheeled on that idiot Jimmy, who was stubbornly refusing to cooperate. "Open the wards! Open the fucking wards before it kills her!" *I should be so lucky.* The real problem was that the little bitch might survive and knock *all* the Ferals out. Then this entire thing was a complete and total waste of millions of dollars.

Jimmy, white-faced, looked from him and his AR-15 to the circle, where Ariel -- and her God damn impossible tiger manifestation -- was dancing around Oz in his Kodiak. The cat wasn't even a third the size of the bear. "You don't need to shoot anybody! Maybe she can knock him out too..."

"Or maybe he'll gut her! Look what they did to Dave!"

The tiger stirred weakly, fighting to get up. Judging from the damage, that motherfucker would be dead in ten minutes or less, so at least he'd managed that. But it was nowhere near enough. "If you don't drop those wards now, *I will make sure you never work again!*"

Jimmy's eyes widened. "All right, God damn it!" The Arcanist gestured, and the wards dropped.

The members of the audience -- those who hadn't run for their lives -- screamed in abject terror. As well they should.

Now let's see how many of these assholes I can 'accidentally' kill, Jackson thought in grim pleasure. *"Friendly fire" is a bitch.*

* * *

Raven stood in wide-eyed frozen terror even as

her every instinct screamed at her to run. Just get the fuck away before that damn bear came after her next, and she ended up like Roger.

The orbiting sigils dropped into the sand as Jimmy broke the ward. Jackson and the guards brought up their weapons -- and pointed them at Ariel and Oz. *Jesus. What the hell are they doing? They'll hit Ariel! Besides, none of the Ferals are responsible for this!*

Ariel turned, and for a split second, their eyes met through her manifestation. "Raven, *sing!*" she screamed. "*It's Jackson! He's the one who's doing this!*"

What? Raven's gaze flew to the billionaire. There was a cold, faint smile on Jackson's face as he took aim. It looked like he was drawing a bead on Ariel, not Oz. *Oh, hell, she's right!*

Raven's terror shattered, broken by the need to save her stubborn, courageous friend. Drawing breath, reaching deep, she gathered every bit of power she had. Power that could save Ariel as she'd been too panicked to save Roger.

This time will be different. This time she wouldn't have to live with the guilt of doing nothing. She began to sing, the words of rock's greatest Bard pouring out of her, backed by all her power, all her determination not to fail again. "Imagine there's no heaven…"

Jackson's eyes widened as he began to fall under the spell of her magic. His finger relaxed on the trigger. He lifted his head and looked at her, a frown of confusion on his face.

"Imagine" had been her mother's favorite song, and Raven had sung it to her as she'd died from cancer. Now she poured all the emotion she'd felt that day into the song -- the sadness, the grief, the longing for more time with the woman she'd loved so much.

Jackson's gaze met hers, and as she watched, his

pupils dilated. Just past him, she saw the other gunmen glance around, overwhelmed by the raw power of her grief, of her love.

She wrapped her magic around them all. She had to hold them, had to keep them from killing…

Jackson's dazed eyes suddenly sharpened, narrowed as he fought her. *She was losing him.* Raven reached deep into her memory of serenading her mother that last time, giving the song everything she had. And took him under again. Jackson's gaze went vague, losing the calculation, the hate, the rage.

Just beyond him, she saw one gunman's head lift, frowning as he looked around as if wondering why no one was shooting. His eyes widened, then narrowed in cold rage. *Fuck, I don't have him at all.* He turned, swinging his rifle to draw a bead on her face. She sang harder, but her magic just bounced off him like rain on a windshield.

Shit shit… He can't hear me. He's deaf.
He's going to kill me.

* * *

Kordell had started toward Zoe, determined to make her stop whatever the fuck she was doing… Then Raven began to sing, and every hair on the back of his neck rose as her magnificent voice rolled over him. He turned…

For one glorious instant, he thought it was going to work. The gunmen were letting their weapons drop.

Except for one guy standing arm's length away. *The one turning to aim at Raven.*

Oh, hell no, you don't! Kordell spun and kicked straight up, his foot slamming up under the weapon's barrel and knocking it skyward. It went off with a thundering boom.

Kordell didn't know shit about the martial arts,

but he could kick like a Rockette.

The fucker almost lost the gun, but somehow he held onto it and whirled toward Kordell, who found himself staring down the black maw of its barrel. *Fuck.*

A gold blur slammed into the man with a roar that made Kordell jump. With a startled yell, the shooter hit the ground flat on his back.

Valeria Sanz snarled as she pinned the asshole beneath three hundred pounds of fangs, claws and muscle.

Something gold and glowing appeared, hovering over the man's face. Craning his neck, Kordell realized they were words, arranged horizontally in the air so that the gunman could read them from where he lay. *"If you move, I'll rip out your throat."*

Damn, Kordell thought. *You can create words with a manifestation?*

The shooter froze, his eyes wide as he stared up into the lioness' furious Feral gold stare. Well, he wouldn't be a problem for a while. But Jackson... Kordell wasn't sure how long Raven could hold the bastard.

He turned to look for reinforcements. Most of the crowd had already run, but several of the contestants had lingered -- including the Bards. "Help Raven!" he shouted, waving his arms at them. "She can't hold them long! Sing!"

For a moment, there was no sound other than the unearthly purity of Raven's voice giving "Imagine" another go. Then two other Bards joined in, and he felt the power of the spell instantly triple.

A heartbeat later, a fourth voice joined, high and pure.

Kordell blinked in amazement. Zoe was singing her heart out.

Chapter Fourteen
Dave

I writhed in agony at the gut wound. *This is a hell of a lot worse than when I died the first time…*

Then I heard Smilodon's familiar basso roar, saw his blazing glow from the corner of one eye, far brighter than my attackers. Ariel, enclosed by Smiley's manifestation, landed on Chris's back. He screamed and reared off me, staggering backward. A heartbeat later, his manifestation vanished, and he collapsed on the ground, out cold.

How the hell did she do that?

Oz whirled on her. I tried to get up and go after him, but the gut wound went off in my side like a hand grenade. I hit the ground again, yowling.

All I wanted to do was lie down and die. Just get the hell away from all this fucking pain. I wasn't going to survive this. The nearest veterinary hospital was on Nassau, five hundred miles away. Besides, I doubted the vet there had ever treated anything bigger than a golden retriever. I was fucked.

Oz lunged at Ariel, slashing a glowing paw at her tiger mani's head. She leaped six feet straight up, dodging the strike, but he dove at her, huge jaws gaping wide to reveal glowing fangs. She twisted in mid-air, and he missed by a fraction of an inch. Ariel hit the ground and darted away, the roaring bear in pursuit.

I could feel her terror even as she taunted him, trying to goad him into a mistake. She had a spell she'd used to knock out Chris and Oz, but she couldn't punch it through the full thickness of the Kodiak's shell. She needed him to thin it, as Chris had when he was attacking me.

I was going to have to set him up for her. But fuck me, this was going to *hurt*.

Still, I couldn't let the son of a bitch kill Ariel. So I gritted my teeth and rolled onto my paws, my fangs clenched against the scream.

What the hell are you doing? Ariel demanded through the collar. *Save your strength! I'll knock him out the way I did the other two.*

You snuck up on the other two, I told her, and braced my legs apart, though all I wanted to do was vomit. I was *not* going to look at what they'd done to my side. Some things I just fucking didn't want to see.

I staggered grimly across the sand toward Oz. As if from a long way away, I could hear an unearthly chorus singing "Imagine." It made me want to lie down and let go, but the bear had to go down first. If I gave up, Smilodon would die with me, and our manifestation would collapse. Ariel would be screwed.

The bear didn't even see me coming. He was focused on Ariel, who darted around him like a Chihuahua snapping at a Doberman. *Keep him looking the other way while I get close enough,* I told her. *I'll distract the fucker long enough for you to get the blade in.*

How the hell will you do that?

I'll think of something. I broke into a labored trot, grinding my teeth against the pain that jolted through me with every step as blood streamed from my open wound. I was leaving a trail. The circle seemed to spin around me, gray speckles whirling at the edge of my vision. I slowed down, worried I was going to pass out.

I focused my attention on the bear's broad, golden back. *One more step, damn it. I can manage one more step. There. Now another one. If I can take him down, I can lie down. All I have to do is take him down and it will be over. All this shit will finally be over. This constant, nagging, grinding fucking* effort *will be done. No more God damn cages, no more God damn pain. Just peace.*

Ariel had forced Oz to retreat toward me by attacking his legs with teeth and claws. He was five feet away now, ordinarily an easy jump. I gathered what was left of my strength…

Golden sparks streamed out of the night to cocoon me in magic. Smiley, generating a manifestation much brighter than it should have been. *What the fuck are you doing?*

Smilodon ignored me as he drove us forward, carrying our weakened tiger body inside the manifestation's shell. *How the…* Ariel must be drawing on the Earth's magical field to help power the mani.

Oz, focused on Ariel, had thickened the front of his manifestation as Ariel taunted him, apparently cautious of whatever spell she'd used to down the other Ferals.

"Manifest a blade!" she told me. *"I'll shoot my spell through it!"*

Which was when I saw the little lunatic was dancing in front of the bear covered in nothing more than a T-shirt and shorts. She was channeling *all* her power into Smilodon.

Oh, hell, I had to work fast before the bear took a bite out of her face. I manifested a human arm and transformed one finger into a long, ice-pick-thin blade.

Heaving onto my back legs, I lunged, screaming at the effort of lifting six hundred pounds of dying tiger. Even as Oz started to turn, I rammed the blade into the base of his skull. Ariel's magic surged through my collar and up the length of my arm. Oz convulsed with a choked scream and went down in a heap. His bear popped like a soap bubble.

For a moment I stared dumbly down at him.

Okay. Okay, that's done. I let myself sag to the sand, trying not to jar my wound. Didn't work. I screamed at the burning, blazing pain.

Ariel jumped over Oz's unconscious body to kneel beside me. Her eyes widened in horror. "Shit, you're bleeding out. Where's that bleeder? We need to plug it with a manifestation." She scanned my bloody side as if she had X-ray vision. Which, given her magic, she basically did. "There!" Spreading her hands over the wound, she stabbed what felt like a red-hot poker into my side as she blocked the rips in my intestines. I'd have cursed if she wasn't using all my magic to keep me breathing.

"Sorry, sorry! Hold on." She threw her head up and yelled, "Tisha, he's gonna need transport!"

"I've already called for a helicopter," the showrunner said, running toward us. "Hoped one of you would be alive to need it. It'll be landing in twenty."

I let my eyes slide shut. "Won't be in time."

"Yes, it will," Ariel snarled. "Don't you dare let go, Dave!" Suddenly my mind was full of her as her fierce, determined will flooded through the collar. "I'm damn well going to keep you alive."

"You're… wasting your time," I panted. I'd used the last of my strength to take out Oz. "You don't have enough power. And I'm… They ripped me up. Lost too much blood."

"Shut up." She started crawling on the sand around me, drawing sigils with fingers wet with my blood.

"What the hell are you doing?" Tisha demanded.

"Smiley and I blocked the worst of the bleeders with patch manifestations. Now I'm going to feed them healing magic."

"Trying to... to kill your... yourself?"

"Shush, you ungrateful cat," she growled, drawing a sigil. I lifted my head an inch or so, managed to get a look at what she was doing.

"That's... that's an Earth sigil."

"No kidding." She was working fast, reaching over me to dip her fingers in the blood pooled on the sand. Which, given it was my blood, made it borderline black magic. I don't think she gave a shit.

"You can't... use healing magic on... on combat wounds. There isn't... isn't time." I'd be dead long before the spell could take effect. That kind of magic was only effective with diseases like cancer, not traumatic injuries.

Smilodon was doing something. I could feel the tiger reaching for her, locking onto her. What's more, something small and glowing was circling my head. It floated past my eyes, and I realized it was one of the Earth sigils.

She'd activated my collar sigils. They'd risen out of the clay glyphs and started revolving around my head. Ariel began to chant. My jaw dropped as I recognized the words, though I hadn't heard them in fifteen years.

She was working the spell Arcanists used to bind Ferals to their Familiars.

But she seemed to be focusing it on *herself*.

"What are... you doing?" I panted. "You're... not a Feral. Your magic doesn't work... work that... that way."

She shot me a glittering look. "But yours and Smiley's do."

Are you trying to put all three of us in your body? I demanded through the collar, horrified. *Because that's not going to work.*

"Then I guess you're just going to have to stay alive -- because I'm not letting you go." As I touched her mind, I realized she meant every word of it. All her life, she'd been alone. Until I'd come along. *She loves me.* And not just because I helped her pain. *Me. She loves* me, *furry or not.*

That's right, she growled in my mind. *I love you and your dirty jokes and your cynicism and your wisdom. I don't give a single solitary fuck what anyone else thinks about it. Every Normie bigot can kiss my ass. Love is rare and precious, and this love is nobody's God damn business but ours. I'm not giving you up. Not now. Not in five years. Not at all. Not until the day I quit breathing.*

And I believed her. She meant every word of it. A crazy joy rolled over me, despite my wounds, despite my pain. *She loves me.*

I loved her right back. That was why I'd been so scared. I loved her battered, wounded soul, her blazing magic, her desperate longing and her loyal heart. She could not let me die any more than I could have let Oz kill her. Which was why I couldn't let go and leave her. It would inflict a wound on her soul that would never heal.

So I grabbed for her, just as I'd held on to Smilodon as he'd dragged me back from death. The pain didn't matter. Nothing mattered except her. Giving her what she needed -- and what I needed every bit as much. Somehow, I was going to survive long enough for the helicopter to arrive and take me to the veterinary hospital. I'd survive the surgery to repair my gut wound. Because I couldn't leave my Ariel alone.

* * *

Tisha watched Ariel as she worked her frantic magic, feeling her heart go out to the girl. She thought of how shocked she'd been when Oz, Chris and Tyrone went after Ariel and Dave.

It had been utterly out of character for the three men. She'd come to know them well over the past months as they'd worked on the show, both during the auditions and when the shooting started. All three of them were decorated war heroes. Ariel was right. *Jackson had done this.*

She turned and looked around the circle. Two of the camera crew had bound the unconscious Ferals with loop after loop of power cable. As the Bards sang, other crewmembers had tied up Jackson's gunmen -- and Jackson himself.

She moved to join Dr. Kingston, who was kneeling beside Chris, drawing another tube of blood. "How's it going?"

The doctor sat back on her heels and started filling out a label, which she then affixed to the tube. "I've got blood drawn from all three Ferals. If Ariel's right, when the Bahamian authorities test these samples, they'll find evidence that they were under the influence of Berserker. Assuming the same thing shows up in the bottles of PowerUp…"

"It will," Tisha said grimly. "I already talked to that damned Alchemist. Sanders admitted he made the potion under Jackson's orders." She turned to look at the big man, eyes narrow. "Now I just need to find out what the hell Jackson thought he was doing -- other than trying to kill innocent people and frame the Ferals for it."

Dr. Kingston shook her head. "I don't understand any of this. It makes no sense."

"Tell me about it. We worked on this project for two years. And he just blew the whole thing all to hell. Millions of dollars -- it's insane. And that's aside from all the people he tried to kill."

She headed for Raven, who was sitting in one of the audience chairs taking a break. The Bards were taking turns keeping the gunmen calmed down until they could be placed under arrest by the Bahamian authorities.

"How's Dave?" Raven asked the doctor anxiously. Ariel still knelt in the sand by the tiger's side, working that spell of hers.

"Still breathing, thank God. Look, I want to find out why the hell Jackson did this, Raven. Do you think you can put him in the mood to tell the truth for once in his God damn life?"

Raven paused, considering. "I could sing 'Your Lies.'" That had been one of her biggest hits -- a song about a woman talking to her cheating lover. Her mouth tightened. "I'd like to know what the fuck he was thinking too."

Raven gestured at Devyn Allison, who was singing 'Peace Train.'" The man sighed in relief and sat down as she began to sing, moving closer to where the big man sat, his arms bound to the chair he sat in.

Jackson stared dreamily up at Raven, obviously thoroughly relaxed. Tisha waited, letting Raven's song take effect. Finally she gestured to Elaine Jones, one of the more ballsy shooters. The woman nodded, picked up her camera and followed Tish as she approached the producer.

"Jackson, I've got a couple of questions," she began. Raven, knowing what she needed, began to sing more softly. "Mind talking to me?"

Jackson gave her a pleasant smile, looking more laid-back than she'd ever seen him. "Sure."

"Why were you trying to kill them?"

Jackson's gaze flickered, a faint frown tightening

his mouth. Raven leaned in, pouring more power into her voice until he relaxed again. "I had to have a reason," he said, his voice calm and matter-of-fact. He didn't sound at all drugged.

"For what?"

"Running for President as a Humanist."

Tisha blinked. Even Raven missed a note. Jackson had always been a passionate advocate for Talent rights, happy to skewer the Humanist Party as fascists. "Why would you want to do that?"

"I've managed to do everything I've ever wanted to do. It's all gotten too damned easy. I need a challenge. Politics would fit the bill." He gave her his supremely confident smile. "I'm going to run for the Humanist nomination for president. And I'm going to win."

"But... why? You're not a Humanist. You've always mocked them as dumb bigots."

"Well, yeah. But the Humanists don't have a good presidential candidate -- the current front runner is a racist bomb-throwing lunatic."

"Why not run as a Constitutionalist? You're popular enough."

He snorted. "Not enough to beat Helen Granger. The party's all but anointed her. Member of the New York Granger dynasty, daughter of a governor, a governor herself. I don't have the experience -- she'd beat me like a drum. But the Humanists... Steve Myer's popular with conspiracy theorists, but only people who believe in lizard men will vote for his dumb ass."

Tisha stared at him. "Jackson, every time you open your mouth, you call Humanists morons. You don't seriously think they're going to support you?"

"Of course, they will," he said serenely. "They

just have to believe I've seen the light. I just need a believable excuse. Then I can make the rounds of the talk shows saying I was wrong, and the Humanists were right all along. They'll eat it up with a spoon."

Suddenly so many things Jackson had done that made zero sense at the time became perfectly logical. "That's why you insisted on the showmance. I told you it would blow up in our faces, but you swore it wouldn't. Because you *wanted* a scandal."

He nodded. "The Humanists wouldn't have watched the show otherwise, but I needed to get them outraged. Outraged enough to watch, so they'd see *this*." He gestured grandly at the circle.

"That's why you hired the alchemist to drug the PowerUp -- so the Ferals would go berserk." She shook her head. "I wondered why you wanted to have just them in this challenge, considering that the whole point of the show was *all* the Talents participating."

He nodded. "I figured once the Ferals killed a dozen or so audience members, me and my boys would shoot them. Then I could tell everyone the Humanists were right all along, and the Talents need to be put in camps..." He hesitated a moment, as if remembering who he was talking to. "Except for you, of course."

"Jackson, the cops would have done tox screens. They'd have caught you."

He snorted. "Not after I paid the right people. But then you and Valeria insisted on that safety ward, and I realized I was going to have to come up with a reason to drop it." Anger sparked in his eyes. "Then there was that cunt Ariel and her fucking dreams. She just wouldn't shut up. When she insisted on testing the PowerUp, I knew I had to arrange a little friendly fire for her and that damn tiger."

Tisha stared at him. "You're a fucking sociopath. Why did I never realize that before?"

He gave her a slow smile. "Because I played you, darling. I played you like a fiddle. I do that. It's *my* Talent."

In the distance, Tisha could hear the *whomp whomp whomp* of approaching rotors. "That's the 'copter." Leaning forward, Tisha said softly, "There's a Bahamian detective on that flight. I'm going to do my best to make sure you go to jail, Jackson. But even if you don't, I will make damn sure you never see the inside of the White House."

Rage flashed in his eyes, but Raven segued into "Imagine" again, and he settled back, the rage fading as he listened. Tisha turned and stalked toward the circle, where the helicopter was just setting down.

Epilogue

Ariel

No armed protestors lurked at the gate when I drove Dave and Valeria to Briggs Feral Sanctuary in my rented van. "Human Heritage's lawyer finally told them to cut it the hell out," he told me when I commented on the bigot-free environment. "Between Kurt's lawsuit and that bombing in Wisconsin, they've decided to lay low for a while."

"Let's hope that continues with Roth out of jail." The former president had served six months in federal prison after his conviction on conspiracy charges two years ago. Former South Carolina state representative Virginia Laurel was still locked up for her role in the plot, while Arcanist contract assassin Adrian Fleming had gotten life for Felony Magical Murder. He'd only escaped the death penalty by testifying against Laurel and Roth.

"Hope Jackson gets time," Valeria said, her lioness rumbling a deep growl.

"If he doesn't, it won't be because we didn't do our part," I said.

While Dave had recovered from surgery, we'd spent weeks answering questions from the Royal Bahamas Police Force and prosecutors. Zoe and Alchemist Nathan Sanders were also cooperating with the prosecution as part of a plea agreement. Billionaire or not, Jackson was now in Her Majesty's Prison in Fox Hill awaiting trial, having been declared a flight risk. I gathered he'd tried a bribe that hadn't gone well. Which wasn't exactly a surprise, considering the leaked recording saying he was just going to buy them all off.

I drove down the winding road shaded by oaks,

maples and pines to the generous parking lot. It was packed, though the park had closed for the night. "Looks like everyone in town is here."

Dave's tail lashed, and I felt his excitement. "Between all the volunteers, the melded Ferals, Genevieve, Kurt, Jake, Erica, and my folks, it'll be a crowd." He turned to Valeria. "And all the Melds are looking forward to meeting you, Valeria. We've never had a female Meld here before."

"Hope they won't be disappointed." It was hard to read the lioness' expressions, but I thought Valeria looked uneasy.

He snorted. "Don't worry about that. You're gonna be a furry Bachelorette with Sam, Reggie and George vying for the rose."

I parked and let the two cats out of the van, and we all headed along the winding walkway past the combination ticket booth and souvenir shop. The sun was setting, and the cool spring air carried the scents of blooming flowers and the musk of wild predators.

Valeria made a rumbling sound of approval, studying the curving enclosures with their sixteen-foot galvanized wire panels. A jaguar paced along the length of one of the enclosures, studying us with glowing golden eyes. "Nice enclosures. Looks like your cats have plenty of room."

"Yeah, Kurt prides himself on the facilities BFS provides. Wait until you see the treehouses we've built for the Melds," Dave said. "Heating, air conditioning *and* Wi-Fi."

A long, moaning roar sounded in the distance.

"Hey yourself, Clarence," Dave called. "I've got a woman of my own now." He sounded downright smug as Smilodon rumbled happily.

Kurt Briggs lived in a big rambling farmhouse

located at the rear of the park. They'd set up a big white tent in the front yard that reminded me of the one where I'd met Dave two months before.

"Dave!" A tiny woman in her sixties ran from the tent, arms flung wide.

He manifested in a swirl of golden light and strode to meet her, lifting her off her feet in a fierce hug to swing her in an exuberant circle. "Mom! God, I've missed you!"

"Lord, boy, you scared hell out of us!" A tall, rawboned man who looked a lot like Dave's manifestation joined the group hug, pounding his son's golden, glowing back. Smilodon, never shy, shoved his way into the middle of the trio, rubbing his chin up and down the woman's hip until she knelt to hug his furry neck. He rumbled happily as Dave's father gave him a vigorous ear scratch.

I hung back, sweat trickling down my spine as I watched the enthusiastic greeting. No member of my family had ever been that damn glad to see me. *What if they don't like me? What if they think...*

A big, furred head butted my arm. I looked down to see Valeria gazing up at me. "Don't be ridiculous. You saved their son. They're going to love you."

"How did you know..."

The lioness flicked an ear. "Even in this crowd, I can smell your anxiety."

Dave pulled free from his folks and held out a hand toward me, a tender smile on his face. "Mom, Dad, this is Ariel Piper. She saved my ass. Ariel, these are my folks, Betty and Eric Frost."

The two turned. Feeling awkward, I stepped forward, extending a hand to shake. "It's nice to meet you, Mr. and Mrs..."

Before I could finish the sentence, Betty ignored the hand in favor of pulling me into a hug. "Ariel! It's so good to meet you." Her body felt warm and motherly against mine, and to my surprise, I felt my eyes sting. "Thank you for bringing my boy back to me," she said as she finally drew away, her blue eyes shining with tears.

"We owe you more than we can say," Eric agreed. "If it hadn't been for you and your magic -- and your determination to protect Dave -- he'd be dead."

"Ahhhh…" I felt my cheeks go hot. I'd been thanked by grateful parents before -- that girl's school leaped to mind -- but it had never meant so much. "It was… It was more a mutual rescue," I said, and had clear my throat. "And if Valeria hadn't taken down that shooter of Gilbert's…"

I turned to gesture at the lioness, only to see her staring in dumbfounded awe. Following her gaze, I saw a huge beast that had to be the most gorgeous male lion I'd ever seen. He was flanked by a tiger and another, slightly smaller lion. This must be Sam, Reggie and George, the three Melds Dave had mentioned.

Magic swirled as they manifested. The big lion's mani was a tall, handsome man, while his friends included a shorter guy who looked like an Olympic gymnast and a third who could have played defensive tackle in the NFL. "You must be Valeria," the lion meld said. "I've heard so much about you. I'm Sam Champlain."

The gymnast shouldered him aside with a charming grin. "George Davis."

"Reggie Smith." The defensive tackle body-checked the other two, hand extended. I thought he might be Black judging from his features, though it was hard to tell with the golden glow.

"Oh. Ah…" Looking dazzled, Valeria manifested, and I realized I'd never seen her full body before. Her mani was lushly female, hair tumbling around her shoulders in a waterfall of curls as she reached out to shake each man's hand. "Hi. It's… it's nice to meet you."

Sam smiled. "Believe me, the pleasure is mine…"

"And mine," Reggie put in.

"But mostly mine," George insisted, shoving Reggie aside. "I can tell we're going to be great friends."

Valeria's smile heated as her gaze kindled with such wicked speculation, I stared. "I'm sure we will be."

"Damn," I told Dave through the collar. *"I think she's got visions of a harem. Hisum? This is going to be fun to watch."*

"That, or terrifying." He looked around and touched my shoulder, gesturing to direct my attention to a couple more people pushing through the crowd. "Ariel, I'd like to introduce you to Kurt and Gen."

"Oh, sure!" I recognized the big, muscular dark-haired man from TV interviews as he walked over, accompanied by a stunning redhead.

"I'm so glad you were able to join us," Kurt Briggs said, giving me a broad white smile.

"We owe you," his wife agreed. "Dave says he wouldn't have made it without you."

I gave them a smile. "Same goes."

"Can you teach me to do that knockout spell?" Gen asked. "That would be damned handy to have against the next terrorist polar bear."

"Sure, though I sincerely hope there won't *be*

another terrorist polar bear."

Dave snorted. "With our track record?"

I grimaced. "Good point."

"Actually," Genevieve said, hooking an arm through mine to guide me into the tent, "I've got this idea. How would you feel about going into business with me... ?"

* * *

I spent the next couple of hours being treated as a hero by the Briggses, Jake and Erica Nolan, and a small army of volunteers, many of them middle-aged women who seemed to universally adore Dave. They were all amazing cooks, judging from the mouth-watering collection of dishes set up on the tent's serving tables.

"So what's going on with that Gilbert creep?" Eric Frost asked his son. We were all dining picnic style on blankets spread out on the thick spring grass.

Dave gave him a tiger grin, all teeth and nasty. "Awaiting trial in the Bahamas. He was ruled a flight risk, so he ain't going home any time soon. Turns out the Bahamian authorities aren't as easy to bribe as he thought."

"By the way," Jake asked, "Who leaked all that video of his confession?"

"No idea. It's a mystery." Dave's eyes widened in pretended innocence, before he snorted. "Though I will say pissing off Tisha Jennings is never a good idea."

"What about Tyrone, Oz and Chris?" Jake asked. "I know those guys, and there's no way they had anything to do with his bullshit."

"They did spend a couple of days in jail," I said. "But fortunately, that alchemist admitted Jackson had hired him to drug the Ferals, so the cops dropped the charges."

Dave's tail-tip flicked. "Now the guys have joined our lawsuit against the son of a bitch. Given the tox screens that show they were under the influence when they attacked us, Tisha thinks we'll end up owning a chunk of Gilbert's fortune, including Hammerhead Productions. She's planning to turn the show footage into a documentary. We're in negotiations with her over our cut. And we've accepted an offer on the book Ariel and I are writing about the whole thing."

Dave's agent had been shopping around the first couple of chapters -- which dealt with the Ford terrorism case -- even before shooting began on *Arcane Island*. When the scandal broke, a bidding war erupted among the big three publishing houses that ended up netting us a half-million advance. Now we were collaborating.

"That's good," Jake Nolan said. He was just as handsome in person as he'd been on TV -- a powerfully built blond who looked ridiculously happy with his lean, dark-haired wife. They were both detectives with the Sheriff's office now. "I don't suppose you'd have cell numbers for the guys? I was thinking of giving them a call. The aftermath of something like that..." He took his wife's hand. "I mean, I was under a similar kind of spell when I went after Jake, Gen and Erica, and I had a hard time dealing. The nightmares..." He shook his head.

"I think they'd appreciate that," I told him. "They were pretty wrecked when they came out of it and learned how close we'd come to dying. I pointed out they were as much Jackson's victims as we were, but it's still been tough." I grimaced. "Especially with the conspiracy theory bullshit circulating on Humanist social media. There's no situation so hellish, that bunch can't make it worse."

"Good thing Raven got the goods on Jackson," Dave said. "He's trying to claim she made him confess to something he didn't do, but the prosecution doesn't think that's going to fly. It's still not clear whether they'll be able to admit his confession, but between Zoe and the alchemist's testimony and all the blood evidence, they think the chances of a conviction are pretty damn high."

"Either way, that political career of his ain't going to happen," I said with satisfaction. "The Humanists wouldn't touch him with a ten-foot pole now."

Dave gave his mom a broad grin. "Speaking of Raven, she wants Ariel and me to make an appearance at her 'Feral Heart' concert in Atlanta next month. We're looking forward to seeing her and Kordell again…"

"Kordell?" Betty frowned. "That's the Primo, right?"

"Right. Raven hired him as her choreographer and dancer. Anyway, she told me to tell you she can't wait to meet you. She's invited you and Dad to be her guests too."

Betty's blue eyes widened. "Raven wants to meet *me*?"

"Oh yeah. All-access backstage pass, with dinner afterward. *And* she's going to put us up at her hotel. Seems she always books a whole floor wherever she stays for her entourage."

"That's Dave," one of the volunteers put in, looking envious. "No woman alive can resist him, not even rock stars."

"Well, of course not," Dave said, with the

smugness I knew was an act. "They know all about my enormous…"

"Eeewww! Too many legs!" another volunteer interrupted, laughing.

My eyes narrowed, and I made sure my voice took on an icy note. That joke was dying a well-deserved death right fucking *now*. "Actually, he's got the perfect number." Turning to his manifestation, I caught his head in my hands and kissed him, so long and passionately, silence fell. It was broken a heartbeat later by whoops and cheers.

Dave went still for a moment, and then he was kissing me back with all the considerable passion in his soul.

* * *

After the meal, I told Dave I wanted to take a walk around the park, supposedly because I needed to digest that massive meal.

It was dark as Smiley and I set off along the well-lit paved paths between the enclosures. Dave manifested to take my hand, his magic seeming to swirl against my aura, sensitizing my skin and sending a delicious shiver of anticipation down my spine.

I had *plans*.

We walked along, listening to the cats' low roars, rumbles, chuffs, chirps and assorted other noises that didn't sound remotely feline. I knew the beasties ranged from Siamese-sized sand cats to an obese, elderly liger almost as big as Kaiju. Eyes glowed at us from among the vegetation that filled the enclosures, and the air was rich with the smell of cat musk and spring flowers.

Dave paused at one of the enclosures and stared through the darkness at the shadowed bulk of one of the treehouses. "That one was mine."

I leaned against him, propping my chin on his glowing shoulder. Smilodon rubbed his chin against my hip, scent-marking me, and I absently scratched his big furry ears. "I'm looking forward to touring the new place tomorrow." The big rambling two-story Colonial was located a couple of miles away. It was going to need some work, based on the video we'd seen, but we meant to make an offer. Once the advance check cleared, we were going to buy it.

"Our own place," he murmured, staring at the treehouse. "After I died, I figured that was the closest thing to a house I'd ever own."

"You're not dead," I growled.

He turned and grinned at me, his eyes lighting. "I'm sure as hell not. Thanks to you."

With a low groan, he took my mouth. The touch of his manifestation sent a delicious burst of magic through me, and I kissed him back hungrily. "I want you," I rasped against his lips. "Is there somewhere we can go? Because I'd rather not make love with your mom in the next room." That wasn't an exaggeration. The Briggses were putting us all up, and his folks had the room beside ours.

He pulled away from me, his eyes kindling. "I know just the place. Come on…" Turning, he tugged me after him.

* * *

The park's Memorial Garden was situated in the rear of the property not far from the Briggs's home. Massive old trees stood, surrounded by beds of what looked like every species of flower that grew in South Carolina. Granite pavers lay here and there among the blooms, carved with the names of the norm exotic cats buried there. Larger bronze plaques marked the graves of Familiars like Kurt's Stoli and Lahr, Fred Briggs's lion. A water feature chuckled softly near a bronze memorial to Fred himself, though he was buried elsewhere.

Dave led me to a wooden pergola covered on three sides by falls of grape-sized wisteria blooms. As we stepped inside, I noticed the glow of an active spell. It came from the circle of stones in the center of the enclosure, some engraved with permanent sigils, others blank so they could be chalked with whatever glyphs you needed for a given working. It looked like an amplification spell.

In the center of the circle lay a round, fat cushion a good ten feet across. I eyed it. "That looks like a bed."

"Weeeellll," Dave drawled. "It may have been used for that a time or two -- not that I know for sure."

I lifted a brow at him. "Uh-huh."

"Either way, it's got possibilities." He tugged me into the circle. I felt the familiar rush of Earth's magic rising to greet us. Instantly, the magical link between us intensified.

I could feel his desire. Beneath that lay wonder -- wonder that I had fallen in love with him. That I'd been willing to anchor his life force with mine even though I'd had no idea what kind of effect that spell would have on me.

We were linked now. He'd told me that he no longer felt those old-tiger aches Smilodon had developed over the past few years. The veterinary surgeon backed him up on that; the man had commented that based on the last set of X-rays, he'd have thought Smiley was only a couple of years old.

Those spells I'd worked in the circle at Hammerhead Cay had been a lot more powerful than even I had anticipated. We didn't know what that meant. It might have given him ten more years, or twenty -- or seventy. But we were going to find out.

Now I stepped against Dave's mani and slid my arms around his waist. "I'm all for exploring the possibilities."

"So am I." The glow of his eyes intensified, and he leaned in, reaching up to cup my face in his hands. I rose on my toes and took his mouth, sighing as his magic burst over my senses, amplified by the sigils around us. Under the hands I'd spread over his chest, his illusionary cotton T-shirt seemed to melt away. I shivered and broke the kiss, gasping in sudden arousal.

Opening my eyes, I saw him shining in the dark, splendidly naked, his long body lean and powerful, need brightening his aura with turquoise blue. He smiled into my eyes, one hand brushing over my cheekbones. His fingertips left delicious trails of pleasure in their wake, raised sparks of turquoise that danced in my aura. "You're so beautiful," Dave said softly.

I stared up at him, dazzled. "So are you." Grabbing the hem of my T-shirt, I pulled it off over my head and dropped it on the cushion. I expected him to look down at my breasts, mounded high by a pretty lace bra.

But he didn't. His glowing eyes remained locked on mine, his gaze so tender, I felt my eyes sting. "I've been alone so fucking long," I told him, my voice ragged. Then I blinked, because I hadn't intended to say that. "Sometimes it seems like always. But you... You're *there* now, and I can feel you whenever I want. You and Smiley." I swallowed. "You don't know what that means to me."

His lips curled into a tender smile. "I've got a pretty good idea." His fingers skimmed my jawline.

"Yeah, my friends and family have always loved me. But like the joke goes, I had too many legs."

Anger stung me, hot and quick. "Nobody had better make that joke again in my hearing. Or they will fucking well regret it."

"Yeah, you made that really clear tonight." He bent and kissed me again, lusty rather than tender now. I sank against him with a soft, eager moan.

Catching the cups of my bra, he tugged them down, then reached around me to unfasten it. I tensed in anticipation as he pulled back and tossed it aside. My nipples pebbled under a sweet, cool night breeze. I groaned in delight as his clever fingers found them, began to tug and tease. His aura spread over me like a river of sun-warmed honey, golden and impossibly sweet, streaked here and there with blues and rose and soft violet. My aching flesh tightened, responding to the currents of his erotic magic.

We'd gotten damn good at this, the last couple of weeks.

With a low rumble of hunger, Dave began to lick and taste his way along the line of my jaw. I shivered, leaning into him, savoring the lush swirl and dance of his tongue. The shifting shades of his aura glowed like the rising sun spilling veils of color across the sky. He discovered my ear, dipping into the exquisitely sensitive hollow. His magic seemed to tighten over my skin, seeking out bundles of nerves close to the surface, making goose bumps rise.

I needed to give him the same pleasure. Craved it. I reached for my magic, the sigils burning on the stones around me amplifying my power as I sent it dancing down his body in swirling currents. I willed them to tease his magical flesh like ghostly hands.

Smiley rumbled approval. So did Dave.

As he began lazily nibbling down the line of my throat, I threw my head back, threading my fingers through his hair. It felt so slick and soft under my hands. That no longer seemed odd to me, though I knew his body was a manifestation spun of magic, soul and will.

It was just Dave.

I closed my eyes, watching the magic surge and roll around us, loving the intensifying glow of the rose spreading over his skin at his pleasure and my own. I danced my fingertips over the lean, carved muscle of his shoulders, savoring the sculpted contours, then working my way down in curving strokes down his pecs, his ribs. Sliding one hand over, I found the apple-round bulges of his biceps, the working cords of his forearms. I could feel fine hairs there. He told me once that he'd noticed those details appearing after we'd begun to make love. We didn't know whether he'd created them, or I did.

A deep rumble of hunger rolled through the dark -- Smilodon reacting to our need. Dave bent me backward, one arm sliding around my waist to support me as he began tasting his way down my torso.

Dreamily, I found the small point of a male nipple just as his lips discovered my own. He lingered there, tongue swirling around the point, teeth nibbling until delicate silver sensations made me quiver. I flicked my thumb over the nubbin I'd captured, strumming it until he growled softly. He closed his lips over my breast and sucked, hard, demanding pulls.

I arched against him as lust crashed through me in a sudden hot wave. Sliding a hand down, I caressed the tight ripples of his abs to the warm thickness of his exquisitely hard cock. I shivered, remembering how it felt thrusting into me. The way my magic and his clashed and melded as we rode, each teasing the other into delight.

He growled softly and switched his attention to my other nipple, one hand skimming down to tease me through the fabric of my shorts. A heartbeat later, his fingers touched bare skin, sinking right through the fabric just as he had the first time we'd made love. He stroked me with fingers and magic, finding the tiny bundle of nerves that were my clit, my G-spot. His aura tightened, tugged as he worked me with his hands until my hips danced.

Barely thirty seconds passed before a hot throb of delight pulsed through me -- a delicious little hors d'oeuvre of an orgasm. "Jesus!" Tightening my grip on his thick shaft, I began to stroke hard, enjoying his shudder, his lean body so delightfully hot against mine.

"You're so wet," he rumbled, and found the snap of my shorts, flicked it open and slid the zipper down. Licking my lips, I pulled back and helped him slide them and my panties down my legs. I kicked my sandals aside, stepped clear as he pulled everything off and gripped my hips. Dave tumbled me onto my back on the cushion and knelt over me, his golden gaze fierce, his face tight with hunger.

Panting, I watched him stare down at me, his gaze a little wide and wild. He shot a look up at me, then lifted my knees and draped my legs over his back. Dave spread my vaginal lips with his fingers and covered my pussy with his mouth. I convulsed with a gasp as his tongue licked out, swirling hot circles around my clit.

Another orgasm flashed through me in a delicious, burning snap that arched my back and tore a strangled scream from my lips.

* * *

Dave

I smiled in triumph at the echoes of her climax burning through the collar.

It wasn't the first time we'd made love since my recovery. Every time she'd used her sexual magic to build my strength still more. Ariel's magic was *potent*, particularly when she called on the Earth's magic. The way she was now.

I meant to reward her for everything she'd done for me -- for *us*. Reaching up, I filled my hands with her soft breasts as I started licking her clit, enjoying the way she rolled her hips against my face.

"Oh, God!" she panted, a note of desperation in her voice that sent arousal pounding through my blood. Her hips pumped against my face as she whimpered breathless pleas. "Fuck me, Dave!"

"Not yet." My hands danced over her body, even as her nails raked my shoulders.

"Dave," she panted. "I want... I want to make love..."

"Working on it," I murmured, lowering my head to feast again. She moaned and hunched against my mouth.

And even though her hands were nowhere near my cock, I felt long fingers wrap around it as another set cupped my balls. She coiled her power tight and began to stroke, long and slow at first, then faster.

As if she'd developed multiple sets of hands, I could feel her caressing my arms where I braced myself between her slim, lovely legs. The currents of her magic danced hot and bright over my skin, shedding rainbow light. My own magic chased it, spilling turquoise and rose sparks.

A wet mouth engulfed the head of my cock, and I damn near came on the spot.

I was rock hard now, and I could smell how wet she was growing as she dreamily rolled my balls between her fingers. I'd lost track of what was her body and what was her magic. Decided I didn't care. She began slowly sucking down my shaft, inch by inch. *Has to be magic...*

I looked up her writhing body. Yep, there was her head where it should be, tossing on the cushion. But that skilled and wicked mouth felt real.

Her lips tightened, sucking hard, and my eyes almost crossed. Nope, definitely not real -- she'd have had to breathe by now, and how could she suck down the whole thing, plus balls?

"Dave," she panted, and yeah, that was her voice. "God, Dave..."

It was a good thing I could will myself hard even if I came, because I could tell I wasn't going to be able to take much of this. But I was damned well going to make her come again too. Alternating sucking and tongue work, I slid two fingers deep and gave her long, slow thrusts. But even as I teased her, I whirled hot swirls of magic over her skin until rose and violet began to chase each other through her aura, glowing brighter and brighter until they burned stark white in a ferocious climax.

"Daaaaaave! Fuck me! Please, please, fuck me!"

I did the mental math, trying to determine if I had the self-control to tease her any longer. *Yeah.* "Not just..."

Before I could get the last word out of my mouth, she scrambled free of my hold and flipped, landing on all fours. She looked back over her shoulder at me, her eyes glittering and wild. Violet, blue and rose massed and rolled over her aura like storm clouds shot with lightning. *"Now!"*

I blinked at the deep thrum of magic that echoed in her voice. Had she'd just done one of my acoustic tricks? As I blinked at her, she dipped her shoulders, raising her ass high like a female big cat begging to be fucked. I heard Smiley's rumble, and the next thing I knew I'd covered her. I strongly suspected he'd done it. But as she rolled her lush hips against my front, I got with the program, positioned my cock with my hands, and thrust. Into wet, swollen heat, so tight I damn near came on the spot. We both groaned as I sank right to the balls.

"Oh, God, yes!" She tossed her head back.

I began fucking her. Slow as I could at first, then harder, *harder* -- long, digging thrusts she met with rolling hips. "Yes, yes, yes!" she chanted, our magic whirling together in delicious little tornadoes of flaming color that brightened by the second.

The orgasm hit me in a white-hot detonation that seemed to blow the top of my head off. For a moment, I went blind from the sheer pleasure of it.

Her pleasure stormed me a heartbeat later, so fierce and bright my entire consciousness reverberated to it. My shout of triumph and love and delight was echoed by Ariel's. Magic rained sparks around us like a snowstorm of light.

Smilodon's roar made my ears ring.

When the last throbbing echoes faded, we peeled away from each other and collapsed on the huge cushion, limp and sated. Exhausted, I wrapped my arms around her and rolled onto my back, enjoying the sensation of her soft body nestling into mine. We lay still, drinking in the peace of the moment as I savored her love, as intense as her magic. As strong and unassailable.

"I guess," I said sleepily, "if I used the words 'Happily Ever After' that would be cheesy."

She stirred and sighed. "Except we're still going to have to deal with those damned Humanists. And the lawsuits. And getting that asshole Jackson convicted…"

I snorted. "Fuck them. We've beaten a lot worse than a collection of cowardly bigots." I cuddled her close. An idea hit. Unable to resist, I reached for my magic…

The guitar riff from "Eye of the Tiger" rang across the park as I started belting out the song. *"Went the distance, now I'm back on my feet, Just a man and his will to survive…"*

Laughing, Ariel started singing along, our voices blending with Smiley's triumphant roar.

Angela Knight

New York Times best-selling author Angela Knight has written and published more than sixty novels, novellas, and ebooks, including the Mageverse and Merlin's Legacy series. With a career spanning more than two decades, Romantic Times Bookclub Magazine has awarded her their Career Achievement award in Paranormal Romance, as well as two Reviewers' Choice awards for Best Erotic Romance and Best Werewolf Romance.

Angela is currently a writer, editor, and cover artist for Changeling Press LLC. She also teaches online writing courses. Besides her fiction work, Angela's writing career includes a decade as an award-winning South Carolina newspaper reporter. She lives in South Carolina with her husband, Michael, a thirty-year police veteran and detective with a local police department.

Angela at Changeling: changelingpress.com/angela-knight-a-26

Changeling Press E-Books

More Sci-Fi, Fantasy, Paranormal, and BDSM adventures available in e-book format for immediate download at ChangelingPress.com -- Werewolves, Vampires, Dragons, Shapeshifters and more -- Erotic Tales from the edge of your imagination.

What are E-Books?

E-books, or electronic books, are books designed to be read in digital format -- on your desktop or laptop computer, notebook, tablet, Smart Phone, or any electronic e-book reader.

Where can I get Changeling Press E-Books?

Changeling Press e-books are available at ChangelingPress.com, Amazon, Apple Books, Barnes & Noble, and Kobo/Walmart.

Changeling Press LLC

ChangelingPress.com

Made in the USA
Monee, IL
21 April 2023